I0591395

PRAISE FOR BRYAN YOUNG

"Bryan Young is an imaginative writer who has a director's eye, a film historian's perspective, a critic's cynicism, and a genre fan's enthusiasm. It's an interesting mix and I look forward to seeing everything he writes."

—Aaron Allston, *New York Times* bestselling author and author of more than a dozen Star Wars novels

THE SERPENT'S HEAD

BRYAN YOUNG

WFP
WORDFIRE PRESS

EBook ISBN: 978-1-68057-336-7
Trade Paperback ISBN: 978-1-68057-335-0
Cover design by Janet McDonald
Cover artwork images by Adobe Stock
Kevin J. Anderson, Art Director

Published by
WordFire Press, LLC
PO Box 1840
Monument CO 80132
Kevin J. Anderson & Rebecca Moesta, Publishers
WordFire Press eBook Edition 2022
WordFire Press Trade Paperback Edition 2022
WordFire Press Hardcover Edition 2022
Printed in the USA

Join our WordFire Press Readers Group for
sneak previews, updates, new projects, and giveaways.
Sign up at wordfirepress.com

DEDICATION

This book is for Aaron Allston, who made me rewrite it.
Twice.

PART I
THE MAN CALLED TWELVE

I

For a world so new to life, it seemed as though Glycon-Prime was dying.

But the stranger in the tattered serape knew better, riding his mount through the expanse of red-soiled wastelands toward life and work. The mounts didn't come cheap, but they were reliable. The stranger reckoned he'd spent most of his reward money on the animal, just to get to the next town and the next job. But he had enough left over to feed himself and buy a few canteens of water, which, in the end, was all he needed.

On these frontier planets, towns and villages were always few and far between. It was always a free-for-all at the beginning, with colonists, merchants, and miners trekking off in every direction and settling wherever they could find a good vein of underground water or ore.

Clip-clopping along, he was a lone figure on the landscape, covered head to toe in the fine red dust of the transforming planet. The stubble across his face made the strong line of his chin fuzzy. His lips, for the most part, stayed closed, tight like a crease in his face. The only bit of color not tainted by the red of the planet were his eyes, horizon blue, and reflecting a steely resolve.

Looking down at his worn, filthy hands, red with Glyconian grime, chapped from dryness, and leathered from sun exposure, he cursed himself, wishing he could have afforded a speeder.

"A speeder would have been faster," a digital voice said, emanating from the strap on the stranger's left wrist.

"What good would faster do if you still haven't found me my next job?" he snapped back.

The computer intelligence didn't respond, only went to work, scouring newsfeeds through the system, looking for a paying gig for the gunsel that programmed him.

His mount, some alien cross between a mule and an alpaca the locals called a dromid, carried his weight easily and didn't need much water. Since it was hairless, revealing strong muscles along the length of its bulbous shape, and tinted red like everything else on Glycon-Prime, the gunslinger could only assume that it was either from the new, forsaken planet or engineered to live on it. Either way, it was surefooted, strong of back, and didn't stink as bad as the mounts on the last planet he'd called home. Sure, it took a week to travel a road that would have taken a speeder only a few hours, but the stranger didn't mind.

He didn't want to see anybody anyway.

"This world seems rougher than the others, Twelve," his wrist-bound companion said. "There's not much work, and according to the satellite data, the weather isn't going to be in our favor for much longer. It's only going to get warmer."

"Just shut up and find me that job, Zeke. Or at least the next town."

"My name is not, Zeke, sir."

"And mine's not Twelve."

"But it's ..."

"You gonna find me that job, or am I gonna have to shut you down?"

"Understood, sir."

Flipping the reins and bringing the dromid to a quicker pace, he tried not to be annoyed. Despite the struggle, the man called Twelve much preferred the nomadic lifestyle provided by bounty hunting on frontier worlds than living in space or in some sprawling, planet-sized megalopolis. Skipping from one dusty town to the next, sending his digital assistant into the networked space of the world so he didn't have to be bothered, he made an eager, honest living, usually on the right side of the law.

It was a living he understood.

Perhaps "living" was a bit of a stretch.

He was surviving.

And when Glycon-Prime had developed into something that more resembled the planet-cities of developed worlds and less like the wild lands, the dark stranger would pick up and move on to another outlying star system and start all over.

It gave him plenty of time to be alone.

"Still no job, sir. But I do have a blip of a town on the map."

"Show me."

Twelve raised the underside of his wrist to look at Zeke. Strapped around his arm was a leather belt about ten centimeters wide that held tight to him and was home to the brilliant computer intelligence and display that made up the whole of Zeke's consciousness.

On the display, Zeke had provided a topographical map of the flat spread of land. Across it ran a dark red line that the man recognized as the route they had plotted to the next major city. Far off to the side was a blinking green dot.

"That," the wrist computer said, "is a small settlement called Nine Mine City, sir."

"Any work listed?"

"There was some work there a bit ago, according to the system, but the last listing expired a dozen rotations ago."

"Hm," the man said.

He didn't always get jobs off the feed. Sometimes small merchants who couldn't afford the listing fee hired him to scare off the mutants; other times the peasants hired him to scare off the merchants.

The feed seemed to be mostly filled with contracts that came from the corporate interests that built the atmospheric processing facilities and agricultural centers. It was easy for them to pay to eliminate problems, but more often than not, it felt like they were the bad guys. Bookies and gamblers were frequent clients, looking to take down debtors. His favorite source of employment, though, was the government. Usually, they had him tracking down a genuine, no-good bad guy.

If times were tight enough, he'd take a job from anywhere, but there was something grimly satisfying about taking down evil men in a life where satisfaction was a constant mirage on the horizon.

As he rocked back and forth slowly on his mount, a thin smile cracked across his dry lips. It was a knowing smile. He was more than capable of being the bad guy, too.

"Twelve," Zeke's voice interrupted, stealing the smile from his face, "shall I plot a route to Nine Mine City?"

He clicked the dromid to a stop, looking off to the horizon on his left. Somewhere, far beyond the curve of Glycon-Prime, he imagined a quaint little town where families settled and the saloonkeeper was honest. Children played in the streets, but a shadow loomed over the streets of the town, and only the light of the mysterious man arriving atop his mount could save them all.

He smirked. "May as well."

After two more days of riding, camping each night just off the wide, smooth ribbon of magnetic speeder trail that served as the road, he noticed the red-gray speck at the end of the line. The contours of a city grew with every step he forced the dromid to take.

A column of smoke billowed from somewhere in town or behind it, leaving a gray stripe against the red of the world.

"Sir," his computer said, trying to get his attention.

"What, Zeke?" he raised his wrist to talk to the contraption there.

"Are you sure this is a city? Wouldn't we have seen some traffic, in or out, if there was some bustle to this place?"

Even from a distance, characterizing it as a city was a hyperbolic stretch. It contained perhaps a dozen buildings, maybe two, half of them houses. And now that he thought about it, there really hadn't been any speeders of any sort on the trail in the two days they'd been traveling.

"You're the computer. You tell me."

"I've not found a trace of outgoing communication from this place for more than a full rotation."

"There's gotta be a reason."

"Perhaps a storm knocked out their communications array?"

Curiosity hit him in the gut like a fist, and he thought back to what he needed. Even if he wanted to turn back, he didn't have enough water to make it back through the desert and back to another town. He had no local money, and his credit had dwindled.

He didn't have much of a choice but to head into the mystery of Nine Mine City, and he knew it.

"We'll find out, I suppose, won't we?"

Another twenty minutes of riding down the trail, and he had finally reached the outlying buildings of the village and was surprised by their construction. Most were squat, adobe affairs, painted white to reflect the sun, but coated in the red dust of Glycon, as everything was. Surprise hit him; a few of the buildings even seemed constructed of old-fashioned wood.

"That seem right to you?" he asked.

"Wood is rare this far out in the galaxy," Zeke responded.

There were no trees on Glycon-Prime, at least not any mature enough to produce wood. Anything made of wood would have had to have been imported by starship, making it prohibitively expensive.

Twelve slid down from his saddle, grateful for the chance to stretch his legs, and he walked the rest of the way in to give things a closer look. Leading his mount by the reins, he wandered closer to the "wood" building, close enough to see the wood grain was simulated on a metallic material.

"See? It's fake," he told Zeke.

Harumphing, he kept on walking. If there was a thing he couldn't stand, it was simulated decadence.

His eyes wandered up and down the empty street, wondering where the action was and why things seemed so deserted. The unnatural silence unnerved him. He sought out the comfortable sounds of motors and electrical workings common to a town and couldn't hear the buzzing that one would find normally.

Ignoring the quiet, he instead focused on the hope of a job.

"Still no work on the feed?"

"None."

If there were a contract to be had in any town, the saloon was as good a place as any to find it. Either the law was there to clean up trouble and perhaps they needed help, or perhaps the trouble was waiting around for an answer to their illicit prayers.

Either way, saloons were the best place to get a drink.

Leading his animal up the road further, he found quickly that the saloon wasn't hard to locate. It looked like every other saloon on the backwater planet, right down to the batwing doors. He wondered why they were so fancied out here in the rim but banished the thought. He had bigger things to wonder about.

He hitched the dromid to a piece of metal railing on the front porch of the saloon and walked up to the threshold. Taking a breath, he slowly swung the door open and walked inside the dim, dingy barroom.

Like the town itself, so too was the bar free of life. The only figure in the room was his own reflection in the paneled mirror behind the bar.

Were his eyes playing tricks?

"Hello?" His voice echoed in the vacant hall. "Anybody in here?"

"I'm here," Zeke said, matter-of-factly, but no other voice responded.

A breeze whipped through the room, kicking up a layer of blood colored sand, carrying it from one side to the other.

Bringing the computer on his wrist close to his mouth, he whispered harshly. "Stay quiet."

Zeke complied; his light winked off angrily.

Twelve wondered if a computer could be offended, then realized he didn't care. Approaching the bar, he thought, perhaps, someone might be hiding there behind it, hoping not to be seen.

Could the whole town be out in the mines?

He knew mining was a key staple to the local economy, but he'd never known a saloonkeeper to leave an open shop to take up prospecting. But if there really were nine mines, the townsfolk could be engaged in any sort of arrangement.

The state of disarray behind the bar told a different story, though, and the stranger discarded that conclusion. The cabinets full of bad liquor seemed picked through, and only a few half-full bottles remained. With no one to object, the gunslinger came around the counter, seeking out a glass not covered in grime. He found one hiding beneath a dishrag and placed it on the bar. Then, he selected the bottle with the fanciest printing on it and with liquid still in it. He uncorked it. Taking a sniff, he decided it was good enough and poured himself a shot.

Slugging it back, he resolved to find out exactly what the devil was going on in Nine Mine City.

II

After the saloon, the man called Twelve's next stop was the general store.

No one in their right mind would leave a fully stocked shop unattended on a place as new and lawless as Glycon-Prime. If anyone had holed up against whatever happened in Nine Mine City, it would be at the general store.

General stores on the terraforming frontier were just big enough to hold one of just about anything you could think of needing, crammed onto less shelf space than you could possibly imagine. Invariably, general stores carried all sorts of supplies, ranging from fluoropolymer ropes and GPS trackers to scoped laser blasters and foodstuffs.

He found a general store just up the road, seventy meters down and across the way.

"There's no guard," Zeke, the computer on his wrist, stated matter-of-factly.

"I thought I told you to be quiet," he said, gruffly.

"When was the last time you saw an establishment in a settlement like this without a guard?"

"It's been a while. Now shut up before I shut you off."

"Understood, sir."

Sweeping his blue eyes back and forth across the speeder trail, he sought any sign that would tell him the story of the place. But aside from being empty and silent, the street didn't seem to be out of order. The speeder trail shone with little use. The red soil-stained boardwalk, synthetic boards, of course, was free of litter and trash.

A breeze swept through from behind him kicking more fine, red particles into the air. The only sound on the wind was the flapping of his serape, blowing more dust into the area in front of him.

He turned on his heels, into the wind, and faced the closed, frosted glass doors of the general store wondering what tragedy could be found inside.

"It could be a trap, Twelve," Zeke said.

"You reading any life signs in there?"

"No."

"Then quiet down like I told you."

Stepping up from the speeder trail to the faux-board-walk, he took slow steps toward the door. His fingers dangled over the laser pistol belted to his hip, ready for anything.

The doors slid open slowly, revealing the shambles of the general store beyond. The shelves had been stripped bare, debris littered the floor, and nothing of real value had been left behind.

Slowly, he drew the laser pistol from his hip, aiming it around the corners of the stripped store, making sure the place was truly empty.

All of the technology, all of the weapons, all of the mining equipment, and, above all, every scrap of food was gone.

"I'll give them one thing," he said, "they were thorough."

"It would seem as though something bad has happened here, sir."

"You think?"

"I wonder what's happened."

"Don't we all."

Slipping his pistol back into the holster, he walked back outside to watch the wind blow crimson twisters of dust along the street and stroke the stubble on his chin.

When he stopped to think about it, the answer was right in front of him. It was probably a rogue band of so-and-sos that were behind all this. He grinned at that though, since that meant there would probably be someone out there willing to pay him to take revenge on their behalf.

He tried more doors along the street, and each of them swooshed open easily. The story inside each hovel and shop was the same as the saloon and the general store.

The remnants of life had dwindled to nothing but the scattered debris of a fleeing people. In all his years traveling the frontier, he'd never seen anything like it. No one sailed across the stars to the edge of the frontier to just pack up all their things and leave their homes behind. They had to have been driven out by force. But by whom? And why?

"Somebody did this to them," the man said.

"The mutants?" Zeke asked.

"They're called Glicks here."

"They seem worse here than other planets."

"Maybe they are."

On every terraformed world there were new genetic anomalies that made their way into humans. On some worlds, the process was slow and beneficial and could take generations. On other planets, a small segment of colonists could be mutated, instantly and horribly. It was something in the atmosphere and terraforming chemicals. Sometimes, the way the terraforming companies did it just changed men. The characteristics changed on every world, depending on the cocktail required to make the place livable, so colonists never knew what they were getting into. That was just the risk of being a pioneer on the edge of space.

They had a different name on every world, but on Glycon-Prime they were known as Glicks. Glicks looked like regular people, mostly, but their features had flattened, their hair fell out, and their skin grew hard, dark, and rubbery. Some folks called them Snakes behind their back. They didn't like that too much. They didn't like much of anything too much.

Being mutated over the course of a few nights on a new world is liable to make anybody a little cross.

Zeke's theory about the Glicks made a lot of sense.

A moment of doubt took the man when he caught a faint sound on the wind that sounded vaguely human. It was a soft sound, pitched high, and mixed with a sobbing rhythm.

"Did you hear that, Twelve? Was that a whimper?" Zeke asked.

"Shhh," Twelve said forcefully.

The sound came from the other side of the buildings, and for all he knew, it could have just been the wind whistling through an alleyway. Steering his dromid by the reins like a leash in the direction of the sound, he could more clearly make out the noise of a child crying over their clopping steps.

I should just turn around right now, he told himself.

But he didn't.

And before his mind could protest any further, he was stepping through the alleyway to the open red prairie behind the buildings of Nine Mine City.

As the sound of a young child sobbing grew louder and

louder, the stranger knew he was moving in the right direction. Then, as he finally reached the end of the street, the
bottom seemed to drop out of his stomach, and he gulped
hard.

Before him lay the smoking aftermath of a massacre.

In a pile behind the town were the remains of what he
guessed was most of the townsfolk, save the crying boy. Even
at a distance of twenty meters, the man could tell their
bodies were charred and blackened from laser burns. He
counted the bodies roughly in his head. More than forty. The
settlement's population appeared to consist entirely of
immigrants. Judging by the creamy-dark shade of their skin
and loose-fitting garb, he guessed they had most likely come
from the Persian space outpost.

But now, there they were, contorted in awful ways,
tossed in a pile without a care. Though he tried not to look
too closely, he saw enough to tell him a story of what had
happened. Laser burns that had fried away enough skin to
expose teeth and sinew. Holes in chests revealed through to
the bodies underneath and behind. Lifeless eyes, wide open
and staring. Their faces slacked into looks of deathly peace,
masking what must have been horrifying final moments.

He was certain it must have been Glicks behind this.
Colonists on their own were prone to savagery of a kind, but
nothing like this. Whoever did this was angry.

Twelve turned his attention to the boy who had
somehow managed to survive. The boy seemed normal, free
of any genetic mutations, and about ten years old. His skin
was milky brown and his hair dark, thick, and coarse. His
nose was a button on his face that the stranger knew would
grow sharper as it grew when puberty set in. He wore gray
coveralls that matched the muted sky and stood out starkly
against the scarlet landscape. The stranger wondered why

the boy wasn't wearing the flowing tunics and headcloths usual for interstellar immigrants descended from the Arabs of old on desert planets.

He shrugged. Perhaps the flowing tunics would come as the boy grew older.

Banishing emotion from his voice, Twelve took a few non-threatening steps toward the boy, slowly. "What happened here?"

Startled, the boy turned, saw the pistols belted to the stranger's hip, and cringed. "Please don't kill me...."

"I'm not going to kill you," the man said gruffly, close enough to the boy that he could reach out and touch him. "What happened to these people?"

"The Glicks," the boy said with effort. "It was the Glicks. They came and killed everyone."

That answered one question, but the level of destruction before him was still more than he'd seen from any mutants and certainly didn't fit with any patterns he'd seen from Glicks. Why would they drag the townsfolk out to the back of town? Were the Glicks holding them hostage, waiting for some ransom that went unpaid?

The boy sniffled again; his sobbing continued.

"Anybody else still breathin', son?"

The boy nodded his head urgently and grabbed the gunslinger by the hand, dragging him to the far side of the pile of smoldering corpses.

Laying in the grass was another young boy, unconscious. He was older than the first boy, just at the edge of manhood. Thirteen, the stranger reckoned. Fourteen tops.

"His name is Nik," the sniffling boy pointed to his unconscious friend. "Do you think he's gonna die, mister?"

The gunslinger knelt down beside the wounded boy, trying to find any sign of a visible wound. His hands moved around the cloth of Nik's traditional, billowy white tunic, searching for any sign of laser burn on his chest. Nik was still breathing, but it was a shallow and unsteady sort of breath. The youngster might have just fainted from the carnage, and no one could blame him for it.

But no, there on the side of Nik's arm was a white and pink blister of laser burn. Was it enough to cause unconsciousness?

No, it was just a graze. The boy's arm had been gravely burned, but that wouldn't have been enough to knock him out. The sight of the slaughter had been enough to put him down.

"It's just a scratch," the gunslinger determined. "Even if it tore something and bled for a couple of days, he'd still be livin'. That laser burn'll hurt for a while, though. Bad. Worse, if he doesn't take care of it."

Taking all of the stranger's words in, the smaller boy paused, then looked up with wide eyes, bright and the color of chestnut, covered in a film of spent tears. "My name's Amir. You got a name, mister?"

"No...."

"I call him Twelve," Zeke blurted loudly, startling Amir.

"Who?" Amir looked down to the light emanating from the stranger's wrist. "You've got an AI on there, Mr. Twelve?"

"I won't for much longer if he doesn't keep his mouth shut." Twelve raised Zeke slightly and held down the button that would power him down.

Before Amir could press him to elaborate, the tang of crashing metal filled their ears, interrupting the conversation and forcing a flinch from both of them. Twelve pulled his right pistol, aiming it at the sound. It came from behind one of the massive atmosphere reprocessors, a box of steel, washed red from exposure. An intake on the back sucked the air in silently. The filter over it, designed to keep the dust out, was the color of blood. The output, an impressive engine thruster-like tube on the top, took the oxygenated air after it had been filtered through an artificial respirator and pumped it right back out into the atmosphere. Just by breathing and planting trees, the colonists were making the place livable and making the atmo-reprocessors obsolete. Once that happened the company would pick them back up, reconfigure them for the air of the next planet to colonize, and it would all start over again.

But that didn't explain the noise. Were the Glicks back? Were they lying in wait to finish off the survivors? Or was it just a piece of machinery falling apart?

The gunslinger made careful eye contact with Amir and put his finger to his lips, pantomiming that the boy needed to remain silent and stay back. He never lowered his aim from the direction of the noise.

Amir nodded his head furiously. Surely, he could be quiet. It was probably the only reason he was still alive.

Quietly, like a cat padding through grass, Twelve approached the atmo-reprocessor. They had such a low breakdown rate, built solid for space travel and the harsh environments of the frontier, so the stranger was wary of chalking the noise up to mechanical problems. Glicks seemed the most likely explanation....

He took slow, careful steps, making his way around the monstrous machine, gun pointed ahead of him.

Coming to the final corner, he paused, waiting for any sound, any indication whatsoever, of what was waiting for him. The indigenous animals were usually afraid of machinery, so he crossed that off his mental list, too.

There was no helping it. He was just going to have to

jump the corner and hope he was quicker on the trigger if danger presented itself.

Gritting his teeth, he counted to three in his mind and, in a flash, turned the corner, gun raised, ready to kill …

… a little girl no older than five years old with thick black hair in two messy pigtails, wearing a sundress in the Persian style, standing alone in the dirt. She clutched tightly to her middle a little brown rag doll with a smear of red grime across its face to match her own.

Her face was pale and her expression blank. She had locked eyes with the pile of bodies and didn't seem able to tear her gaze away.

The stranger let out a breath of annoyed relief and holstered his laser pistol.

"You scared us, little lady."

She said nothing. A massacre would be a wretched thing to see for a kid at any age.

"Why don't you come back on over here with us?" the stranger asked cautiously. Careful not to touch the little girl, he led her back to where Nik was lying, still out cold, with Amir standing over him.

He turned her around, facing her away from the dead remains of the townsfolk.

"She got a name?"

Wide-eyed, staring at the pile of bodies, Amir didn't respond.

"Son? She got a name?" he repeated.

"Oh. Yeah. Lila," the boy said, distracted by the sight. "Her name is Lila, Mr. Twelve."

"Don't call me that. Just tell me where everybody else is."

"It's just them and us," Amir dropped his head. "They got everybody."

"You sure this is everybody? This town looked like a whole lot more folks put their roots down here than this."

"The mines dried up. My pa calls this place a *sher metrew*," Amir said.

"A ghost town?" the stranger guessed.

The boy bobbed his head up and down. "We were moving on soon."

The gunslinger tilted his head, taking in the sight of the corpses once more. "I think things have changed, son."

He watched the boy turn his head, trying hard to avoid looking at the pile, knowing that somewhere in that smattering of meat and bones were his loved ones.

But the boy couldn't help looking at it any more than the stranger could. It was there. It wasn't going away.

Water leaked out from the boy's eyes, slowly at first, then like a waterfall. The boy sobbed. "It's not fair, my parents gettin' killed like this."

"Life isn't fair, kid."

Amir turned and kicked a rock into the empty desert beyond them. "We were fixing to leave today," he said fiercely. "We were packed and everything. They killed my parents and took our speeder van full of everything."

The boy kicked another rock, sending it sailing even farther than the first. "Guess I'm not going anywhere, now."

"You can't stay here," the man said firmly.

Then the gunslinger walked back to his dromid, Amir following behind.

"Why can't I stay here, mister?" the boy asked as Twelve unbuckled the thick leather strap that tied down his saddle pack to the dromid.

"Because you shouldn't." The stranger pulled from his bag a water canteen and walked back toward Nik and Lila, Amir in tow.

Screwing the cap off the water container, he stood over Nik and poured out a steady stream of liquid onto his face. The boy gasped, sitting upright almost immediately, screaming, "Miri!"

The stranger assumed the boy must have been delusional.

But Nik kept spouting that word over and over, his eyes got wider, his voice hoarser with concern. "Miri! They have her! Where'd they take her?"

Nik took in the familiar faces of those around him, but when he caught sight of the stranger, he shut his mouth, recoiling. He probably noticed the pair of laser pistols on Twelve's hip as he pulled back, staring at them like they were a predator ready to eat him.

Amir knelt down to reassure the disoriented boy, speaking in a hushed and kindly tone. "It's all right, Nik."

Nik's hysterics bristled the gunslinger. He found himself suppressing the urge to roll his eyes and leave the lot of them right then and there.

"Is she all right?" The wounded boy just wouldn't let it go. "Is Miri all right?"

"She's gonna be," Amir looked up to the stranger. "This man here's gonna help us."

"Now hold on a minute there, son. I haven't said anything about helping anybody do anything."

"But you have to, mister," Amir clasped his hands in front of his chest, almost like he was praying.

"I don't have to do anything."

Immediately, the stranger found himself facing a much more terrifying and effective weapon than any energy blaster: the puppy-dog-eyed faces of children begging for help. The worst was the youngest, the little girl so petrified and shellshocked she hadn't spoken a word. Her gaze pierced him.

"I reckon we can talk about it later," he forced himself to mumble.

"But it's my sister, Miri," Nik said. "They've got her! They took her!"

The stranger motioned to the charred remains of the townsfolk. "The ones who did this took her?"

Both boys nodded.

The stranger grew silent. Perhaps he was too cynical, but what other reason could there be for a pack of Glicks to take a girl that age? He wondered what reason the two boys, inno- cent to the urges of men, would give for her abduction. Or maybe he just wanted them to tell him, in their own words, what happened. Or maybe he just had a mean streak in him. "Why would they take her?"

Amir shrugged. "I didn't see it happen."

The gunslinger turned his gaze to the older boy, who held on to his burned arm as he spoke, as though putting pressure on it would stop the singing pain of the burn.

Nik spoke through cringing tears. "I was right there when they took her. We were running like everybody was. They were herding us back here, shooting everyone. After they killed my *maader* and *pedar*, they shot 'em while they were trying to protect us, Miri grabbed me, and we started running."

The boy stopped and took a breath, looking around at the mess of bodies in front of him. Nik closed his eyes, as though he were trying to unsee the images, but the stranger knew the images would never go away.

The boy continued, "They had speeders everywhere, and you couldn't hear anything except their turbines and the screaming. We made it out back here and one of them said they needed to grab one for the Santa Madre, and so two of them grabbed Miri and started dragging her off. I grabbed her and pulled her back, but that's when they shot me."

Nik looked down to the burn on his arm while the stranger pondered the story.

The details were curious, not at all what he'd expected to hear. He assumed she was just another prize for the men, but that didn't seem so likely anymore.

Nik looked back up at the stranger through a film of water in his eyes. "What'll they do to her, mister?"

"I'm not sure."

"But what about us, can't we help her?"

He looked over their faces again, trying hard to ignore the feeling tugging him to stay. He imagined that his empathy was a person in his psyche he could shove out the door when he wanted to be left alone, but it wasn't as corporeal as that.

It was more like an emanating spirit that infected him whether he liked it or not. He'd gone nameless and spiritless for so long, but there was nowhere he could run from himself.

Reflected in each of the children's eyes was the frightened terror of a lost child. The hurt was permanent. They were lost forever. Their parents would never find them.

He couldn't replace their parents, nor would he ever want to. But something nagged at him, some old forgotten piece of humanity he hadn't used in a while, laying dusty on a shelf within him.

Dusting that feeling off, the least he could do was set them on the right path, right?

III

Miri was terrified and alone.

For hours she'd been in the dark, a hood covering her face. Plastic tie straps had been affixed to her wrists which were pinned brutally behind her back.

Her hijab had been lost in the struggle, so she was almost grateful for the hood. The last thing she wanted was to feel the shame of her captors staring at her, uncovered.

She was confident the darkness she was consumed by was the cramped shelter of a speeder's rear compartment. It was warm, and stifling, but the climate controls kept her at least cooler than she would be outside.

The last thing she remembered seeing before her dark captivity was her brother, Nik, getting grazed by a blaster in his forearm. He grabbed the wound and hit the ground, tumbling. Just before that, she quite distinctly remembered one of the Glicks pointing at her as she ran with Nik under one arm and saying, "That one ..."

And another replying, "For Santa Madre?"

And then, no matter how far and fast they ran through the din of screaming and death, the blaster bolt that tagged Nik was faster.

Miri remembered screaming, and she remembered thinking distinctly to herself that screaming wouldn't help her situation, that it would only draw unwanted attention to her, but she couldn't help it. She hoped, at the very least, that her screaming had allowed them to forget about Nik, who hit the ground with his hurt arm.

Maybe he wasn't dead after all. And if she could keep their minds on her, maybe they wouldn't walk over to him and blast him any further.

Rough hands snatched her from behind, wrapping strong arms around her middle and yanking her backward toward their speeders, and all she could think to do was wish and pray that Nik had survived.

If she'd been able to somehow keep him alive, it would be worth whatever torment and torture the Glicks had in mind for her.

Laying there, hands bound in the dark, stuffed into the cargo compartment of a speeder, she had plenty of time to wonder who or what Santa Madre was, exactly. She'd never heard of Santa Madre, when people spoke of the Glicks, names or titles were rarely mentioned, save for the one they called the Serpent's Head.

Before Miri could think too hard about her predicament, the compartment she'd been stuffed into opened, letting her feel the heat of the Glyconian sun hit her directly. Even the dark black cloth of the hood seemed to brighten with the light.

She could feel no less than two pairs of hands wrap around her limbs and pull her. The palms were dry and rubbery, and she wondered if her captors were wearing gloves.

"Where are you taking me?" Miri struggled beneath their touch.

They responded only by tightening their grip around her shoulders and ankles and hefting her awkwardly from the compartment.

Miri's stomach lurched as they carried her from room to room, upstairs, and winding through narrow hallways where she could feel the Glicks bumping into walls around the sharp turns. She tried twisting and turning out of their clutches, but their grip was far too tight and escape seemed hopeless.

Even if she could get away, she didn't even know where it was they took her. Where would she go, and how would she get to safety?

Visions of getting lost in the red desert, blindfolded with her hands tied behind her back, filled her head.

Trying to put the clamping pain of pressure out of her mind, and the deadened sensation of her arms dangling beneath her, Miri instead focused on her surroundings, hoping she'd be given some clue that would help her escape. Not now, but at some later point.

Listening for clues, her heart broke. Not one person, human or Glick, spoke the entire time.

In some of the larger rooms, she could hear the vague outlines of conversations, but it seemed as though the sound she heard most often was hushed silence as she came through rooms, dangling awkwardly from the grip of those that carried her.

Finally, a door whooshed open, and Miri could feel a blast of intense heat from inside the room. She wondered if it was actually a door to the outside. It seemed warmer than the sun, yet the light felt softer and somehow more pervasive through the cloth than the bright spotlight of solar rays she'd experienced while she was still outside.

Tilted upright, they planted her roughly into a chair, pulling her arms up so they could slip the chair against her back and keep her hands tied behind her.

When she'd settled into the chair, resigned to meet whatever fate they'd planned for her, Miri felt a hand grasp the hood at the top of her head. Catching much of her hair through the black cloth, the hand snatched it upward, removing the covering from her face.

Miri flinched with the light piercing her eyes; everything was washed out in red and white bands of color. Her eyes tried focusing, but the strain of adjusting from dark to light forced a vein to throb in her head.

Aside from the throbbing, she felt the nagging worry of her hair uncovered build in her. She felt almost topless without the hijab, not knowing where she was or who would see her. She'd been disoriented enough, and the last thing she wanted was to feel worried and even more uncomfortable.

Soon, the scene sharpened into focus.

She could not have ever predicted the sight before her.

The red light and warmth came from infrared heat lamps on the far side of the room. Directly below the lamps was a rock and a creature sunbathing atop it.

Miri guessed it to be a snake, but she knew the mound of rubbery green flesh was too big to be a snake. And why would a snake be in a tattered dress? The dress itself was frayed at the edges, and the field of whitish cloth was painted red in the light.

The creature's breathing could be heard from across the room, like a hissing respirator, venting gas.

A coldness found itself lodged in Miri's breast, a chilling feeling that told her she was a mouse tossed into a cage for a meal. That lump on the rock would soon have her weight added to it, swallowed whole by the monster.

As the reptilian creature stirred, tears leaked from Miri's eyes, knowing this would be the end for her. Her thoughts turned to Nik, hoping he'd at least made it out safe.

The monster uncoiled further, revealing new details, namely a jumbled patch of untidy black hair, greasy and unkempt.

Miri had never seen a snake with hair.

Soon, the mound yawned, like a cat, revealing its stretching limbs that were those of a frumpy humanoid. Miri wanted to see its face but could only see the tousle of hair. Its arching back was turned to her.

"Hello?" the young girl said meekly, hoping she wasn't actually intended to be a meal for the beast.

Slowly, the creature's head turned toward her, revealing horror of a kind Miri had never even imagined before. This was no snake, and Santa Madre was no pet, but a Glick, mutated further than any Glick Miri had ever seen. Instead of the wide rubbery features that looked generally human, Santa Madre's snout had elongated, and her skin had turned green and scaly. Her eyes had bulged out and drifted to the sides of her head, peering out with black eyes like a doll's. Around her neck rested a string of shining pearls, reflecting back the red light in shimmering glints. At the ends of her arms were shriveled hands, and at the ends of those were fingernails sharpened to points.

Smeared across her dried lizard lips was a sloppy coat of red lipstick, as though a child had applied it.

Santa Madre's breathing slowed into a bass-filled

purring that caught in her throat. She flicked her tongue through razored teeth.

Miri couldn't tell if the tongue was forked or not, but it would be no wonder if it was. There seemed to be no humanity left in this woman at all.

Or so she thought.

The thick line of her vast mouth curled up into a smile, revealing the points of her teeth in a fiendish grin.

"They've brought me a new one," Santa Madre said in a low tone, her voice coarse but oily. She slithered forward off her rock and ambled toward a frightened Miri, making a wide circle around her.

When the snake-woman moved past the point of Miri's peripheral vision, Miri tried twisting her head around to see what fate might meet her, but she could not contort herself in such a way. She couldn't see Santa Madre, but she could feel her hot breath on the back of her neck in time with the revving of her breath. Whipping her neck the other way, Miri could see her own outline reflected in the wall, an immense mirror.

Behind Miri, she could make out the grotesque silhouette of Santa Madre, reaching up with a hand. The sharpened point of a fingernail gently scratched up Miri's back until it reached her neck, and then she could feel the strength of Santa Madre's wrinkled fingers coil around her throat.

At the back of Miri's head, she could feel a brush bury its teeth into the back of her head and come down roughly, taking a clump of her raven black hair with it.

"You seem sturdy," Santa Madre said, her every *ess* sound long and drawn out, like a snake. "Perhaps you'll last longer than the others...."

IV

After a quick and cursory search for any supplies they might have missed, the stranger left Nine Mine City, followed step for step by the three reeling children. The younger boy, Amir, suggested they stay and look for anything else that would help, but the stranger insisted they hightail it for now. Maybe they'd find something useful, but the place had been picked over pretty clean, and there was no telling what kind of surveillance the Glicks might have left in their wake to make sure they'd done the job right.

The man called Twelve, three children and dromid in tow, filled his canteens in the groundwater well at the center of town and walked deep into the outskirts, doing his best to cover their tracks and avoid attracting any attention that might draw the marauding Glicks onto their trail. The last thing he wanted was them coming back to finish the job.

The kids cried silently on their forced march through the Glyconian desert, only settling when the stranger stopped them in a low valley a few miles from the city and out of sight from the road. Zeke had marked the spot on the map, even though his vocabulator had been shut off, temporarily at least.

"Here's home tonight," the stranger said to the kids.

The hill on one side of the spot Zeke had chosen would obscure their view from the road, and the massive atmoreprocessor they sat in the lee of would obscure any other view of them at a distance.

From his saddlebag the stranger withdrew a brown, waxy cylinder about fifty centimeters in length and as big around as a credit chip. He had only a few left and hadn't planned to use them anytime soon, but he was confident the kids could use the comfort of a campfire.

Since there was no natural litter on such a new planet devoid of old plant growth, they had artificial flame logs that would burn hot and clean, just like an old Earth campfire, through the whole night.

Using the power charge from his left pistol, the stranger lit the log, creating a brilliant, crackling fire. Though it produced no smoke, it smelled like a campfire just like on Earth proper.

The kids huddled around the warm flames, drying their eyes and trying hard to put their minds somewhere else.

When Lila's stomach rumbled audibly, the stranger realized what it was that would really calm them down.

Going back to the pack on the side of the dromid, he pulled out a full day's worth of protein rations. They were in airtight plastic bags that were spongy to the touch. With the knife he kept tucked away in his boot, he cut the tops off the packets, pouring the brown goo into the small tin pot tied to the leather saddlebag. Then he went back to the children, circled around the flames.

"Hold this," he told Nik, handing him the pot to cook over the fire.

Even this small task was still too much for the disconcerted Nik. The stranger nodded to Amir, who took the pot from the other boy and dealt with the cooking himself. He was just as hungry as anything.

A slight grin crept across one side of the stranger's face. The food would be a good distraction. If he could get the kids fed and asleep, then he could be on his way, and when they woke up, they could go their way. He found no sense in getting too mixed up with them.

But all the same, something gnawed at him. Maybe he wasn't such a good guy if he wanted so badly to escape. The grim smile faded from his face, and he wondered what sort of person he really was deep down in his core.

He could talk it over with Zeke another time.

They all ate in silence. Lila and Amir took to the food slowly, eating with the sort of despondence he'd expect from kids who had just witnessed a massacre. Nik ate, but begrudgingly so.

Like a kettle of warm water, the stranger could feel Nik's rage bubbling up, just a little bit at a time. Each bite of the meal Nik took was another minute stolen from the effort to rescue his sister. The rage burned beneath him, and the bubbles grew more and more frequent. The boy finished his food and had nothing to do but simmer, watching everyone else eat.

And, like that kettle, he finally boiled into a high-pitched whistle. "I can't take this anymore," he yelled as he stood. "I'm gonna get those damn Glicks that took my sister."

His hands had curled up into fists, his shouting was directed at the sky.

The stranger wasn't sure what he could possibly say that

would mollify the boy short of, "Let's go." But the gunslinger had no intention of going anywhere.

"Why don't you take a seat there, son." Twelve tried to insert a quiet reassurance into his tone.

It didn't work.

Nik ignored the man, instead taking a threatening step toward the fire. "We've got to go get her. They could be killing her right now!"

"It's no use to set out tonight. Following a trail at night is a quick way to get yourself lost."

Nik took a step toward the fire and kicked, launching a melted piece of the artificial log toward the desert hill, red embers floating up into the air in its wake.

"Somebody's gonna get hurt if you don't take a seat." A low menace filled Twelve's voice.

Nik couldn't help but listen that time. He collapsed back down to the ground, sitting cross-legged in the soft soil. Then, after a long moment, he broke the silence softly, the wound plain in his voice. "Are you gonna help me get her back?"

But the man said nothing.

Amir asked this time, just as quietly. "You are going to help us, aren't you, mister?"

Not knowing what he could do that would actually help and keep him paid and fed, the stranger kept his mouth shut.

He looked to Lila, who hadn't said a word since he'd met her. Her eyes were wide, reflecting the fire against a glaze of constant tears.

"We'll talk about it in the morning."

"No. It's best settled tonight." Nik's voice grew again, both in confidence and volume.

"You've had a long day, kid. We'll talk after a good night's sleep has cooled your head."

Amir spoke this time, a voice of reason compared to the older boy. "Mister, we're just kids and you gotta help us. You may have helped us so far, but it would be just as bad as killing us yourself as to let us fight the Glicks all by ourselves."

"He's right," Nik said. "You'd be killing us yourself. You have to help us find her."

The stranger held steadfast, saying nothing. He knew what his path was, and as much as he wanted to help these kids, he didn't see them as part of that path.

He walked alone.

"We'd help you find your sister." Amir seemed like a calm and quiet boy, wise beyond his years.

The stranger laughed, gently. Caught with his heart in his throat, he said, "I reckon you would."

"So you'll help us?" Amir took a step forward, his eyes growing big.

Defeated, the stranger let out a deep sigh. "We'll see."

Nik got down to his knees, like he was praying to the mysterious bounty hunter. "We'll find her. We're sure to do it with your help."

"Why don't you wait to thank me till the morning. Now hush up and let's get some sleep."

V

The cold, blue night reached its middle.

The twin moons of Glycon-Prime provided two spots of dim white light in the field of midnight that made the nothingness across the landscape easy to see. For the most part, aside from the occasional hills and berms, the landscape was long and flat, stretching out to the curve of the planet. The occasional sapling, planted by settlers, broke the straight line, but other than that, this planet was barren. Well, not quite barren. Barren implied an inability to produce life, and this place was certainly making a go of it.

From the rise of the hill, not far off to the east, one could see the black outline of Nine Mine City. In better times, it would have been lit up bright like a proper village.

But now it was dead, as were all of its former inhabitants. Well, most of its former inhabitants. Three of the four survivors of the Nine Mine Massacre slept uneasily in bedrolls they'd pilfered from town before they'd fled with their lives.

The stranger rolled to his other side, pulling the flap of

his sleeping bag over his shoulder, and turning his back to the kids. He didn't want to look at them while he charted his course and, more likely than not, decided their fate.

"How can you leave them to fight the Glicks on their own, sir?" Zeke, the voice from his wrist computer, asked.

"I thought I turned you off," the man said quietly.

"You did. What's the worst that could happen if you help them find the missing girl?" Zeke asked.

Entertaining the thought for just a moment, he wondered what would happen if he did ride up to the Glick encampment with three underage children in tow. "We'd all get killed, more than likely. You saw what those Glicks did."

"Is that why you can't sleep, Twelve?"

"Do I need to turn you off again? You're gonna wake the kids."

Maybe it wasn't the decision weighing on his conscience keeping him awake, but because Nik had spent every moment since he'd fallen asleep whimpering and muttering his sister's name. "Miri ... Miri ... We're coming, Miri...."

Over and over and over again.

"Miri ... They've got you ... We're coming ... Miri ... Miri ... Miri ..."

Soon, the name was echoing in his own mind with just as much determination, and it was driving him crazy.

He found himself packing his bedroll back onto his indigenous mount. He tied his cooking pot to the saddlebag and tucked his knife back down into his heavy work boot.

He felt a tingle on his wrist and just knew that Zeke wanted to say something, but before Zeke could, he whispered down to the computer. "They'll be much safer without me."

"Sure," the computer said, as unimpressed as a digital voice could sound.

"There any rewards or jobs on the feed for the Glicks who did this?" he said, trying to remove the doubts from his mind, convincing himself he'd stay if there were money in it.

"Negative, I'm sorry to say."

"Well then, that's that."

"If you're sure."

"As anything."

Showing his age with a groan, the stranger pulled himself back up onto the back of his dromid, clicking three times with his mouth and digging his heels into the animal's side.

"Let's go," he whispered to the animal.

The dromid let out a wet noise, passing air between its smacking lips, before it obliged.

"Shhh," the gunslinger said. If his conversation with Zeke hadn't woken them, surely the riding animal would.

The dromid trotted just a few steps out into the night before stopping dead in its tracks.

"What are you doing?" Twelve tugged the reins and slapped the back of the dromid's neck with them. "What in the hell is the matter now?"

He looked up to see what the matter was, and suddenly he felt caught, like a fugitive in the spotlight in the midst of a prison break.

Standing there in front of him, blocking the dromid's path, was Lila. In her tattered dress, clutching her doll close to her, she stared up at the stranger.

There was a sadness in her eyes, shame and disappointment. Her sad resolve melted the man's countenance. His gaming face transformed into one of unabashed shame.

He could feel the self-hatred simmering in his desperation to leave. He could see in her face that even if he tried to convince her he was leaving to take up the hunt on his own, she wouldn't believe him. How could she?

An ache grew in his heart, and he knew what he had to do, though there was no profit in it.

But what was profit?

Lila's brow furrowed, as though she was insisting he head immediately back to bed.

"All right, all right," he muttered, trying not to wake the rest of them. "I get the picture. Enough already. I get the point. I can't fight all of you, now can I?"

Lila cocked her head to one side like a scolding mother.

That thought killed him. This was probably the final lesson she'd learned from her mother. Lila was on her own now, and that fact ached further into his bones.

"Go on, go back to bed."

She didn't move.

"Fine. I'll stay," he said, feeling guilt weigh him down.

But she still didn't move.

"I'm staying, aren't I? Get back to bed."

She didn't budge from her spot until he turned the dromid back around and unpacked his bedroll once more.

Twelve knelt down, ignoring the creak in his knees and flopped down into his bag. Then, confident he wouldn't be getting up for the night again, he kicked off his boots. "Are you happy now?"

Finally, Lila looked down to the ground, tightened the grip on her doll, and retreated back to bed.

Zeke buzzed at low volume. "Welcome back, Twelve."

The stranger harumphed and curled into the sleeping bag, covering himself over and hoping the firm grip of sleep would take him quickly.

None of them stirred again until morning.

VI

The red sandstone landscape of Glycon-Prime never looked more vibrant than in the steel-gray of morning, just before sunrise.

But the gunslinger guessed the children derived no joy from the view.

For breakfast, the stranger fed them dry rations from his saddlebag and let them each take a single swig of water from one of the skins dangling off the back of the dromid.

"So, mister, let's go find my sister," Nik, the older boy, insisted as he clutched the laser burn on his arm.

"Relax, would you kid?" the stranger replied, exasperated and walking away, back to his dromid.

Nik followed him the whole time, relentless. "She's still out there. You said we'd do it in the morning. Well, it's the morning."

"There's some things we have to do first."

"Things? Like what? What's more important than finding her?"

BRYAN YOUNG

The man fished a tube of ointment from the bag and handed it to the boy. "Rub some of this on that burn. It should heal up soon enough."

Nik snatched the tube and put it between his teeth while he undressed the makeshift bandages over the burn on his arm just below his right shoulder. It was a mottle of pink and red, raw from the dry bandage that had sweated to it overnight.

Twelve looked away from the wound, ashamed of himself. He hadn't wanted to waste the ointment on these kids if he was going to leave. But seeing the boy spread the white paste over the seared flesh, cringing every time he applied too much pressure, made the man's heart sink.

He was better than depriving children medicine. Wasn't he? A small voice in the back of his mind scolded him for not tending to the wound the night prior.

The gunslinger took the tube away from the boy and tied the bandage back on the boy's arm.

"Thank you, sir," Nik said.

"You're welcome. Now here's the rest of this tube. You'll need to put more of this stuff on later. But you hold on to it, in case something happens, then you'll have it no matter what."

Nik took the tube, nodding his head the whole time. "Now are we going to save my sister?"

"You want to walk all the way there?"

"No...."

"You want to eat dirt when you're hungry on the way?"

"Well, no...."

"Then we're gonna need to head back into town and see if there's anything those Glicks left that we can use." Twelve cursed himself under his breath. Had he thought for a minute he'd have been leading this expedition of children, he'd have made that search before they left. "Maybe we'll find a speeder or something."

The younger boy, Amir, raised his hand like he was in school. "Well, mister, there aren't any speeders in town, they took 'em all as far as I could tell. But I'm pretty sure they didn't take the dromids from the Croker's stable."

"That'll do, son," the stranger said, forcing a smile.

Amir smiled back, clearly satisfied for being a help.

"The sooner we get packed, the sooner we can find your sister. Now, let's get to it."

He could see that Nik wanted to argue, but instead caught his breath and set himself to the task of helping Lila collect her bedding and roll it up tight.

Amir carefully rolled up his own sleeping bag. Each of them in turn handed the rolls to the stranger so he could tie them to the saddlebags on the dromid. The man then tied the tin pot back on the bags, letting it dangle and bob with each step the hoofed dromid took.

Once everything had been packed and set back in its right place, the stranger lifted Lila up, doll and all, and placed her in the animal's saddle.

Wishing he had reins and bits for the kids as well, the stranger set out with the boys following behind on foot.

The hike back to Nine Mine City seemed much easier than the hike away. Leaving the city, the children seemed as though they were carrying the weight of the events on their backs. Coming back to the city, they seemed to have left much of that weight back at the camp.

Keeping an eye out for any change in the village, the stranger was reasonably certain no one, Glick nor colonist, had made their way through since the massacre.

"Zeke." Twelve raised his wrist computer to his face. "Any communications in or out of Nine Mine City?"

"Negative, sir."

"Any chatter about it elsewhere?"

"Negative, sir."

"You think we're good to go, then?"

"You're asking for my opinion?" the computer asked, almost gleefully.

"No," the man half-smiled, lowering his arm back to his side.

It seemed like the coast was clear and they'd have the run of the place.

As they entered the town the same direction they left it, he wondered what the town, still abandoned, would look like a hundred years in the future. He could see the sky as a deep, beautiful blue, rich with the new makeup of the atmosphere. The saplings and plants that had been put into the ground were overgrown and intertwined with the shattered windows of the buildings. The buildings themselves were caked in soil that had turned more brown than red from all of the foreign nutrients and plant matter that had seeped in over the years.

"The Croker's house is down this way." Amir grabbed the man by his dusted red serape and tried dragging him toward the western edge of town.

"Hold on, now, son," the stranger said, turning to Nik and Lila. He pulled the young girl off the mount and set her back down on the ground. "Why don't you two head home and grab anything that might be useful. Can you do that for me, Lila?"

"All right." Lila eyed him suspiciously. He'd have to work to earn her trust if he wanted it.

"Don't worry, I'm not going anywhere but with your friend here." The stranger put a hand on Nik's shoulder, which felt unnatural to him. "You're gonna have to watch over her. You got that, son?"

"Got it," Nik nodded.

"Hurry up now, we haven't got much time."

"Come on, Lila," Nik led her off to the other end of town.

Amir took a hold of the stranger's serape once more and led him west. "It's this way, Mr. Twelve."

"My name's not Twelve."

"Well, that's what your computer said it was."

"He says lots of things," the stranger exhaled. "You doing okay, son?"

"What do you mean?" He never slowed his pace, meandering through the vacant buildings with purpose.

"I mean, you know ... you've ..."

"I won't lie, mister, it's been a hard couple of days."

The boy's elegant understatement almost elicited a laugh from the hardened gunslinger, but he bit his lip and let the boy lead on.

Amir had led the gunslinger directly to the Croker's stable. It was one of the few simulated wood buildings in the town, and it must have been erected at great expense. It was said that wood made animals more at ease with their surroundings, but the stranger had always been ruffled by that explanation. Dromids weren't from Earth proper and wouldn't know wood from concrete.

"You think they killed the animals?" Amir looked up at the stranger, his eyes wide.

"It's possible."

"I don't know why they would kill 'em. But why would they kill everybody else, either?"

"It doesn't make sense to me either, son."

The impressive faux-wooden door of the stable wasn't locked or latched, but it was big enough that it took the both of them to pull it open. As the door creaked outward, the pungent odor of straw and fecal matter that followed the Glyconian pack animals around like a rain cloud hit them with full force.

Amir took the lead, checking stalls one at a time, searching for a live dromid that could carry his weight, and probably Nik's, too.

The stranger moved toward the back of the stable, looking into each stall as he went, hoping that whatever animals might have been left hadn't died in the night or been shot down by the Glicks.

"Back here, kid."

Success.

In the second-to-last stall was a sickly old dromid, huddling in the corner, starving. It hadn't been fed in at least a day, maybe two or more. By the looks of it, it might not have eaten in at least a week. It was shaky on its feet, and its skin was sticking to its bones. Even through the fur they could see the outline of its rib cage.

Amir walked into the stall and rubbed his hands over the coarse hair of the dromid's face and head. "It's all right, boy," Amir shushed at the animal, soothing it. "We'll take care of you. We're here now. We'll make it all better."

"You shouldn't make promises you don't know how to keep," the stranger warned.

"We'll keep this one," Amir said, determined.

"We'll see."

"We need him, don't we? Then we'll keep him living as long as we can. And we can't do anything to him worse than what's been done."

The little fellow had a point.

If they couldn't find a speeder, this was the next best thing for transportation through the desert. They'd have to do as right by the creature as they could.

"Lead him out," the gunslinger told Amir. "Let's get a move on."

Amir obliged, leading the dromid of skin and bone out of the stable, but the stranger lingered.

"Zeke?"

The wrist computer blinked to life. "Twelve?"

"You've been scanning things. What is it you think happened here?"

"I've picked up nothing unusual. Everything seems consistent with what we've seen."

"Which is what, exactly?"

"The Glicks attacked. People died. I can't, with any certainty, ascertain any reason."

"Me neither. And I don't like thinking there's no reason. There's got to be something."

"You never know with Glicks, sir."

"I know." The man took one last look around the stable from where he stood, sighing. "Well, keep a look out for anything. I want to know what we're up against."

"Very good, sir."

Zeke winked away on the screen, leaving Twelve alone in the stable with his thoughts, which drifted to Nik and Lila, wondering how they were getting on in their quest to scrounge supplies. Then a part of him wondered why. *If anything happened to them it'd be two less brats I'd have to deal with.*

Nik didn't want to spend a minute longer in his family home than he needed to. Seeing his house, a pang of sorrow filled him, and he realized that the comfort of his home came not from the physical space, but from the people.

And all the people that made this home, his *maader*, *pedar*, and sister, were gone. Dead or kidnapped.

"We need to hurry this up, Lila," Nik told the little girl. "The longer we're here, the harder it's going to be to find Miri."

"We'll find her," Lila said, meek but confident.

Every inch of the space and every shattered artifact told him a story or conjured a memory of a time when things made sense and he was loved and comfortable and had nothing to worry about.

But he was the head of the family now, and it was up to him to make things right.

Moving past the front room, the family room, not wanting to cope with the flood of memories he'd have there, he led Lila straight to the kitchen's pantry.

But as they scrounged for dried food and rations, those memories ate at Nik all the same. Trying to banish the image of the family room from his mind only brought those memories closer to the surface. He could see the wide box of the living space, and imagine clearly his parents seated on the couch, he and his sister, Miri, crouched on the floor on either side. His father told the tale of the sword hanging on the wall above the entertainment unit, pristine and beautiful. The sword was thin, sharp, and slightly curved. The handle and scabbard were ornate, made with steel and elegantly decorated wood.

His father told stories to the whole family that night, but when the subject of the sword came up, he always seemed to speak directly to Nik.

"This is a Bedouin sword," his father had said, smoothing the hair of his black bristle mustache as he spoke to the family. "It's been in the family since we first left Earth proper. We're a frontier people, Nik. All of the true Arabs are. Nomads, for a thousand years. We'll always be on the frontier, moving forward across the galaxy, living like no one else can. My father had my name etched on this blade when he gave it to me when I moved on and came to Glycon-Prime. One day, when you decide to move on and colonize another planet, I'll etch your name on it also, and then you can give it to your son."

Hearing his father's voice in the deep, dark places of his head caused a cold shiver to course through Nik's body.

Banishing the memory, Nik focused on collecting dried food from the pantry Nik's father worked his hands to the bone to stock. Lila held open a sack they'd pulled from a cabinet, and Nik stuffed it with plastic containers of food, bags of preserved food materials, and cans of vegetables until the sack was half-full and the pantry was bare.

Lila cinched the cloth bag closed, and Nik took it from her, hefting it over one shoulder, where the weight of the food sagged down, hitting the back of his knees with each step toward the living room he took.

He found it there, mounted to the wall above their entertainment unit. Just where his father had put it ...

The sword ...

Setting the provisions down on the floor, right in the spot he'd always sat, he moved the couch over to the wall. The legs of the couch screeched lightly on the hard floor as he dragged. It weighed next to nothing since it was manufactured on another world and shipped to Glycon-Prime. With the couch in place, Nik carefully crawled up on top of it as Lila looked on.

Reaching up to the wall, he grabbed the sword, pulling it down, surprised by the weight. It seemed heavier than the couch.

Nik didn't quite know when or where it had come from, exactly. His father never elaborated in the stories, and he'd never caught the interest in family ancestry his father had. He didn't even know if they were really even Bedouins. The Persian space outpost seemed a melting pot of people from the region. He only knew that it had been in the family for generations; passed down from father to son for a hundred years or more.

Pulling it from the scabbard, he was surprised by its glimmer. Etched across the sturdy, sharp blade were the names of his forebears.

He spent a long moment looking up and down the names until he found his father's name, Abdullah, and the blank space below it.

Then, after a long moment, he spoke, still staring at the sword. "Lila, it's time to go."

He didn't notice that she'd been at the door's threshold, lugging the bag of supplies on her own, watching his every move in silence.

Hefting the sword with one hand, he leapt down from the couch and reached out to Lila with the other. "Give me the bag. I'll carry it."

"All right," she said quietly, letting the top of it go.

"Go ahead," he told her, nudging Lila out the door.

She took steps down the front porch and walked toward the street, giving Nik the last moment he needed in his old home and his old life.

Nik shut the door behind him and moved on.

Lost in his thoughts, Nik, with Lila in tow, made it to the

middle of the main street, where Amir and the stranger were already waiting for them.

Amir and the man were each mounted on their own dromid. Amir's weight alone sagged the spine of the second mount, but that's all they had to work with.

The stranger said nothing when they arrived, arousing Nik's suspicious nature. Suspicions or not, he didn't feel as though he had much of a choice in his situation. His family was dead, he was only twelve years old, and the stranger was the best chance he had to save his sister.

With silence from the stranger, Amir spoke enough for the both of them. "Nik, we found another dromid, so we won't have to walk. You and Lila can both ride with me. And wait, Nik ... is that your dad's sword?"

"Yes."

"What good's a sword?" Amir asked, petulantly. "Why not get a rifle?"

"Because I don't have a rifle."

"Your dad didn't have a laser pistol or an energy rifle or nothing?" Amir asked.

"No. Didn't yours?"

"Well, no, but ..."

"Then shut up about it. I've got my father's sword, and I aim to bring it."

The stranger growled. "Will the two of you quit your yapping and let's go. I thought you wanted to save your sister."

"Yes," Nik said. And without another word, he slid his sword between the saddlebag and the dromid, securing it as best he could. Then he did his best to boost Lila up to the top of the mount with Amir, then climbed up himself.

"The trail left by the Glicks leads west," the gunslinger said. "Let's go."

And so, the four of them set out, riding with the hot sunrise to their backs.

Every thought in Nik's head was bent on his sister. "I hope she's okay."

VII

Through the plate metal door of her prison cell, Miri strained to make out voices in the hallway beyond. Pressing her ear to the steel, she found it cool to the touch; a relief after the hours of baking in the red room with that horrible ... thing.

Even hours after the guards had pulled her out of there, she could still feel the intensity of the lights on her, almost as intense as the gaze of Santa Madre.

Pushing her ear closer to the door, she couldn't make out the voices beyond clearly, only that there were voices, raised and loud. Were they shouting from across a distance? Or angry? Was this whole compound under attack? Or was this business as usual?

Miri couldn't tell.

There were no easy answers for Miri about where she was being held or what was happening to her. Her head still ached from the pulling and tearing that the monster had done with the brush. When Santa Madre had satisfied her desire for hair brushing, the horrible creature had pulled Miri's hair into two too-tight ponytails. For being so tight, they were ragged, uneven, and stray hair frayed everywhere.

Miri shuddered when she remembered what happened next.

Santa Madre had hovered over her, her breath hot and coppery, and roughly applied a coat of makeup to the frightened girl. The monster twisted a tube of bright red lipstick, melting in the heat and sweating, and smeared it across Miri's lips and rubbed it into her cheeks. The only thing Miri could think of as the moist color touched her lips for the first time was that it had first touched the scaly lips of Santa Madre, and that thought caused her to cry and almost made her vomit.

That wasn't all that happened.

Miri didn't even want to think about the rest, but couldn't help it. The entire scene played out in her mind over and over again. Everything she saw seemed to serve as a reminder for the ordeals she'd endured over the last rotation.

Miri looked down at all the makeup smeared on the baggy sleeves of her clothing where she'd tried to wipe it all off as soon as the guards had pulled her out of the oversized terrarium and cut her bonds.

She wanted nothing more than to keep her face covered and hidden, and to get all of the infected cosmetics off her.

It was some time the night before that they'd tossed Miri into the cell, small, cold, and bare.

After an hour of looking for any way to escape, she'd finally collapsed from exhaustion on the metal slab of a bed.

When she awoke is when she decided she needed to listen for any clues to her captivity, but none of it made sense. They hadn't put her to work, and they hadn't killed her. The men hadn't made any advances, and no one seemed to look twice at her, except with pity. No one had even spoken to her, save the slithering voice of Santa Madre.

Santa Madre.

Miri decided there was no way Santa Madre was just a Glick. Glicks used to be human before the new atmosphere affected them. She had never seen a colonist so badly misshapen and twisted, both physically and mentally.

Santa Madre must have been something new, something this world created on its own, because Miri had never seen such sinister darkness in a human before. Even the Glicks that ran down the townsfolk had some of their humanity left; Santa Madre was something different altogether.

Her heart thumped in her chest, and she wondered if she were actually dead and this was someone's idea of hell; her hijab ripped from her in front of strangers, played with like a doll by a monster, no one acknowledging her existence, her family dead, and no one alive to help her.

"I will not despair," she told herself.

Tears came, slowly at first, and she had to tell herself again.

"Someone will come. Someone has to come," she whispered, trying to convince herself, deep down in her heart.

But in that deep down place, she was confident no one was left. She'd spend the rest of her life with her soul torn apart by the indignities of Santa Madre.

Her mind raced back and forth between hope and despair, not able to decide which made the most sense.

When the voices on the other side of the door grew louder, Miri had to forget all about her dilemma and simply recoil from the door before it opened.

The door zipped open, and her hands snapped instinctively to her face, as though she could hide if she couldn't see them.

Standing on the other side of the door were a pair of Glicks. They were dressed in black uniforms with green trimming. Each had a laser pistol slung across a belt that bisected the one-piece uniform.

Glicks didn't have much in the way of facial expressions, their skin was so rubbery that it seemed to cause them too much effort when they did react to something, but these two looked almost as though they hated what they were doing to Miri.

"What do you want from me?" she screamed.

But their only reply was stepping into the cell, looming over Miri like a menace.

"What are you doing to me?"

Keeping her face covered with one hand, Miri flailed with the rest of her body, kicking and shouting.

"Leave me alone!"

When the Glicks reached her, they put their hands up in front of them and reached down into the mess of kicking girl, working to restrain her.

"Don't touch me!" She could feel their hands grabbing at her limbs, trying to find a solid purchase, but she wriggled and writhed as best she could, keeping them from putting her down. From the corner of her eye, she spied the laser pistols and wondered if, in all of her flailing, she could snatch one of them and turn the tables.

One of the Glicks finally grabbed the hand Miri had been using to cover her face and lifted it up in his direction. Of course she resisted, trying to pull her hand back down, but she twisted directions and her free hand shot out toward the pistol on his hip ...

... but her arm was caught in midair by the other Glick.

"No," she whimpered.

With both of her hands trapped, the kicking Miri did

with her legs didn't do much to help, and soon enough the rubbery fists of the Glicks were wrapped around her ankles and wrists.

Without a word, they stopped there, keeping her held down. She twisted and turned her body, making it as difficult for them as possible, but their grips held fast.

Miri gritted her teeth. "What are you doing with me?"

Resigned to the fact that they were going to do something horrible, and she was already ashamed, she closed her eyes, not wanting to see what came next.

That's when they lifted her up.

"What?" She opened her eyes, seeing the ceiling getting closer to her.

The Glicks hefted her toward the door.

"Where are you taking me?" Panic filled her chest, and she doubled the twisting and turning of her torso. There weren't many places they'd possibly be taking her, but only one made sense.

She didn't want to believe it, but by the time they'd reached the cell door, she knew where they were going.

"No! You can't! You can't take me to her," Miri said, wishing she was wrong. "You can't! Not again!"

VIII

The gunslinger and his young wards spent the better part of an hour trotting along the speeder trail.

The hooves of the dromids clip-clopped in a steady beat on the paved roadway that had linked Nine Mine City with the rest of the world. Raising a hand to call a stop behind him, the man called Twelve pulled the reins of his dromid and stepped off the side of it.

The dromid fell to its knees, exhausted, curling up into a laying position for its rest.

"Go ahead," he told the kids trailing him. "Get on down. Water these dromids up. Give 'em rest, and we'll get going again in a minute."

One by one, the three children slid off the side of the dromid, each hitting the ground with a dusty thud. First Lila, the little girl. Then Amir, the kid with his head screwed on straight. He grabbed the little girl by the hand and led her around to the saddlebags for the water canteens.

Finally, the eldest boy, Nik, plopped down to the ground, producing a cloud of red soil on impact. Even doing something simple like dismounting the dromid was filled with an anger in him that gave the gunslinger pause.

Nik reminded the man too much of himself at that age.

A scary thought.

With the kids and dromids taking a rest, the gunslinger turned to the horizon, stretching his legs over thirty paces before reactivating Zeke with the press of his finger.

"Zeke ..."

"Twelve. What can I do for you?" Zeke said, his voice tinged with excitement. Maybe the damn thing was happy to feel useful.

"Anything up ahead I should know about?"

"I've not intercepted any transmissions that would indicate a trap, if that's what you mean."

"That's what I mean," Twelve said. "What's the next town like?"

"Stelio City?"

"Is that the next town?"

"Indeed."

"Then what can you tell me about it?" The gunslinger gazed out over the curve of the red horizon, wondering if the town was there, somewhere in the distance, just a speck he still couldn't quite see.

"Only that it's the same as others on Glycon-Prime, only more so," Zeke said.

"Any jobs?"

"Oddly, no. It seems as dead as Nine Mine City. No jobs. No outgoing communication I can detect."

"Hmm ..."

"From what I'm piecing together from elsewhere, reading between the lines, it seems as though there's a lot of Glick activity centered in this entire region."

"So, whatever's going on, whatever they're up to, we're

close to it." Twelve rubbed his chin and looked back at the kids, dirt and sweat-stained from their travels, but not broken from their trials.

"It would seem so, sir."

"All right. Let me know if you hear anything else."

"As you please."

Resting his hands on the laser pistols at his hip, just below the line of his serape, the gunslinger kicked dirt on his slow walk back to the kids and the dromids.

When he returned, Lila broke her silence to simply proclaim that she'd named the steeds. "This one is Bluey," she said of the emaciated one she'd been riding atop.

Of the dromid Twelve had been riding, she said, "that one's name is Tornado."

Despite the fact that Bluey wasn't blue, and Tornado was neither fast nor fierce, no one argued.

"Mount back up," the man said. "Let's get a move on."

"How are we gonna find my sister, mister?" Nik asked, though it took a while for an answer to come. The empty space between talking was filled with the steady beat of hooves.

"Haven't you been listening?" Twelve asked. "We're tracking the Glicks who did it."

"How?" Amir asked.

"Everything leaves a footprint, be it on sand or on satellite. Whatever they've been planning, we're getting close to the center of it."

"And what happens when we find 'em?" Nik asked.

"Then we'll make 'em pay," the stranger said matter-of-factly.

That answer seemed to mollify Nik, and he fell silent.

For what seemed like hours, the only sounds were the

steady hoofbeats of the dromids until Amir broke the long quiet, "Mister, you got a wife and kids?"

The stranger ignored the boy, trotting along on his mount and pretending not to hear him.

Amir, though, was insistent. "Don't you have any, mister?"

The stranger kicked the back of the dromid, quickening its pace, doing his best to put at least twenty meters between himself and the kids.

In quiet anger, they rode and rode without a rest for quite a spell. The stranger never quite let the kids catch up to him, though they tried. Amir had tried to spur Bluey to quicken his pace, but Bluey could barely keep himself moving forward as it was.

Up ahead on the trail, alone as ever, all Twelve could think about was how much he'd rather not remember anything. It astounded him how much time it took to bury something so deep he could be numb to it.

"Why didn't you just tell them?" Zeke asked, quietly.

"Why don't you mind your business?" he replied.

A glimmer in the distance distracted Twelve long enough to ignore the next question from Zeke. The computer asked twice more, which seemed like nothing more than a buzzing in Twelve's ears.

"You don't always have to be so guarded," the wrist computer said after a time.

"Hush," he said, seeing a glint on the horizon.

Dismounting Tornado, he hit the ground on his feet and took a few steps forward, squinting in hopes of seeing more detail in the distance. The rise he stood upon led down into a valley of red dust and below them was the outline of another sparse town.

"Is that—" he said.

"Stelio City," Zeke said before the gunslinger could finish his question.

"Stelio City?" the man repeated, shaking his head and letting out a breath that might have been confused for a laugh. "Every minor outpost with a population of twenty gets to call itself a city on the frontier."

"The population is actually closer to nine hundred, sir."

Behind him, he could hear the kids hopping down from their perch, then he turned to see them all off their dromid, giving the poor creature a rest. Then, as a group, they approached him cautiously, quietly.

A pang of guilt hit him in the gut when he saw their wincing walk toward him. Had he given them a reason to be scared?

"I'm going to go check it out," he said, trying his hardest to sound soft and fatherly, pointing to the town below. "Maybe I can get a bead on the Glicks that took your sister, son."

Nik's face hardened and he spat on the ground. "*Neek hallak*, you're gonna leave us here, aren't you?"

The gunslinger smirked. The boy was terrible at swearing in his family's tongue, but the sentiment was appreciated.

"Settle down, will you? We're going to find her, and we're going to get her. We'll do it a lot faster if I don't have to stop and reassure you that's what we're doin' every five minutes."

He stopped and turned back around, scanning the immediate vicinity with his eyes. About a hundred meters to their left, well off the speeder trail, he found what he was looking for. A satellite relay tower, reaching up to the sky, its communications dish pointed out toward a thousand other star systems.

"You see that tower over there?" the stranger asked, pointing to it. "Go hide over on the other side of it. It's bigger than it looks from here. You'll be able to hide behind it well enough. Rest your dromid. Feed him some. I'll be back along as soon as I can find out more. But I can't have you down there to worry about."

Amir got between Nik and the stranger, putting a hand on the older boy's chest as though Nik was going to start something. "Don't worry about Nik, sir. We appreciate the help."

"Good," the man said. "Now get down to that relay tower, like I said. If you want to keep my help, you're gonna have to trust me. I'll be back as fast as I can."

"Fine," Nik relented, throwing his hands in the air and turning.

Taking the initiative, Amir grabbed Bluey's reins and led him off the trail. "We'll be there, sir. You can count on us."

"Good."

Jumping back up onto his mount, the stranger started on his way down the long, lonely road to Stelio City.

IX

For a frontier outpost on the edge of space, Stelio City seemed to be doing rather well; it was certainly much more advanced and lively than Nine Mine City ever was. The city's boom must have begun a decade prior, when colonists had first begun to arrive on Glycon-Prime. The buildings of Stelio were taller than in Nine Mine and painted in brighter colors to offset the rolling crimson landscape. More technology was apparent; lights and digital signs were strung about, and more speeders than dromids filled the main road.

The man called Twelve found that outposts on infant worlds were always easy to navigate. Everything was always set up along center roads that ran in all four major directions out of town, which gave traveling colonists something familiar to latch onto.

"According to the map, the saloon is up ahead," Zeke chimed in from his wrist.

The saloon, right in front of him, was a garish two-story affair that had made its money doubling as a casino. A gaudy, flashing digital sign advertising booze, girls, and gambling was mounted above the awning that covered the porch leading to the saloon's entrance. Fancy electric signs were the surest indication of the decadent decline of a place.

"I'm not sure I would have found it without you, Zeke." The gunslinger smirked sarcastically, "Thanks a lot."

"You're perfectly welcome. What's your plan?"

"Plan?"

"Please don't tell me you're going in there to interrogate a bottle and shoot up the place."

"I'll probably shoot the place up first. Now shut up while I'm in there."

"If you insist."

Tying his dromid to the edge of the saloon's porch, the stranger came up the steps to the door and strutted in with all the confidence of an angry champion.

A swell of pride matched his anger in a way he hadn't felt in a long time. He decided the part of furious hero, exacting revenge for kids and common folk, suited him.

His swagger carried him all the way to the bar where a dumpy little man, fat from a life of wealth and excess, stood, waiting to offer a drink and snatch a credit.

At the sight of the stranger, the overweight barkeep's eyebrows crinkled together, nervously. His forehead sprouted beads of stinking sweat. The nostrils beneath his sharp, hooked nose flared, and his posture grew defensive.

The stranger knew he looked like trouble, and it showed on the barkeep's face.

Being midday, the only other patrons in the bar were a group of Glicks playing poker in the dimly lit back corner of the establishment.

The gunslinger eyed them on his way to the bar, hoping to inject venom into his gaze.

"I need a whiskey," he said, kicking his right foot up on the bar's metal foot rest. "And I need some information."

The sweaty little man obliged to the whiskey, pouring a shot of the brown liquid out quickly and corking the bottle back up in a flash.

The barman's accent was thick and wheezy. Each syllable he spoke sounded as though he were scraping the bottom of a gravel pit for them. He shrunk behind the bar as he spoke, "What is it I can help you with?"

"You know anything about a group of Glicks who did that god-awful thing to the folks in that outpost a piece down the road? Nine Mine it was called." The gunslinger accentuated the word "Glick" like it was from a pit most foul.

"It is not my business to know such things," the bartender stammered, his eyes darting significantly between the gunslinger at the bar and the group of Glicks in the corner.

The gunslinger took the hint he didn't need.

The chatter had stopped, and from the corner of his eye, he could see he drew the attention from the crowd in the back. Their ears perked up, and suddenly their game just happened to be played out.

Anything the stranger had to say, they'd be paying attention.

He turned toward the dirty Glicks, their tough features drawing tightly with their angrily squinted eyes.

"Maybe," the gunslinger said slowly, enunciating each syllable, "you fine gentlemen could tell me where I could find that group of no-good cowards and snakes that murdered all those innocent men, women, and children back in Nine Mine City."

One of them bristled and hissed at the mention of the word snake. Another pounded the table with his fist. A third muttered through his thick, stretched lips, "They had what was comin' to 'em."

The fourth in the group clearly had the most sense and tried to calm the others, not wanting trouble. His voice slithered like most Glicks, but there was a smooth and easy confidence behind it. "What's it to you, stranger?"

"My employers, they got their folks killed back in Nine Mine and I've come to do 'em," the gunslinger growled.

"The only thing you're doin' right is finding your way into a shallow grave," said the Glick with the least sense.

A sick feeling of joy spread warmth through the gunslinger's body. A slow, worrisome smile crept across his face. "That some kind of threat?"

The threatening Glick doubled-down, standing up to meet the stranger's intimidation. "You better believe it."

The stranger's voice remained calm as he slowly bared his twin laser pistols from beneath his serape. "I don't take too kindly to threats. You see, I just don't think they're funny."

The rest of the Glicks stood in solidarity with their mate, roughly tossing their chairs back behind them. The loudest shouted back, "You won't think it's very funny when they're tossin' dirt on your face."

The gunslinger's smile broadened unnaturally, baring his teeth. "You know the one thing I do like about threats?"

The Glicks backed away from the table slowly, their fingers dancing and twitching to snatch their guns up into their palms. The leader spoke, calm and cool, "What is it you like about threats?"

"That the people who make 'em don't live very long."

The Glick opened his mouth, about to speak, but his words trailed off as his elbow pulled up, sliding into place over his gun, his fingers yearning, reaching, grasping for his energy pistol ...

... but it was too late.

The gunslinger was faster.

Much faster.

With the blinding speed of an orbit-breaking starship, the stranger had unholstered his left pistol and pulled the trigger, turning the chest of the offending Glick into a smoking red and black hole with a single azure bolt of light.

"Any of you other child-killers want to make a threat?"

When no one responded, and the Glicks stared, dumb-founded, the gunslinger smiled at the prospect of more violence.

"My God!" the bartender shouted from behind the gunslinger, just before a glass shattered as he dove behind the counter, most likely to stay out of the line of fire.

The stranger cocked his head to the side, staring the new leader of the Glicks right in his beady, black eyes.

"Go ahead," Twelve said. "Do it."

The Glick's skin glossed over with a nervous sweat, making them look more like the slimy snakes of old Earth than the stranger had ever seen.

Looking at the three remaining Glicks, he could tell which one was the fastest and would need to be taken down first, then the other two would fall. It was the one in the back, not saying anything. There was a resolve in his eyes and a quickness in his reflexes that the stranger could read like a newsfeed.

Next was the one on the right and a step closer. His elbow looked like a greased hinge, he'd be fast on the draw, but something in the way he held his hand, with a twinge of frightened hesitancy, told the gunslinger that he'd be a safe second target.

The last one was easy to decide. The one who did all the talking and taunting was always the slowest. Anybody who fancied himself powerful at the barrel of a laser gun but wasn't that good with it had to rely on his mouth to get him out of the stickiest situations.

But no amount of talking would get any of the Glicks out of this situation.

That didn't stop the talker from trying. "We can be reasonable...."

"You don't think that time's passed?"

"You never know. Maybe we'll surrender. We'll give ourselves up to the authorities."

That was an empty promise, and the stranger knew it. The authorities stuck to the spaceports, where civilized society did the same.

"Today, I am the authorities," Twelve said.

That's when the snake in the shadow made his move. He was fast, there was no doubt of that. He had time to get his laser pistol from his holster and raise it up no farther than a forty-five-degree angle.

His shooting arm and throat had taken the full force of a pair of blue laser blasts.

The second-fastest had actually reached his gun, but wasn't able to pull it, taking a fast blast in the torso.

The talker was the last to go down, still speaking. The blazing heat of the bolt fried into his face at the mouth.

In the space of a blink, the stranger had fired three times with his already drawn left pistol and a fourth with his right. And each of them in turn crumpled to the floor to join the fourth of their number.

With a flourish, the stranger flipped his laser pistols back into his worn leather holsters and turned back to the bar.

From behind it, the bartender slowly raised himself back

up, peeking from beneath the bar at first, assaying the damage to his establishment.

"Now that it's a little quieter in here," the stranger said to the bartender, "maybe you can help me out and answer my questions straight."

The dirt in the air had collected on the bartender's shirt where he'd been sweating, around his neck and peeking up from between his fat arms. His face dripped with perspiration and his voice quivered with anxiety, "If I help you, they'd certainly kill me."

The stranger slid his empty shot glass across the bar, nodding for a refill. "Well, how are they gonna know you helped me unless you told 'em?"

The fat little bartender used his dishrag to wipe the sweat from his jowls, then poured another shot for the gunslinger, trying hard to ignore the question.

"I'm certainly not going to tell 'em you helped me. So I don't think there's all that much to worry about here." He took his drink with his left hand and made a point to finger his pistol with the other.

This menacing gesture unnerved the wheezing bartender, and the sweat he'd sopped up returned just as fast.

"Tell you what," the gunslinger assured him, "I'll make sure anybody who does know you helped me out won't be living for much longer."

Weighing his options, watching the stranger's grip tense around the butt of his pistol, the bartender cracked. "They have a fortress, down by the river off to the north of the town. But please, I tell you—I beg you—do not go."

"Why all the concern for this particular brand of mutant scum?"

"They will most certainly kill you." The bartender wrung his sweaty dishrag in knots with both hands.

"I aim to do a lot more killing than that. Who's in charge out at this fortress?"

The fat little man's face bled white.

"Come now, it can't be all that bad." The stranger took a swig of the alcohol before him.

"It's worse than that." The bartender squeezed his rag tightly enough that his knuckles turned white. "His name from before he came here was Josef Guerrero...."

"And what's his name now?"

"The Serpent." The bartender's back lurched with a shiver at the mention of the name.

"The Serpent? He's a Glick then, I take it?"

"Aye. The atmosphere rebreathers changed him horribly and made an already angry man downright diabolical. His men are called serpents, but he is the Serpent."

"I think you've seen for yourself how I deal with snakes."

"I beg you," the bartender smashed his palms down on the bar, "we'll all suffer if you anger him. He has many followers and ..."

"Followers?"

"They are devout. Fanatical and angry."

"Aren't we all? What's their deal?"

The barkeep pursed his lips, coiling his arms back toward his body.

"It's all right," the stranger assured him. "You're safe with me."

The bartender's eyes darted back and forth, and he craned his neck back, making sure the doorway was clear. Then, he whispered lowly, saying only a single word: "Revolution."

"Revolution?" the gunslinger said.

"Shh … Don't say it loudly. They want to take the world back from the company, as punishment for their transformations."

"How many are there?"

"There's an army of them at the Serpent's fortress. They've heard his call and have been coming from all over Glycon to join in his fight."

"Hmm," the stranger stroked his chin.

"His reach is far and influence wide, he will find out about your plans. And when he finds out, he'll kill you. Or worse, he'll give you to Santa Madre as a plaything."

"Is that so?"

The bartender nodded.

"Why did they massacre Nine Mine?"

Through a wheeze, the fat man shrugged. "He's unbalanced. Anything is possible. Perhaps they refused his goods. Or simply looked at them wrong. He's irrational. But here in Stelio we try to be peaceful."

This gave the stranger pause. "Any law in this town?"

"He is on the Serpent's payroll."

"I see. And what of this 'Santa Madre'?"

"I've said too much already. They're sure to kill me."

"Fine." The gunslinger turned, heading for the door, a plan percolating in his head. "Go ahead and tell them I was going to kill you if you didn't talk. And that you know I'm coming for them."

The bartender called out to the stranger before he left the bar. "And if they ask, who shall I tell them is coming?"

But Twelve kept walking, making no reply whatsoever.

X

itting in the lee of the soaring relay tower, waiting for their protector to return, Amir did his best to keep his mind from turning back to its grief. But every time he closed his eyes, his thoughts drifted to his parents. He'd cry, then try hard to think of something else.

It was difficult to wrap a mind around the finality of death; doubly so for one so young. All he could think of it as was a never-ending blackness, but comfortable. Like sleeping through a wonderful dream and not having to wake up in the morning.

Amir pushed the thoughts of death and the unknown out of his mind and focused his worry on the others. Lila had barely spoken a word since the massacre, save the few she spent naming the dromids.

Amir's father had told him many times over his decade in existence that he'd always be fine when he'd been hurt because youngsters healed faster. "Youngsters have extra spirit in them," Amir's father would say, "and they always heal, twice as strong as before."

Amir had only heard it applied to physical maladies, but it didn't take much to assume the same held true for the heart. Lila was quiet, sure, but she'd be fine eventually. He assumed that when she was grown, after this whole ordeal was over, she wouldn't remember any of what had happened.

If Amir and Nik would only be so lucky.

Nik was the one Amir worried about most. He was over the edge, concerned for his sister to the point of heartsickness. Sitting there with a clenched jaw, the older boy was balling up fists of red soil and clumps of sparse grass, then tossing them and starting over. Amir was convinced Nik was liable to do anything. In fact, Amir was impressed that Nik hadn't screamed up into the sky, mounted the dromid they'd found, and lit off into the desert on his own.

Nik had always been impulsive like that for as long as Amir had known him. Amir had first met Nik on the shuttle to Glycon-Prime, and they'd played together then. But that was so long ago he'd barely remembered it. No, his most defining memory of Nik came years later.

They were older and had nothing better to do. Nik had gotten into an argument with his father and had convinced Amir to flee into the Glyconian desert with him and start their own city.

They were gone for all of four hours.

It was the longest either of them had been away from home on their own.

Amir took in a deep breath and wondered when the stranger would return, but his thoughts were interrupted by the sound of a clearing of a throat off to his right.

Snapping his head in the direction of the noise, Amir saw that the stranger had appeared, almost as if he'd teleported across the landscape, seated atop his mount, and weary from the travel.

"You came back." Amir scrambled to his feet.

Nik did likewise, tossing two fistfuls of dirt back to the ground on his way upright. Then, he spoke with a speed that made him barely comprehensible. "What happened out there? What happened to Miri? Do you know where they've got her?"

"They're not too far from here," the stranger said.

"And that's where they're keeping my sister?"

Amir stepped between Nik and the mounted gunman, hoping Nik wouldn't blow up. "Of course she's there. Where else would she be?"

"That's a good point, kid," the stranger nodded. "Where else would she be?"

"What's that supposed to mean?" Nik said, stepping closer to Amir, trying to move around him and get closer to the gunslinger and his dromid.

The gunslinger ignored them. Instead of answering, he walked his dromid up next to the relay tower and the other emaciated dromid, Bluey.

With a sigh he dismounted his dromid and, with his back turned to them, rifled through his saddlebags.

"Did you hear me?" Nik said. "What's that supposed to mean?"

Amir took another step over, doing his best to stay between Nik and the gunslinger. The last thing he wanted was for a fight to break out. Mainly because he knew if a fight broke out, Nik didn't have a chance in hell of winning.

The gunslinger withdrew from the saddlebags a bulging cloth, rolled up like a bedroll, but much thinner. He carried it to near where Lila sat.

"Take a seat, fellas," he ordered them.

Twelve got down on his knees, then dropped down to rest himself cross-legged in the dirt. He set the coiled cloth before him on the ground, unrolling it to reveal the contents held inside.

Lila paid little notice until the stranger picked up one of the containers and handed it to her. "Here, eat this, darlin'. It'll make you feel better."

Amir glanced over to Nik, who probably didn't even realize he was licking his lips. Relief hit him. The food would keep him distracted enough for the time being.

The boys didn't need to be told twice to eat. Amir and Nik sat down around the feast of warm food packets and processed jerky that the stranger had given them and went to work quickly, tearing the packets open with their teeth and eating the hearty contents inside with loud slurps.

Rations like these, straight from the colonizing ships, were rare and expensive. They were chock-full of all the vitamins and nutrients one needed to go long stretches without sustenance. They also contained all kinds of inoculations against the bacteria and diseases that were specific to the planet.

Glycon-Prime had a nasty bacteria that made the flus on Earth look like a mild sweat. But the food prevented it, more often than not.

Sucking the paste into his mouth from the plastic tube, Amir was convinced that there was no more delicious, rich, or hearty a substance on Glycon-Prime. He'd had the rations before, but they hadn't tasted this good.

"These must have cost you a fortune," Amir said through a mouthful of paste.

The stranger ignored Amir's observation. "I'm going to be honest with you kids," he said as he grabbed the water

74

skin and took a hefty draught, before passing it around the circle. "Things aren't looking the best they could."

Amir gulped down some more of his mush before looking up with fright in his eyes. "What does that mean?"

"It means that if they still have her, she'll be at their fortress."

Nik looked up from his tube and wiped his mouth, then spoke for the first time with a glimmer of hope in his voice. "So let's go get her then."

"It's not that easy, son," the stranger said.

"They've got her," Nik said, tightening his hands into fists and raising his voice. "Who else would? We watched 'em take her. Now we know where. What's not easy about that? It's the simplest thing in the world."

Amir recognized the tone in Nik's voice. Trouble was coming, and he was sure of it.

"This fortress isn't some unmanned outpost on a tropical beach," the stranger said. "It's a place of war, guarded by an army of snakes. Each one of 'em is armed to the teeth and just as eager to kill you as look at you."

Nik's shoulders hunched, his body admitted defeat, but clearly his spirit couldn't. "There has got to be some way."

"I didn't say there was no way to get her. I said it wasn't going to be easy."

"I'll do anything I have to." Nik clenched his jaw.

"I understand you miss your folks," the gunslinger said. "It hurts fierce, and it hurts for a long time. I promise, we'll do what we have to."

"Please, mister," Nik said through gasping tears, "please help me get my sister back. She's all I got."

"We will, son," the stranger said quietly. "We will."

Amir watched Nik and the stranger fade into quiet and Lila lick the rest of her paste from her fingers. He could feel his stomach full and satisfied, which made him wonder what Miri was doing, how she felt, and what she was eating.

He imagined they were starving Miri in a prison cell somewhere in their fortress, and he felt guilty for eating so well.

"I don't think I can eat any more," Amir said.

"What's wrong?" Lila asked him in her soft squeak of a voice.

"Nothing," Amir said. "I'm just worried about Miri."

XI

I t's almost ready," Santa Madre said. Though her words seemed innocent enough, they sounded ugly, coming through her throat like a cough.

Santa Madre's terrarium was no more comforting to Miri than the last time she'd been a forced guest there. The lights were no different than before, bright red and creating a sweltering heat, but the rest of the room had been rearranged.

The horrible old snake herself was wearing a tattered wig at a crooked angle and a dress that left the rubbery, dark skin of her arms and back exposed.

Santa Madre stood off to the left. Her back was turned to Miri, but it was obvious something was going on. The Glick stood at a counter, and Miri could hear sounds of her preparing something, clinks of metal and the banging of utensils.

"It's not hot enough yet," Santa Madre coughed. "It needs more time."

Miri tried to smell what might be cooking, but the only things she could smell were feces and sweat. Turning her neck toward the warming rock she'd first seen Santa Madre on, she could see smears on the walls around it she hadn't noticed before. Back in the corners, colored red from the lights, were stinking mounds of waste. The urine slid down, collecting in a pool in the center of the room, right under the table Miri's chair had been tucked up to.

"Almost ready, Maggie," the beastly woman said.

Miri wondered if there had been a Maggie, or if she'd been told Miri's name and Maggie had just come out. Miri didn't recall giving anyone her name, so she assumed there must have been a Maggie before, if nothing else, just in the mind of Santa Madre.

"Why am I here?" Miri struggled against the binding around her hands.

Santa Madre didn't seem to hear Miri. She simply went about her business, stirring something in front of her.

Miri could hear a bubbling sound and twisted her head around to see. She could make out a cloud of steam rising from in front of Santa Madre. She must have been boiling something.

Miri's mind raced through possibilities, but none ended pleasantly. Though Miri could feel growling pangs of hunger in her stomach and a deep, dry thirst in her throat, there was nothing Santa Madre could prepare that she'd willingly eat or drink.

"It's almost ready," Santa Madre said absently, paying no attention to her captive.

With a heavy limp in her step, she moved away from her workspace and toward a cabinet further down the wall.

In the space Santa Madre left, Miri could see indeed a sizable black pot, pouring steam through the top, churning loudly. A white froth peeked from the top of the pot, bubbling and boiling over. Finally, it crested the lip and boiling water streamed down the sides of the pot, sizzling as it hit the heat conductor surface Santa Madre had been using to cook with.

Miri's eyes darted back to Santa Madre, who'd come over to the table, clinking an armful of glass cups of various sizes, spilling them out over its surface. Some were worn and chipped, filthy too, covered in grease spots and grime. Others seemed like new, but there was nothing Santa Madre could do to force Miri to trust in their cleanliness.

"What is this?" Miri asked.

Santa Madre, who'd begun arranging the cups on the table, finally looked up. Her eyes, already black, darkened as they focused in on Miri for the first time. Through the mess of caked on lipstick and rouge, Santa Madre enunciated slowly with her gravelly voice. "It's time for tea, Maggie."

The creature that must have impossibly been human once, went back to her work, arranging the containers on the table in a circle as though other guests might be arriving for this tea party.

Smelling the rancid, burning water on the heat element, listening to it sizzle, and thinking of all the raw sewage tucked into every corner of the room, the last thing Miri wanted was to have a tea party.

"But I don't want tea," Miri finally said, meekly, searching herself for strength. She wanted the statement to feel bold and confident, but it squeaked out of her like the frightened girl she was.

Santa Madre paid Miri no mind, shuffling the cups around on the table as though the setting still wasn't quite right. She moved cups from one side of the table to the other and made sure that the dirtiest, slimiest one with the most jagged, chipped rim was placed directly in front of Miri.

"I. Don't. Want. Tea." Miri repeated. Stronger this time. Louder. With much more vehemence in her voice.

"Eh?" Santa Madre looked up, taking her greasy palms off the glass intended for Miri. "What's that?"

"I don't want tea," Miri said once more, practically shouting.

Santa Madre, shuffling her hands together in front of her, blinked at Miri.

"Is Maggie going to ..." Santa Madre coughed, mid-sentence, and licked the leaking mucous from her lips before starting over again. "Is she going to be a bad girl?"

"I ..." Before Miri could say another word, Santa Madre had closed the distance between them and had wrapped her claws around Miri's cheeks, squeezing them together.

Their faces inched closer together.

The smell of rotting flesh and sour mucous blasted into Miri's nose and mouth with every angry breath Santa Madre took. Miri could feel Santa Madre's sharp nails scratch into her skin, and all the strength she'd found for defiance withered.

Miri only hoped that the punishment for bad girls was that they wouldn't get their tea.

"You don't get to be a bad girl, Maggie." The gravel in Santa Madre's voice deepened, and she brought her face even closer to Miri's, staring into her with her black eyes. "It'ssss not allowed."

Looking into Santa Madre's eyes, Miri could see the finer detail of them and see that they weren't quite completely black, but more of a deep, dark purple. The only true black was a slit in the middles from top to bottom. At a distance, the colors would be indiscernible from each other. Rimmed around her eyelids, where lashes must have once been, was a flaky crust of white giving the area around her eyes all the outward appearance of snakeskin.

After a particularly nasty, rattling wheeze, the mutant coughed in Miri's face again, showering her with bilious spittle.

"It's time for tea," Santa Madre said. "And you have to like it, Maggie."

She let go of Miri's face and greedily snatched up the cup she'd placed in front of the poor girl. Holding it in both hands, Santa Madre turned and limped toward the boiling kettle still erupting off to Miri's left.

"It'ssss hibisssscusss," the mutant said as she dipped her hand and the cup into the bubbling hot liquid.

With the cup full, she turned toward Miri, limping back to the tea party she'd laid out. The hand she held the cup in was dripping with steaming liquid up to her wrist, and boiling tea was overflowing from the cup.

Santa Madre didn't even notice the heat.

"Open wide ..." she brought the cup closer to Miri's face.

Miri sucked in a breath and held her lips closed as tightly as she could.

"It'ssss no good, Maggie. You must be good." With her free hand, Santa Madre reached up and pinched Miri's nostrils together.

Miri panicked, the loss of breath was too much for her, and it only took a moment of resisting before her mouth popped open to take in a deep breath.

That's when Santa Madre swooped in with the steaming cup of tea, trickling boiling hot liquid into Miri's mouth.

The burn didn't come instantly.

It wasn't until Santa Madre had poured a whole mouthful of the tea that the heat and the taste hit Miri.

At first it didn't taste like anything. The temperature seemed to slowly rise until it was too much to take, and then the taste of flowers and sewage hit the burning roof of her mouth. Santa Madre finally let go of her nose, and that's when the smell got worse, and the notes of fecal matter rose to prominence.

Reflexively, she spit it all out in a spray that showered Santa Madre in the liquid, running the makeup down her rubbery face.

"You were ssssuppossssed to be good, Maggie. And you're very bad, now...."

Through the searing heat and pain on her tongue and the roof of her mouth, the only thing she could think of was how badly she wanted to escape.

But she'd need a plan first.

"It'ssss time to show you how to behave ..."

But even before a plan, she'd need to survive Santa Madre's infernal tea party.

XII

At their camp, far away from the speeder trail, the gunslinger sat at the fire created by the artificial logs, watching each of the children toss and turn, trying their best to sleep. The kids had eaten a hearty meal of rations and had each, in turn, grown silent and tired, leaving the stranger the first watch of the night.

A breeze came across the desert, cooled by the river that passed by Stelio City and snaked off to the east. To Twelve, the chilled wind felt like a good and simple pleasure, drying up the sweat on his exposed flesh.

To his left, Lila and her doll were wrapped up tight in a blanket, curled up next to the fire. Exhaustion had attacked and she had surrendered to its demands of sleep.

Across the fire, Nik tried to sleep. He'd tucked his knees up into his chest into some kind of fetal position, lying on top of his bedrolls. His eyes weren't closed; he merely stared into the fire, and his eyes darted across the flames rapidly. His mind was elsewhere, undoubtedly lost in worry for the fate of his sister.

To his right, Amir, the middle child in this new orphan family, propped his head up with his hand and elbow. With his other hand, he drew circles in the dirt. Once the circles cluttered each other out, he'd smooth the dirt over and start again. Perhaps the boy was worrying, but he'd been dealing with it better than any of the trio.

The stranger was worried enough for the lot of them. He knew what had to be done, and he knew how he needed to do it. He thought long and hard about what the fat, little barkeep told him, that this may well turn into a suicide mission.

And he could hear Zeke in his mind, echoing the sentiment. But Zeke was just a back-talking artificially intelligent jerk. What did he know?

The stranger stood, slowly, then softly spoke. Most of the gravel in his voice was gone. "Amir."

Amir turned toward him. "Yes, sir?"

"I reckon you and I will take a little trip and see what there is to see."

"Where are we going?"

The stranger kicked soil over the fire and kept his voice soft. "We're gonna go see what we're up against."

And, just as the stranger expected, Nik rose from his prostrate position, taking offense. "What? What about me? I'm going, too."

"I need you to stay here." The gunslinger adjusted the straps of his pistol belt, tightening them. He didn't need to, but it seemed easier to deflect the kid if he was doing something rather than nothing.

"What?" Nik said. "She's my sister, I should go."

"You're the eldest. You have the most responsibility, and these two are as much your responsibility as they are mine. I need you to stay here and watch over Lila. She's got to be safe, or she'll be taken just as sure as your sister was."

Nik's jaw locked, firm. "Fine. But I'll need a laser pistol."

"You don't get a laser pistol."

"You don't trust me enough to give me a gun? I've been shootin' plenty with my ..."

"No. It's not negotiable. I've been far enough in this life with a laser pistol strapped to my hip, and they've done me far more harm than good." Twelve couldn't look the boy in the eyes as he spoke, instead drifting his gaze down to his boots, shuffling more dirt over the remains of the log. "You ought to learn how to get along without one."

"But what if somebody comes out here?" Nik asked.

"No one will. Besides, you have that sword of yours. You'll do fine on your own. We're out in the middle of nowhere. When you hear me whistle in the dark, whistle back. I'll find you easy enough. You hear anybody comin' that doesn't whistle, grab Lila and get up on Bluey and head out in a hurry. If it's safe, come back in the morning."

Twelve knew the boy didn't like the idea of staying. He wouldn't have at that age either. But Twelve also knew that being given the responsibility of taking care of the younger girl, being the head of the camp, and being treated like an adult, was alluring to the boy.

"Let's go, son," the stranger said to Amir, turning from the fire and walking toward the dromids.

Amir came to Tornado and tried his hardest to climb aboard the dromid without help. The stranger bent his knees, reached out, and lifted the boy up into the saddle.

"Thank you, sir."

Grabbing the reins of the pack animal, the gunslinger led them out into the desert, heading right for the fortress on foot.

They disappeared into the night, hoping Nik could keep a cool head and just sleep the worry away. A good night of sleep was exactly what a boy with a head that hot needed. It's something they all needed, but sometimes—this time—other matters were more pressing.

The gunslinger, leading the dromid, double checked the map on Zeke's bright face and matched it against Zeke's compass.

"You're going the right way," was all Zeke said.

After walking along for a while, the nearly barren desert they'd called home gave way to a dry patch of prairie.

The change didn't surprise him.

He hadn't been on Glycon-Prime long enough to know the place as well as he would have liked, and the landscape of a terraforming planet was wont to change as frequently as the seasons.

He usually arrived on a colonizing freighter and circled the world until he was sick of it and hopped on another ship. Sometimes it would take him years before he wanted to leave, but the red dirt and mutated denizens of Glycon-Prime had him thinking about that next freighter already.

His stomach fluttered. If the boy hadn't been up on the dromid, well within earshot, he probably would have asked Zeke why he felt like turning coward and leaving a planet in such dire need of heroes.

He could already imagine what the wrist computer would say. "I don't see the logic. What would you leaving have to do with Glycon-Prime having a hero or not?"

Twelve wondered if he could get Zeke's programming changed so he was more agreeable, but then abandoned the thought. Zeke was Zeke, and as much of a pain as he could be, he was a help and a companion, no matter how bizarre that idea might have sounded. Through thick and thin, he had something ... no ... someone to talk to.

Not like the Glicks.

Maybe the atmosphere did something more to the Glicks than just alter their appearance. It seemed obvious to anyone why a person would get mean after a transformation as horrendous as the one Glicks survived. It certainly wasn't anything they'd signed up for when they'd come out to colonize. But there was something more to it. Something in the air on Glycon-Prime must have turned on their vicious gene.

That was the only way to explain the threat they were facing.

The stranger's thoughts were interrupted by Amir, who spoke in a quiet squeak. "You really think it's out here?"

"Yes," he replied softly.

"You think we'll really find Miri?"

"We'll try."

"We'll do it, mister. Sure as anything."

"I hope you're right, son."

They started up a rise in the landscape, inching their way closer to its summit. The increasing vegetation as they went, though still sparse, told the stranger they were getting closer and closer to running water. And, as they reached the top of the rise, the pair of them could see out over the valley a twinkling of lights from the Serpent's fortress, a mighty construct that dwarfed the raging waterway next to it. Huge spotlights circled back and forth around the perimeter as though it were a prison.

Ostensibly, the responsible architect had a strong predilection for industrial design embellished by spikes and sharp angles. It looked like something from a much darker world with much larger threats than Glycon-Prime had to offer.

Even at a great distance and in the dark, the stranger could make out a mounted gun on the top of the fortress wall. No one on a speeder would be able to get closer than a thousand meters of that place without getting blown to bits.

The gunslinger's voice turned to a whisper. "I think maybe it's best if we leave the dromid here, son. We'll sneak down on our own and take a look around."

Amir slid off the side of the beast and hit the soft soil below him with a thud. Dusting himself off, the small boy came around to the gunslinger's side. "What's the plan, mister?"

"We'll sneak on down there and look around for ways in and play spot-the-guard."

"Yes, sir."

Crouching low, they walked slowly down the slope, remaining as silent as they could be. In the spongy dirt of Glycon-Prime, their footsteps made little sound.

They couldn't help but marvel at the size of the fortress. As they got closer to it, its appearance only grew larger.

They covered about a hundred meters of space before the gunslinger slowed his pace and crouched down, low to the ground.

"Shh ... Get down here and don't make a sound, son."

Amir dropped into a prone position immediately.

From their vantage point, they could see shadows and movement in the windows and could make out figures walking along the top parapet wall. Glicks hovered around some of the entryways, too.

"Now, we're gonna play that game. We'll get a little closer, and we're gonna count who we see."

Amir nodded firmly, not making a sound.

The gunslinger made the count in his head and the boy on his fingers.

One and two patrolled the top, manning the giant gun if the alarm sounded and they were required to do so.

Three was a guard standing in the dark on the ground directly below the first two.

Four and five could be seen patrolling the perimeter of the second floor, walking from one window to the next, taking long looks outside each time.

Another pair stood outside the main entrance that opened out in the same direction as the river's flow.

Others were scattered about.

"How many did you count, son?"

"I've got twelve."

"Me too."

"How many do you think are in there sleeping, mister?"

"That's a good question. I'd guess at least twice that. Maybe more."

That's when Zeke finally interrupted, and for a computer he seemed close to annoyed. "I'm not sure why you didn't ask me to just scan the building."

"Well, scan it then," the gunslinger said. "Just be quiet about it."

"I have," Zeke said, lowering his volume. "And I count no less than thirty life signs, though I admit my own scanning signal is far too weak to penetrate the fortress very far."

Amir looked down at the stranger's wrist computer as though Zeke were a person with eyes to stare down. "So, you're telling us what we already knew, basically?"

"Well, I have more easily verifiable data," Zeke said.

"You're a real hero, Zeke."

"There is something else, sir," the computer said.

"Spill it."

"Well, there seems to be a massive heat spike coming

from somewhere inside the fortress. It appears to be limited to one room."

"What is it?" Amir asked.

"Unknown. It could be a reactor, a weapon, a really big heat lamp. There's no telling for sure without getting closer."

"Fine. Now shut up, and we'll take it from here," the gunslinger said, before a noise interrupted him.

A mechanical and high-pitched whine could be heard in the distance, whirring loudly. It was the unmistakable sound of a speeder engine. It came from behind them, over on the other side of the ridge.

Terrified the driver in the speeder would discover the dromid standing idly at the top of the ridge, or worse, crash into it and give away their position, the gunslinger turned his head back to see what the damage was going to be.

The noise grew louder as the vehicle sped toward the ridge, blasted over the top, and came back down the other side, racing toward the fortress. Alarm klaxons sounded from the building, and all of the spotlights trained themselves on the speeder, following it on its way in.

It was a great relief to Twelve and Amir that the speeder whizzed right by the dromid and their own position without so much as glancing in their direction. With the bright spotlights from the fortress focused tightly on the speeder, it was no wonder the driver couldn't see anything of consequence out in the dark.

Twelve glanced up and down the building, hoping to see how the guards reacted to new arrivals, and could see the two guards up on the roof, mounting themselves on the big gun, aiming it in the direction of the oncoming speeder.

The speeder itself was a newer model, curves all the way around. In the bright spotlights, the speeder appeared to be colored a military green along the top, trimmed in a gunmetal gray. Sitting in the cockpit were a pair of the biggest, ugliest, meanest-looking Glicks the stranger had ever seen.

Attached to the sled of the speeder were huge square crates of material. The gunslinger assumed it was a shipment of ammunition, power cells, or whatever other explosives the Glicks would be collecting in their war against the provisional corporate government of Glycon-Prime. On the other hand, it could have been something as innocuous as rations. Either way, it was being used to fuel this rebellion.

The speeder got close enough to the fortress that a wall on the broadside opened up to allow the speeder entrance. With the doors opening, it gave Amir and the stranger a perfect opportunity to see inside.

Their eyes widened at the sight.

"This might be a little harder than I thought, son."

XIII

Nik sat in the dark with his back against the metal box of the tower's base. Over the hours Amir and the stranger had been gone, the night had only grown colder and lonelier.

The only sound that accompanied his otherwise silent vigil was the gentle snoring sounds coming from Lila, and the creaking sounds of Glyconian insects in the distance.

Twice since they'd been gone did he think he could hear footsteps approaching the camp, but in both cases it had turned out to be nothing more than the underweight dromid, Bluey, shifting its weight in the sand.

He'd been told the insects made a sound a lot like the grasshoppers on Earth did, but these were of a much lower pitch and slower in speed. His mother told him it was much more eerie than the crickets she'd been used to, and to illustrate the point, she'd pulled up an audio file of the sound on her computer console comparing crickets. The Earth crickets that neither of them had heard in person sounded very much like a sweet song you could fall gently asleep to. The crickets of his mother's youth croaked, grimly, but not unpleasantly. The Glyconian crickets, the same that were out in force while Nik stood silent guard over Lila in the desert, sounded much more like the ominous soundtrack to a murder.

The deeper and more homicidally melodic the sound of the insects grew, the tighter Nik clutched the hilt of his familial sword. He stared down at his hand gripping the Bedouin heirloom, wondering when his hand had grown so angular and old looking. A pair of veins he'd never noticed before ran over the top of his hand, and he thought for the first time he was turning into an actual adult.

The idea of being grown up filled him with the dread of responsibility.

In front of him, in the sand, he'd drawn Miri's name with his finger. Over and over and over again. Whether he liked it or not, he was responsible for her, and it was eating away at him. Nik wondered if anyone were ever truly ready to become a man, then he remembered the answer in something his father had once said. Their neighbors had just found out they were going to have a baby, and the would-be father had said over and over again that he wasn't ready for the responsibility.

"No one ever is," Nik's father had told the young man. "If we wait until we're ready for anything, we never will be. But once a thing happens, we rise to meet that challenge. I didn't feel ready to have children when my wife first told me she was pregnant. I didn't think I was responsible enough. But because she was pregnant, I decided I'd put aside my anxiety and do my best. Now I have two wonderful children that I wouldn't trade the galaxy for."

His father's words echoed in Nik's head. When he'd heard it said, Nik had never thought he'd find relevance in those words at all, let alone so soon. Sure, he wasn't having a child, but he was dealing with the unexpected, unsure of himself and his capabilities, but doing his best to rise to that challenge.

Thinking about his father and hearing his voice play in his head soothed the boy. As painful as it was, it felt good to remember.

Nik couldn't tell which pain was more severe, the ache in his heart for his lost loved ones, or the healing wound on his arm. One was corporeal, the other emotional, but both had the power to hurt.

Reaching across his body, he undressed the burn on his shoulder to look at it, but he couldn't see much. The paste Twelve had given him had taken away the sting, now it was more of a dull ache. The flesh had faded from a bright red to a tender pink, slimy from the remnants of the medicine and sweat from the bandage. Nik poked at the mottled skin, expecting to wince with pain, but the hurt was manageable.

Twelve's medicine was working well.

Nik slathered on a new layer and tied a cloth back over it, hoping to forget about it.

Whiling away his time trying to stay awake, the boy stared up at the stars and constellations. Twice, he saw meteors streak across the night sky.

He'd never seen the stars and the twin moons so bright and clear. Even in the small town of Nine Mine City, the lights of the community drowned out much of the sky's brilliance. From cities, skies always seemed at their darkest and most unforgiving. Nik supposed that was true of any city on any world, then wished his family had moved to any other city than the one they'd chosen.

To distract himself, he spent what felt like hours giving random star patterns names, connecting the dots into new combinations of constellations.

It wasn't more than an hour or two before he nodded off for the first time, and when he awoke suddenly, he had no way of knowing how long he'd been out.

It must have been quite a while because the smaller of Glycon-Prime's two moons was two-thirds of the way across its arc in the sky, and the larger moon found itself straight across the horizon, setting low against the landscape.

"They should be back by now," he told himself over the dim symphony of insectoid chirps, doing an excellent job of suppressing the jolt of panic he felt when he woke.

Standing up, Nik stretched his legs and took a lap around the encampment. Perhaps he could catch the glint of twin moonlight on his approaching comrades.

If only he knew which direction was which and which direction they'd eventually be coming from.

Since the camp was in at the bottom of a rise on two sides, he could see no light from the speeder trail. They were sloped far enough away that he couldn't even see the milky haze of light above Stelio City. Since he'd failed every lesson at telling time or direction by the lunar orbits, he was unnervingly lost.

The sound of the Glyconian crickets, the dim of the night, and the black of landscape made him feel very small, turning and turning about, wondering what it was he was supposed to do.

"*Ebn El Qah'ba,*" he said out loud. "Where are they?"

Swearing in the family tongue started a reaction in Nik that sent his head swimming. The disorientation he'd already experienced only compounded the phantom feeling that he might be getting in trouble for using such language.

No one was around to hear his transgression. Lila was safely asleep and even if she could tattle, who would she tell?

The gunslinger? Nik's parents wouldn't storm into the camp and slap him across the mouth.

Even something he'd learned to dread, that sting of his cheek, was something you could miss.

Swallowing the emotions, he took a deep breath and did his best to balance himself. He could get through this, surely. A small voice inside him told him the worst was coming, though. It would hit him, like a speeder crashing into the side of a building, exploding in flames.

"Please," he said quietly to Amir and Twelve, knowing they were nowhere within earshot. "Please, come back. Don't make me come out there after you."

His bravado was real.

Resolving then and there to find them if they didn't return by morning, he knew he'd have to storm the fortress by himself, sword in hand, if that's what it took.

But what about Lila? The quiet voice in the back of his head asked him.

A whistling sound in the distance allowed him to put off that decision for at least a while yet. Relief washed over him, easing his shoulders and relaxing the tension in him.

He whistled back, too gently though.

The night whistled at him once more.

Louder this time, with more force, he passed the breath between his pursed lips and let out a warbling shriek.

They had to have heard that.

Turning back to the little girl, Nik covered up Lila with another blanket, protecting her from the cold, hoping to over-accentuate the good job he'd done protecting her in the absence of his comrades.

Nik tried hard to contain his curiosity, biting his bottom lip to keep himself from speaking until they gave their report. He had nothing to say, and they'd seen where they were holding Miri.

They finally appeared, stepping out of the curtain of blackness. The hoofbeats of their dromid served as a percussion section for the crickets' strings. Silently, in his typical fashion, the gunslinger led Tornado, Amir riding still, to the other dromid across the encampment.

Amir, exhausted, practically fell off his mount, then grabbed a sleeping roll and went directly to lie down.

The gunslinger used the charge pack in his laser pistol to restart the fire that had been put out before they departed on their mission.

And still, no one spoke.

The pain in Nik's lip rose, the longer the stranger went without speaking, the harder Nik bit.

Frustration forced him to bite even harder. How could they keep their mouths shut for so long? How could they keep him waiting in suspense?

He watched as the man called Twelve settled in around the fire, warming his hands as though there wasn't a thing wrong in the world and nothing was at stake.

Finally, Nik had bitten down so hard that he'd pierced the skin in his lip. He could taste it hot on his tongue when he finally broke the silence. "Well?"

"Well, what?"

"Well? What's going on?"

"I think we can manage," the gunslinger said after a long, thoughtful pause. "It won't be easy, but maybe we'll manage."

"What did the fortress look like?"

"Big and nasty, like you'd expect a place like that to look. Definitely not inviting. Lots of guns. Lots of men. Lots of armed speeders—"

"—a tank." Amir jumped in.

"A tank," the stranger concurred.

Amir tried to bring hope back to the conversation. "But I think we can do it. I could think of a hundred ways we could get closer. We can do it, can't we, mister?"

The gunslinger's eyes darted about, as though he were going over all the variables in his head and making rough calculations. "It's possible."

"I think our chances would be better if we all had guns," Nik blurted.

"No," the stranger said firmly. "Killing a man isn't always the answer. We're outgunned as sure as anything. We'll have to outthink 'em." He stopped, then pointed to Lila, fast asleep. "And really, how much good you think it would do to put a gun in that little girl's hands?"

"Killing 'em would be answer enough for me," Nik said.

"Revenge isn't noble. I can guarantee your parents wouldn't want blood on your hands on account of them."

"It's not on account of them. It's on account of Miri. At least I've got you three. Miri's in there alone. And they're doin' who knows what to her. Killing them is definitely answer enough for that."

Amir piped in; the sound of his high voice grated at Nik. "We've been talking about it, Nik. Haven't we, mister? We've got a great plan and it's just ... it's pretty clever. I think every-thing'll turn out just fine."

"The boy's right. I've got a plan. Now get some rest, and first thing in the morning we'll break that place wide open."

Whatever Nik wanted to do, he knew he'd have to wait till morning. He still couldn't figure out what direction was up or down, let alone which direction to head in order to charge the fortress on his lonesome.

Begrudgingly, he surrendered. "Fine."

"Get to sleep, now," the man said.

And that's what they all did.

But Nik's sleep was fitful, and he had a powerful dream that would stick with him for the rest of his days.

In his sleep, he found himself in his idea of the fortress, down in the cellar.

Vermin crawled along the nooks and crannies, and there was a thick, mildewy moisture in the air. "Dank" wasn't strong enough a word to describe it.

Though he didn't know how, he just knew that he was in the Serpent's sprawling complex, deep below it. A dungeon. Sounds of a distant torture being conducted echoed throughout the great stone walls. It was a combination of screaming and delighted laughter.

Someone out there was enjoying the harm they were inflicting.

Finally, he came to a thick metal door with a small window above the level of his head. Bars covered the opening. A slot at the foot was there, presumably to slide just enough protein slop through to keep prisoners alive long enough to torture them even more.

Though he wasn't sure how he got there, he found himself on the inside of the dungeon's cell.

His sister's cell.

Miri's cell.

That's where he was.

She was there. Alive. Calling out for help, but he couldn't touch her. Tears had cleaned tracks through the dirt caked onto her face.

Her dress was torn and tattered, smeared with more of the same red dirt that was ubiquitous across the planet.

"Please, Nik," Miri whispered. "Please help me. Don't let

her near me. She's awful and crazy and I'm sure she'll kill me. Allah, Nik, anyone, please just help me."

His heart broke, shattering into a million pieces that he could see spilling out onto the floor in front of him. Watching the beads of heart-shaped glass tumble along the ground, he could feel himself shifting into a more ethereal form.

Reaching out to his sister, Nik tried to touch even just her fingertips, just to let her feel comforted. But he was no longer real and had no physical form. He was a stray, conscious vapor watching this all unfold in his dreams.

As transparent and translucent as he was, he could feel the tears come down his own face.

"Miri," he called out, but she couldn't hear him, either. They were so close to each other but so wholly separate.

That's when the door opened, and a white bar of light shone itself on Miri's frightened body.

She spoke lowly, her voice cracking in pain and anguish. "No … Please don't. Not again. Not with her … Don't hurt me! Not with her!"

The silhouetted outline of a burly Glick filled the door-way. Terror washed over Miri's face, the tears washing away even more of the dirt. "Please. Not again. Not again!"

That's when the dream ended.

And he knew for certain, for the first time since she'd been taken, that she was alive.

Deep down, he just knew it.

She was alive.

And the plan had to work.

PART II
THE PLAN

XIV

J ack Peters had been reluctantly elected sheriff of Stelio City three months prior and had since learned to enjoy the benefits of his office. When he got drafted for the job, he hadn't realized there would be so many.

His desk was cherry wood, not the fake varnished simulated wood you often found on a frontier world. This was a hunk of heavy wood flown halfway across the universe at an incredible cost.

Sitting at his lavish desk, Sheriff Peters whiled away his time cleaning and oiling all the moving parts of his vintage six-shot ray blaster. Those were even more rare than real wooden desks.

He was a satisfied man, though. His family was safe and well provided for, and, for the most part, his cooperation meant that the people of Stelio City were safe. It was his job to ensure they were all protected, by any means necessary. That was the oath he took when he accepted his office, and it's what he spent every day doing.

And the people of Stelio City had little to worry about these days.

Sure, there was that spot of trouble out at the bar, but that didn't have to do with any of the citizens of Stelio. As far as the sheriff was concerned, it didn't have anything to do with him. He stayed out of the business of Guerrero and his men, whether they were on the giving end or the receiving end. And the last thing he wanted to do was round up a posse to hunt down a laser gun fighter that didn't seem to be a threat to anybody in Stelio.

Sticking your neck out sounded to him like a good way to get killed.

He did his part, letting the Serpent know what happened. And unless Guerrero put him on the payroll with hazard pay, what else could he be expected to do about it?

Peters had no love for Glicks, but the more he had to deal with the Serpent personally, the more he understood their position. Or at least he understood the influence their money paid for.

He told himself over and over again that he'd do whatever he needed to in order to make sure the people of Stelio were safe. It was like a meditative mantra.

And that's when the buzz of his door alarm sounded.

"Keep your cover on. I'm coming," he grumbled.

With deft hands, he clicked the parts of his disassembled ray blaster back together. Once it was whole again, he tucked the weapon into the shoulder holster under his left arm, where the vintage handle could stick out, showing it off for all to see.

The door alarm buzzed again, and he could hear the soft knocking of hands on the outer metal door of the sheriff's office.

Putting on his best smile like a disguise, he clicked the button to engage the motors in the door. It whirred open, splitting from the center in two equal, vertical halves. There, behind the door, were two small children that he'd never seen before in his life. They were caked in the red dirt of the world, filthy in every way. Dark circles under their puffy red eyes punctuated their exhaustion.

There was an odor about them, too, but it wasn't the stink of the desert that bothered him. It was trouble Peters smelled.

"What can I help you boys with?"

The younger boy pointed at himself, then to his close-to-teenage friend. "My name is Amir. This here is Nik."

"Well, it's good to meet you, Amir and Nik. I'm Sheriff Peters. What kind of problem is it you boys are having?"

The younger boy spoke with the matter-of-fact air that only a child could produce. "Well, sir, we witnessed some murders."

The older then added, nervously, "And we need to report a stolen person."

"A murder and a stolen person? You boys have been busy," Peters said. Skeptical anxiety grew over the sheriff like a cloud. "Why don't you guys take me out to where this murder happened, and on our way you can tell me all about this stolen person."

The boys turned and led him around the front of the steel box of a building. Tied there was a gaunt, battered dromid that may as well have been at death's door. How it ever bore one or both of those kids was a mystery to the sheriff. The poor creature didn't flinch when the older boy clasped his hands together, giving the younger boy a boost up to a riding position.

The sheriff stopped them before they could take this any further. "Wait a second there. What're you jumpin' up on that dromid for? You can throw a rock from one side of this city to the other. No need for a dromid."

The younger boy looked back to the sheriff and widened his eyes so they caught the light in their wetness. "Because, sir, the killin' happened over in Nine Mine City."

"Now hold on a minute there, boys." Peters backed away from them. "You've got yourselves a sheriff out there, so why in the world would you come all the way out here to report it? Is this some kind of joke?"

The younger boy's eyes widened, and his voice became earnest. "Oh, this is no joke, sir. No joke at all."

"That's right." The older boy puffed his chest up. "We didn't report it to our sheriff because he's dead, too."

That statement shot a shiver of fear down the sheriff's middle. He could only assume the sheriff of Nine Mine City had also operated under the protection of the Serpent, and even with that protection, he'd still been killed. "If the law was killed, why didn't your folks come on down? They wouldn't send kids; this must just be for a laugh."

"Our folks didn't send us, and they couldn't come, neither," the older boy said.

"They were killed, too, Sheriff," the younger boy added.

A hundred possibilities ran through the sheriff's mind, and he assumed this could be some sort of test. "Did Guerrero send you boys?"

The older boy grabbed the reins of the dromid and hopped up onto the beast, right behind the other boy. Then his voice grew cold. "Guerrero the Serpent? No, sir."

The younger boy maintained his matter-of-fact attitude. "He's the one guilty of the murders and the kidnapping."

"We came to have you arrest him," the older boy said.

"And who was it that was allegedly taken?" Peters said, anxiety rising within him.

"It was my big sister," the older boy said with a venom in his voice. "And we aim to get her back. Now do you want to get in your speeder and follow us out to their fortress so we can get her back, or not?"

"Whoa. Whoa. Just hang on a tic. You boys have been grossly misinformed." The sheriff took a few cautious steps toward the boys with his hands raised in open palms. He added in all the oily and slick bravado of a lying politician, hanging on to every one of his syllables. "You two just don't get it. You see, Josef Guerrero might be a Glick, but he's one of the finest and most upstanding citizens on this entire planet. And I can give you my personal guarantee that he's not responsible in any way for any wrongdoing whatsoever."

The young boy smiled. "You're a liar, sir."

"He's got you in his pocket, doesn't he? You're as crooked as he is." The older boy spit at the sheriff's feet.

That left the sheriff's mouth agape. Never in his life had he been talked to with such disrespect, let alone by children.

Peters could feel the fire in his eyes burn with the rising redness in his face. He half expected steam to come shooting out of his ears and his hat to blow off.

"Now, you two get down off of that damn dromid right now," the sheriff growled. "I'm hauling the both of you in for slandering two fine and upstanding citizens of Glycon-Prime."

"Go ahead and try," the older boy said, lilting his words with attitude. Then he clicked through his teeth and jabbed his heels into the mount. "Git, Bluey. Let's go."

Despite its size, and the weight of the boys crushing

down on it, the dromid was much more fleet of foot than the sheriff would have guessed. Carrying them at its top speed, it was easily too fast for the sheriff to pursue on foot.

"Damn it," he said, breathlessly.

Those boys were going to cause him a mess of trouble.

XV

At dusk, the streets of Stelio City were deserted. Sheriff Peters, fearing something bad on the horizon, thought to quell any potential harm to himself or his constituents by calling for a general curfew. Of course the owner of the saloon objected, but once the sheriff explained what had happened in Nine Mine City, the saloonkeeper was all too happy to oblige.

The only light on the street, however, came from the saloon. Just because there was a curfew on the street didn't mean people couldn't enjoy the beverages, games, or the company of the saloonkeeper's women throughout the night.

Personally patrolling the streets, Peters kept his eyes and ears open. He imagined himself as a winged predator, ready to swoop in on any wrongdoers, snatch them up in his talons, and crack them open with his strong beak.

He was dying to see those kids come back so he could lock them up and turn them over to the corporate government. At least that way they'd be out of his hair and probably sent to another world to work off their childhood in a foster home.

He heard the planet Minos was looking for colonists now. Maybe they'd end up out there. That wouldn't be such a bad life for a kid. And maybe the mutants out there wouldn't be as harsh.

Peters didn't relish hurting kids and didn't want to, he just wanted them gone. He wanted them long gone before the Serpent found out about them, because if he caught wind of all this, he'd certainly want them taken up there to his fortress and killed. Brutally, most likely.

Or handed over to Santa Madre.

Peters shuddered.

He wouldn't wish that fate on anyone. He'd seen the body of the last little girl they'd brought up there. It was a shame what happened to Guerrero's mother, but in the sheriff's mind that was no excuse, no excuse whatsoever.

Sheriff Peters didn't want the blood of these kids on his hands either, but if there had to be a choice, he'd clearly choose what was best for himself and for the people of Stelio City.

And if Guerrero's grand plan worked out, and there wasn't going to be a corporate government anymore, Peters would have to get this situation sorted fast if he was going to get these kids away from here.

As he walked up the speeder trail running through the center of town, he marveled at how far this city had come since he'd been elected sheriff. In six months, it had grown from four buildings to thirty. That he could keep the Glicks from Guerrero's gang in line and behaving meant they could spend the money the Serpent paid them in town.

It was quite a boom.

Towns on frontier planets were make or break, and the

decisions Peters had made regarding the Glicks were what put Stelio on the map and kept it there.

Walking by the general store, Sheriff Peters was happy to see the proprietor pop his head out of the window. "Howdy, Sheriff."

Peters tipped his hat. "Emmet."

"Everything all right?"

"Everything's fine," Peters lied. "How's things at the store?"

"They'd be better without this curfew." Emmet wrung his hands together.

"I understand how you feel, but believe you me, it's a necessary precaution."

"What's all the hubbub about?"

"Just some rabble-rousers blowing through town, causing trouble. I want to keep you all safe. And if they blow back through town on the curfew, it gives me a reason to hold 'em."

"I see."

"Well, I'll be along." The sheriff tipped his hat once more. "Have a good evening, Emmet."

"Let me know how it goes."

"Will do."

Emmet closed his shop door back up, locking it tight as the sheriff walked on to continue his rounds of the main street.

Peters took a deep breath of the dirty air, imagining what Glycon-Prime would be like in a decade when the terraforming was complete. It would almost certainly be much more lush. The tree saplings that had been planted at regular intervals down the center street would be reaching higher to the sky and twice as thick. The sky itself would be a more comfortable and soft blue during the day. The planet would become more a luxuriant paradise and less of a florid dust bowl.

It was only a matter of time.

The sheriff checked the chronometer on his wrist. The hour was late. "Hm. Maybe those boys won't be coming back tonight after all...."

Realizing he could be just as ready for them from his office, more so than the street, he picked up his pace, walking double time to the jail.

Opening the door, he looked around one last time at the speeder trail.

The coast was clear.

No signs of trouble.

No one on the road.

No one outside.

Nothing on the horizon.

Maybe I'm worrying myself for nothing, he thought.

The sheriff took a step inside, and the door slid shut behind him. He wiped his brow, removed his hat all in one motion, and put the hat up on a hook next to the door.

Stress coursed through his veins, ending in a deep throb in his temple. Wishing to ease the growing headache, he sat down in the contour-fitting chair behind his desk, kicked his feet up, and took a long, deep breath.

His eyes drooped, though he fought to keep them open. Another few deep breaths and his mind drifted to thoughts of a nice, warm bed.

A loud snore woke him, jolting him back awake.

Peters convinced himself those boys were long gone and he could go back to sleep. Why would they stick around when they knew their lives were in danger? It would be ridiculous. But, then again, they were kids. And never in the history of human beings had kids ever been the most sensible creatures.

Another deep breath, lost in thought, and Peters nodded off to slumber. Things were black and then suddenly he was lying out in the sun on a grassy hill. The grass was a soft bed beneath him.

Moments to relax on the frontier were few.

He could almost see a kite floating high in the sky, carrying him up and over the horizon.

Clouds rolled in, slowly at first then faster and faster, black as night. Three successive bolts of lightning crashed into loud all-consuming blasts of thunder.

Something was wrong; he was frightened and wet from the rain. His body tingled with electricity, and he knew that more thunder and lightning was coming.

Jolted by a bolt of electricity that arced through his entire body, killing him, he snapped awake once more from his nap.

"Huh?"

Looking around, all he could see was the empty office. Beyond that, the empty jailhouse echoed with quiet.

What he mistook for thunder was actually a firm, repetitive pounding on the door that led outside.

"Who is that?" he shouted.

But there was no answer.

Hopping to his feet, Sheriff Peters dashed to the door and pressed the button to open it. The halves of the door split open, showing him the street and buildings across the metal sea of speeder trail. Sticking his head out of the entryway, Sheriff Peters snapped his head back and forth, searching for the culprit.

The street was vacant, and the only sounds were the droning buzz of the atmospheric reprocessors in the

distance, matched with the low, pulsing music of the indigenous insects.

Lying there in front of him, resting at his feet, was a sheet
of flimsy stone paper; its edges fluttering around the rock
that held it down.

Sheriff Peters bent over, picking up the rock with one
hand and the note with the other. Examining the rock for
any significance and seeing it had none, he tossed it aside
then turned to the note, reading it.

Then he read it again.

Crumpling it in his hands, he boiled with worry and
anger.

There wasn't going to be any peaceful solution to this
situation that he'd be pleased with. And these kids certainly
weren't going to take no for an answer.

Guerrero would have to hear about this.

Peters simply didn't have a choice. It was time to fire up
the speeder.

The lush interior upholstery of the sheriff's speeder was
vintage cowhide from Earth proper, and it was just another
reminder of his patronage to the Serpent. As he fired up his
speeder, the electric turbine engine barely made a sound as it
turned over initially, but then whirred to speed after a
moment. It was housed in a massive cylindrical compartment
at the rear of the conveyance that gave it the lift that let it travel
across the speeder trails, desert sand, water, or anything else.

Like a rocket, Peters was off to warn Guerrero, sweating
profusely the entire time.

The look of the fortress was cause enough for alarm. It
was menacing, even from a distance, reminding Peters of
some Gothic abattoir. To Peters, there was nothing worse
than approaching the fortress at night, not knowing if you'd

accidentally be identified as a threat and blown out of the sky.

It had happened before.

That was a hell of a mess for the sheriff to fix, because, of course, the Serpent had forced him to take charge of the cleanup operation. It was stressful and frustrating, but the more frustrated the sheriff became, the more he settled into his leather upholstery, comfortable in the plush seat of his office.

He'd shut up and do his job, hoping he didn't draw the ire of Guerrero with this visit. He wasn't always the most calm and rational man, but that's just the way Glicks were. But he was a rich, angry Glick, which is what made him all the more dangerous.

And at this time of night ... with bad news ...

Sheriff Peters's stomach tied itself into a knot of indigestion and dread.

As Peter's speeder approached the fortress, the massive doors in the side of the stronghold opened up expectantly, granting the lawman passage. Getting into Guerrero's inner sanctum would be another trick altogether.

Peters parked his speeder in line with the others in the expansive warehouse area. All of the speeders in Guerrero's speeder pool were equipped with heavy weaponry.

And there, in the back corner, was actually a tank. It was old, at least twenty years, a relic from the uprising on Orion. It was stolen company property and had almost certainly been used to put down the very sort of uprising Guerrero was hoping to incite.

The thought of all the killing to come added another thick knot to the sheriff's stomach.

That was his best reason to keep the Serpent happy. It

would be the only way to keep the people of Stelio City safe during the coming coup.

Guerrero's pending revolution might have been the worst kept secret in that whole quadrant of Glycon-Prime. It was hard not to notice the influx of Glicks coming from all over the region, assembling at the fortress, enlisting in the Serpent's private army. It was even harder to ignore the delivery of things like that old Orion tank.

Even Peters had been forced to play the game, caching all sheds full of ammunition in Stelio. That's probably what this hubbub in Nine Mine City was all about, they wouldn't play by the Serpent's rules.

Leaping out of his speeder, Sheriff Peters went straight for the staircase that would take him up to the second level of the fortress and get him that much closer to giving Guerrero the bad news. Blocking the way up, however, was a Glick, moist with the heat, making him look more like an oiled snake than a man.

The sheriff tried to walk around him, but it was no good.

"Stop there." This guard seemed to have embraced the stereotype that Glicks were snakes. His voice dripped with venom, and he hung on to every *ess* sound in his vocabulary. "Where is it you think you're going, lawman?"

"I've got an urgent message for your boss."

Folding his arms, the Glick looked the sheriff up and down. "Why don't you give me the message, and I'll deliver it for you."

"You can if you want. But it's bad news."

That was enough to back him down. No one wanted to deliver bad news to the Serpent. Guerrero must have never heard that old yarn about not shooting the messenger.

The guard stepped aside without another word, allowing the sheriff to walk up the stairs and turn the corner.

As Peters rounded the corner, a blast of warmth hit the sheriff, almost as though he were baking in an oven. The wave of heat grew warmer as he walked through the corridor and by the metal door the heat radiated from.

Sheriff Peters shivered in the heat.

He knew what lurked inside. The sheriff supposed he could understand why Guerrero would want to keep her close to him, but keeping her in the room right next to his own office was too much. Passing through the increased temperature in the hallway served as a reminder of how uncomfortable things could be in Guerrero's company.

Peters remembered back to the first time he'd been escorted into Guerrero's office, marched in with an armed escort. At least now he was trusted enough to not need the escort. But when he had arrived, Guerrero was staring solemnly through the one-way mirror that connected his office to the sanctum of Santa Madre.

The sheriff had been shoved deeper into the room and closer to the glass, where he could see Santa Madre twisting the neck of a young girl no older than five or six. The young girl had been filthy and crying, and it seemed as though Santa Madre could no longer stand the screaming.

When it stopped, Guerrero had said simply, without turning to look at the sheriff, "Pity. It looks as if we'll have to find something else to keep *mi madre's* time occupied."

Peters put the thought out of his head and barreled through the corridor, shutting his ears off to whatever screams might be emanating from Santa Madre's quarters.

Beyond that, Peters came to an old-fashioned and impossibly expensive oak door that led into Guerrero's office. He rapped gently on the door, but the feel of the genuine hard wood under his knuckles felt unnatural. He was used to the cold clink of steel on anything but his desk.

A strong but sinister voice answered from the other side. "Enter."

The sheriff opened the door with trepidation, taking in the surroundings as they were revealed to him. The room had been rearranged since his last visit, most likely to accommodate Guerrero's acquisitions. The wall on the right side was covered with brilliant red-velvet drapes that seemed to glow in the soft light of the room. Peters let out a breath of relief. The curtains, if drawn, would offer a view of Santa Madre and her vile existence, and that was the last thing the sheriff wanted to see.

He was nervous enough as it was.

The rest of the walls in Guerrero's office were covered over in wood paneling. Mounted on the walls every few feet was a relic from the history of Earth proper.

A fish mounted on a block of wood was next to a belt used by one of the astronauts in the first Martian explorations a thousand years prior. Next to that rested a chunk of driftwood from the shores of some dried-up Earth river or another. Each piece of Earth memorabilia grew successively more lavish, all the way around the room.

Peters could only assume it was Guerrero's bid to cling to what little shred of his humanity that he could.

The carpet was thick and lush and a dream to walk on.

A desk occupied the center of the room. It was massive, putting the sheriff's own to shame, and of a glossy mahogany that must have cost a fortune to ship across the galaxy.

It made Peters wonder how Guerrero made his money, and how he continued making money, that he could afford all of these reminders of a planet he'd probably never seen.

The room was deep, and far behind the desk was a pair of

wicker chairs with their backs to the door, facing a stone fire-place. Seated in one of those chairs was the Serpent.

The sheriff never got used to how small a man Guerrero was. Over his short stature and gaunt frame hung a fine white suit that offset the dark, vulcanized skin he'd grown.

Perhaps in an attempt to appear both civilized and impossibly rich, Guerrero sipped booze from a crystal tumbler and was reading an ancient leather-bound book. Peters had never actually seen one in person. Books to him were read on a screen.

Guerrero let out a low hiss, disgusted already. Though his voice never reached a volume higher than quiet, his words were soaked in an angry arrogance that couldn't be faked. "And so, Sheriff Peters from Stelio City, what is it that is so important that you feel the need to be honored with my presence?"

The Serpent clapped the book shut and laid it down on the end table next to his chair, along with the booze.

Sheriff Peters fished out the single sheet of flimsy, stone-ground paper from his pocket and accentuated his words with it. "I got this note. You really need to know about it."

"I can't imagine anything in that note that would warrant disturbing me, Peters. Surely you could have simply sent a message digitally. Besides, I pay you much more than you're worth to deal with these problems for me, should they arise."

Peters wasn't offered a chair, so he remained standing, still mostly to Guerrero's back.

"Well, it's these kids," Peters stammered. "They're just kids. Your people didn't finish the job in Nine Mine City. They've been hanging around my town, asking questions, and ..."

"What is your point, Sheriff?"

"What?"

"The point. Come to the point. I grow tired of your prattle. Get to the point or get out. What is it the note says?" Guerrero asked imperiously.

"They want to meet you down on the road a couple of kilometers south of Nine Mine at noon tomorrow. They want to talk about what happened."

Guerrero laughed, which made Peters uneasy. There was nothing pleasant about the sick laugh of a madman.

"You need not have wasted my time. Since you have proved yourself so incapable of handling something so simple and ridiculous, I'll dispatch a pair of my own men to ensure there are no longer any survivors from Nine Mine City."

Peters hung his head.

"And Sheriff, I would suggest you not return unless you have something truly important to tell me. Trust me when I say your life depends on it."

As if to add an exclamation point to the Serpent's sentiment, the scream of a young girl could be heard, muted by the thick one-way mirror and unseen through the red curtain.

Naturally, the sheriff's head snapped to the direction of the sound and every proud thought of being a fair and just dispenser of the law and protector of the weak shrunk within him.

He could hear the screams as he backed out of the Serpent's office, and he could hear them all the way back down the hall and on the way to his speeder. Even on the road, heading back to Stelio City, he could hear them, burned forever into his memory.

XVI

The first Skinner had ever heard of the Serpent's army was in a hushed tone at a bar on the other side of the planet. Having been brutally mutated by the planet and having had his family turn on him, Skinner decided he should join up and do something meaningful with his suddenly meaningless life. And to get payback for his mutation, just like the rest of the Serpent's army.

That was months ago. New Glicks arrived every day from all over the planet, eager to join up for a cause, eager to be accepted by a group just like them, and eager to get revenge. Each of them had a different set of skills they brought from their lives before they were Glicks to add to the cause.

For his part, Skinner had been a brewer. But every Glick in the Serpent's army was expected to take arms and take orders from their stoic leader.

Now, Skinner sat shotgun in a speeder from Guerrero's fleet, flying across the sparse Glyconian landscape in the noonday heat, tasked with killing a pair of kids.

It wasn't exactly what he'd signed up for, but if this was a means to an end, Skinner wasn't going to argue. No one liked a man who balked at an assigned duty.

In the driver's seat of the speeder was a fellow named Sanchez who had been with Guerrero since before they'd arrived on Glycon-Prime and before any of them had turned Glick, before any of them had even known what a Glick was. Sanchez wore a tinted shield that wrapped around his head and eyes to cut out the sun and wagged his tongue out the slit of his mouth.

"Step on it, would you?" Skinner said. "Let's get this done and over with as fast as we can."

Sanchez said nothing, but grunted lowly and increased their speed, gluing Skinner to his chair.

Soon enough, at the top of the hill, two dots appeared on the side of the road, just where they said they'd be. Speeding up the rise, Skinner could make out more and more detail of the boys the closer they got. Behind them stood their timid dromid, looking around nervously. The taller boy held his hand over his eyes like a visor, squinting to see them.

The boys themselves were a sight to see. Their skin was milky brown, their hair was dark and their clothes billowing, like most of the Arabian settlers from Nine Mine City.

But they were young.

Much younger than Skinner had expected. When he'd thought of "kids" he'd assumed they would find teenagers on the edge of adulthood out for vengeance, not actual children.

But it didn't make a difference.

Skinner knew what they had to do, and they would do it.

The speeder slowed rapidly under Sanchez's control, stopping expertly in front of the boys in a cloud of dust.

The younger of the two boys, no older than eight or ten,

inhaled a breath-full of dust and coughed before asking, "One of you two Josef Guerrero?"

Skinner turned to Sanchez to see the same surprised look on his face. Their half-grins at the misunderstanding led to a deep burst of laughter that came from the bottom of their bellies.

"What's so funny?" the older boy asked them as he pulled the reins on his dromid to calm the unsettled creature.

Skinner took a breath, ready to answer, but before he could say anything was interrupted by the echoing ping of a laser bolt. Startled, he looked to his left to see that Sanchez's laughing had ceased; where his face had been was replaced by a smoking maw of blaster-burned flesh.

Confusion took him. Neither of the young boys had pistols at all, let alone any leveled at him. Working to unravel the mystery of the laser bolt's direction, Skinner reached across his chest for the laser pistol holstered neatly under his left arm but was stopped by the sound of a blaster bolt followed by the sizzle and smell of frying flesh.

One clear thought came to him in the midst of all the commotion, and that was the fact that there was more going on here than the extermination of a couple of kids. This was an elaborate ambush, planned from the get-go.

Through his epiphany, Skinner continued reaching for his pistol, but found the burning flesh was his, and he could no longer move his arm without excruciating pain. He'd been tagged in the shoulder and immediately tried clutching the wound with his left hand, but that only made a sharp sting jolt his wound.

Through the sound of his own shrieking, he could hear the younger boy ask him loudly, "Now are you gonna surrender, mister?"

Skinner took in a deep breath, still clutching the hole in

his shoulder. The laughter that had been so easy a moment before was nowhere to be found. Instead, that feeling of confidence was replaced with a painful worry that radiated from his shoulder and tightened his chest.

Fear ate at his confidence when he noticed a man in a serape and a hat aiming a pair of battered laser pistols at him from a distance behind and to the left of the dromid. He must have been there the whole time.

The gunslinger's face wore three days of stubble, and his eyes were wide, deranged, and serious.

What little confidence Skinner had left melted away with every menacing step the gunslinger took toward him. The man with the guns kept one of them trained on Skinner while he holstered the other and let a length of cord that had been coiled around his shoulder fall into his free hand.

Behind the approaching avenger was a dirty-faced little girl, quietly clutching a tattered doll and taking careful steps as well, watching everything unfold before her.

"What is this?" Skinner whined through the hurt.

But before the Glick had time to protest further, a gun was pointed in his face from mere inches away. The coil of cord the man carried got tossed to one of the boys, and the gunslinger's hand reached up and grabbed Skinner by the collar of his sleeveless work suit.

"Get outta there," the grizzled man said through gritted teeth, then tugged Skinner harshly by the collar, dragging him out of the speeder and wrestling him to the ground.

Skinner's wounded shoulder hit the red Glyconian soil first, shooting pain through his body with every stinging piece of grit that rubbed into the open, burning sore.

The gunslinger dragged him across the dirt, pulling open the blaster burn and scraping dirt into new cuts on Skinner's head and face as he pulled.

Skinner, squirming in pain, could feel a knee in his lower back and the point of a gun dug into his head.

"Don't move," the gruff voice said, but he couldn't know how much it hurt.

"Toss me that cord," the voice commanded the boys, who obliged him.

Like a trained lawman, the gunslinger forced Skinner's arms back behind him, stretching the wound on his shoulder and causing a searing sensation that triggered another scream. Carefully, the man wrapped the cord around Skinner's thick wrists, digging in with his knee every time Skinner tried squirming away from the pain. Then, the man led the cord up Skinner's back and wrapped it tightly around his neck, tying it in a very clever slipknot.

Skinner could feel the grasp of choking death every time his hands moved, even slightly.

That wasn't the only way to choke, though. The man left a long leash connected to Skinner's neck that he grasped tightly.

"Get up," the gunslinger tugged on the cord, tightening the grip around Skinner's throat.

Skinner pulled his knees up underneath himself and worked to stand, quickly, before he was strangled by the cord.

When he got to his feet, the gunslinger stood behind him. In front of him were the two boys, slack-jawed and blinking.

The younger of the two spoke, "You gonna kill him then, mister?"

The steely voice of the man in charge came from behind. "Not yet. He knows plenty about what we want to know."

"I know nothing," Skinner pleaded, spitting blood onto the Glyconian dirt.

"Why don't you kids take this speeder and head back to base," the gunslinger said. "You don't want to see what comes next."

The younger boy gulped. "What are you going to do to him?"

"Find out what he knows."

"How?"

"He knows how. Now you kids need to git. Now. Nik, you take this speeder, and you know right where to take it. Get a move on."

"You sure you'll be okay, mister?"

"I said git."

The gunslinger made Skinner watch the kids climb into the speeder, dump Sanchez's body over the side and onto the magnetic trail, and drive away.

It was excruciating to watch, knowing that the gunslinger was simply biding his time. Every minute that Skinner stood there, working hard to suppress the pain, watching those children he was sent to kill get away in his speeder, he knew the gunslinger was staying his hand until they left.

It was a psychological game.

The interrogation had begun already.

With the kids safely away, the gunslinger led Skinner by the neck to the dromid the kids had been handling.

"Where you taking me?"

The gunslinger tugged on the rope, taking the wind right out of the Glick's throat. "If you're gonna talk, it better be to tell me what I want to know about the Serpent's fortress. Anything else and you're just wastin' the last of your breaths."

Without letting go of the rope, the gunslinger hopped up

onto the mount. He tugged on Skinner's neck, signaling his desire for the Glick to follow closer.

"You better keep up, you slithering bastard, else that neck loop's gonna get a lot less accommodating."

The gunslinger clicked his heels into the side of the animal, and it started its long brisk trot into the empty parts of the desert, where no one would hear anything.

"You know why I sent 'em away, don't you?"

Skinner took long, unenthusiastic steps, dragging his feet in the mixture of red sand and darker soil.

Maybe it would be better to just collapse and let the dromid strangle the life from him.

But no, maybe there was still a chance to get out of this. Skinner would just need to wait for the right opening. There had to be a chance....

"I sent 'em away because I didn't want those poor kids to see all the no-good, nasty, horrible things I'm going to do to you. They've seen more than enough for anybody. They already watched their folks get killed on account of you and your buddies. I'm impressed they didn't try to kill you themselves."

The gunslinger tugged on the cord attached to Skinner so he could reach into his saddlebag. Then, he withdrew a canteen and took a long, thirsty draught of it. He made sure to spill water out the sides of his mouth and down in front.

Skinner licked his lips.

"You know what I can't figure?" the gunslinger asked.

Skinner spat what moisture he had in his mouth in the direction of the gunslinger and his dromid.

"I can't figure why you would leave those kids alive in the first place. That was a big mistake. Boys grow up to be men, they have their ambitions of vengeance. The misfortune you've found yourself in currently is that these boys are more tenacious than most."

Skinner's foot caught a lump of soil, tripping him into the dirt. He struggled to get back to his feet before he could choke to death.

"You know what your bigger problem is?" the gunslinger asked.

The loose red soil clung to the sweat and dirt all over Skinner.

He winced in pain.

"The bigger problem is they found me."

Up a steady rise, they came to a circle of satellite relay poles and communications array towers atop the hill.

"This'll do." The gunslinger pulled up on the reins of his dromid, stopping the entire procession. The animal brayed loudly, clearly happy to stop.

Skinner narrowed his eyes, looking around, wondering what secrets this place he'd been brought to held. It must hold some significance. Would there be implements of torture hidden in one of the relay towers? Would he be tied down to one of them and tortured slowly?

"What are we doing here?" Skinner asked, nervously.

The gunslinger yanked on the cord again, choking the Glick. "I told you to shut it unless you were telling me what I wanted to hear."

While Skinner gagged and coughed dryly, trying to catch his breath and somehow loosen the loop around his neck, the stranger tossed a length of cord up around one of the maintenance footholds high up on the communications tower closest to him.

With the cord leading from the Glick's neck up to the post in the tower about ten meters up, the stranger took the end he held and tied it up to his dromid's saddle.

"This is how it's gonna work, fella. I'm gonna ask you some questions. If you don't answer them, I'm gonna have my dromid here start walking."

Skinner tried gulping but couldn't quite force the mix of blood and saliva down his throat through the tension of the cord.

"But that might not be all I do." The gunslinger reached down into his boot and pulled something out.

Until the man stood up, Skinner couldn't determine what it was. It seemed to be a handle of some sort. The gunslinger stood up and extended a blade from the handle.

If Skinner were still truly human and had human facial expressions, panicked dread would have come over his face like a raincloud. But since his skin was all rubber and sinew, the only kind of looking he did was ugly. "Cut me all you want, but I'm not saying anything."

The gunslinger grinned like a predator about to get his dinner, taking slow, careful steps toward the Glick with his knife held up menacingly.

"I think you might be wrong about that. You're gonna tell me what I want to know. And the first thing I want to know about is Santa Madre."

XVII

Noontime was the hottest time of day on any world, and the pioneers of Glycon-Prime knew it was the worst for them. The sun cast a brilliant orange and yellow light that covered the sky and was so bright that no one could even look near it for fear of blindness.

Despite a hundred scoldings to the contrary, Amir had found himself trying to discern the shape of the sun at midday many times throughout his life. Never in all that time did he ever find a definitive answer. He always came up empty with a massive white splotch burned into his vision for a half an hour hence.

And that's what he found himself doing, back at their encampment, sitting in a circle with Nik and Lila, wishing they had a more permanent home than that spare patch of dirt.

Amir's mind drifted to the gunslinger and what he was out there doing, on their behalf.

Even staring right into the hot sun, under its glowing,

oppressive warmth, the thought of the man called Twelve gave Amir a chill.

They knew so little about him, but it wasn't like there were people more trustworthy or with a more transparent background lining up to help them save Miri and exact their revenge.

Nik must have been thinking the same thing when he blurted, "I wonder if he's wanted."

"What?" Amir asked.

"Twelve," Nik explained. "I bet the law wants him, and that's why he doesn't want us to know who he is."

"Wanted men don't help kids like us."

"I guess it doesn't matter as long as he's helping us."

"He's a good man, Nik," Lila interrupted them, breaking her silence. "Even if he doesn't know it."

"We'll see," Nik said, not believing.

They returned to their silence, waiting nervously for the gunslinger.

Amir felt a tension he couldn't quite explain, and he was sure it stemmed from the feeling of conflict between Twelve and the Glick. He'd never been the best at dealing with confrontation, and he was sick thinking about how much worse their confrontation must be getting.

Whenever his parents argued, he'd curl up into a ball on his bed and cover his ears, hoping it would stop sooner rather than later. And he'd never try to get in the middle; the thought of doing so only filled him with dread.

His anxiety wasn't helped by the fact that every so often, carried along on the wind, they could hear a moan or a scream, never able to discern if it was just a trick of the breeze, or the torture being conducted in their name.

After a time, the haunting sounds stopped with the

breeze. The afternoon grew still and silent, more so as the day gave way to evening.

They each lessened their anxiety in different ways.

Nik spent his time clutching his sword.

Amir paced in circles, making unnatural sounds with his mouth, and pretending over and over again to shoot at the Glicks.

Lila alternated between napping and staring out at the desert, waiting for their protector to return.

Words were few between the three of them. If they spoke amongst each other, they'd be forced to face the shared reality of their plight. They'd been orphans for less than three turns of Glycon-Prime, and not once had they talked of it to one another.

Who knew if that day would ever come?

"He's been out there most of the day," Nik said eventually, as evening was upon them.

Amir kicked a clod of dirt into a fine spray in front of him. "I bet he gave that lousy Glick what was coming to him."

"I wonder if he talked," Nik said.

"Oh, he talked," Amir heard a voice from behind them say.

It was Twelve.

Each of the children whipped their attention around to see him. Amir wondered why the gunslinger covered his right hand over with his left. The bulk of Zeke on his left wrist seemed to be shielding the kids from something; some ugly truth he seemed genuinely ashamed of.

"So, what did you find out?" Nik shot up from his seat. "Is my sister alive?"

Nik's breath stopped, waiting for an answer. Amir found his own breathing had ceased, too.

"She's alive," Twelve conceded.

Relieved, the boys both gasped, sucking breath back into their lungs.

"Thank you," Nik said, exhaling the breath and wiping the sweat from his brow with his forearm.

"Don't get too hopeful, that's just the good news," the gunslinger said. "There's plenty of bad news left to go around."

At the mention of bad news, Nik staggered forward a half step, shuffling his feet underneath him to keep from losing his footing.

Amir's heart thumped in his chest so hard he could feel it pumping blood through his neck. He could even hear it, pounding rhythmically on the inside of his ears. He asked the one question he didn't quite want the answer to, "What's the bad news, mister?"

"She might not have much time left."

"What does that mean?" Nik asked. "Why not?"

"Santa Madre," the gunslinger folded his arms and lowered his head.

"What's a Santa Madre?" Nik balled his hands into fists.

"Don't worry about Santa Madre. I'll take care of her." The gunslinger looked down, averting his eyes as he spoke.

Amir wondered about Santa Madre, and what it was the gunslinger wasn't telling them about it.

Nik's voice, struggling with anger, squeaked with emotion as he spoke. "How do we get her back then, mister?"

"We're going to rile things up."

"How do we do that?" Lila asked, not looking up from her doll.

"We're gonna start some trouble." Now that he wasn't obscuring some bit of truth, the gunslinger looked up, engaged with the situation, looking at each of the children right in the eyes as he spoke. "Amir, you saw it. They've got an army up at their fortress. If we can stir up enough trouble in Stelio City, they'll invade, and I'll be able to slip in on my own, unnoticed. I can take care of Santa Madre and get Miri out of there."

Nik took another step forward, his voice straining and cracking even further. "I should be the one going to get her. She's my sister."

Twelve unfolded his arms and reached out to put his left hand on Nik's shoulder. "Your job's going to be hard enough, son."

Amir's eyes scanned down the gunslinger's right arm, over the dusty serape and down to the hand he'd been obscuring as he spoke. Amir understood why he'd covered it; it was splotched vermilion. The dust of Glycon had collected on the blood dripping from his fingers. Amir's eyes widened and all he could think of was the carnage from Nine Mine City.

The gunslinger paid no notice and kept talking. "There's going to be plenty of vengeance, but you're not a soldier. What you are is the oldest, and these other kids are going to need you. Especially since your work is going to be dangerous."

Nik lowered his head, frightened.

"We're going to do this, son, even if it's the last thing we do. I promise."

Nik's head came back, courageous and confident this time. "What do we have to do?"

Twelve smirked, careful not to raise his bloodied hand, holding it unnaturally to his side. "That's the spirit."

The gunslinger pulled his left hand from Nik's shoulder and paced as he talked. "This Serpent's been building an army."

"We knew that," Amir said.

"Well, our little friend let me in on a little secret. Guerrero's been stockpiling munitions in all the surrounding towns for the coup he's planning against the Corporate Authority for turning him into a Glick. That's why his men leveled Nine Mine City. Your folks didn't want anything to do with it, and his men got carried away when they were 'sending them a message.' So, you three are just loose ends that need to be tied up."

Twelve moved around the encampment slowly, deliberately, until he reached Lila. Lila sat in the sand, morose, tired, clutching her doll. The gunslinger crouched down and reached for her with his left hand.

He pushed the hair from her face and tucked it behind her ear. "Well, I know where their stash is in Stelio City."

"So?" Nik didn't follow.

But the circuits in Amir's head were firing at one hundred percent capacity and he grinned, watching the plan come together from the side.

The gunslinger stood; his joints creaked as he did so. "Where's the first place you think Guerrero's army is heading if something happens to their ammunition?"

"To deal with it?" Nik asked, scratching his head, straining to make sense of the plan.

"And while they're gone, if all goes well and your sister's still all right, I can slip in and grab her, no problem."

"So," Amir smiled, rubbing his hands together, "let's blow something up."

XVIII

I t's time for your nap," Santa Madre hissed from her
rock.

To Miri, her hands cuffed in front of her and resting
in her lap, a nap sounded like a dream. She'd been in the
humid prison for hours, doing her best to follow each of
Santa Madre's commands. If she disobeyed, anything was
liable to happen.

The first time Miri had told Santa Madre no, she was
slapped across the face. The second time, Santa Madre
slashed her sharpened nails across Miri's arm. The third time
was a fury of punches and kicks all across Miri's body.

Santa Madre made sure that Miri understood that
disobeying her whims wasn't an act of defiance, but an act of
lunacy with very real, very painful consequences.

Seated in the center of the room, Miri listened for the
sound of the guards opening the door behind her. If she was
off for a nap, they'd be sending her to her cell to rest and
recuperate from her most recent play date with the hideous
matron, wouldn't they?

But the sound of the door didn't come, only Santa Madre did. Getting closer and closer, the oversized Glick limped toward Miri, reaching out with her claws.

"Come. Now. Over here," the beast beckoned.

But Miri didn't budge, unsure of what was expected of her and what was really going on.

"It's time for your nap," Santa Madre repeated.

With no indication she was leaving the room, she looked around once more, wondering what might be used for her nap. There was no bed to speak of. Miri wondered if Santa Madre was kept in here at nights or if she too was transferred to a cell, treated as much a plaything for the Serpent as Miri was for Santa Madre herself.

"Now." The slithering hag hissed, reaching out for Miri, grabbing the girl by her bound wrists.

"I'm not tired." Miri struggled against Santa Madre's grip. Not purposely, it was just a reflex, but Miri instantly realized she'd made a grave mistake.

Santa Madre's eyes widened, and her face tightened, wrinkling her skin in a way that reminded Miri of reptilian scales. The matronly snake swatted Miri's hands away and reached for the girl's head, taking hold of a fisted patch of her hair. Santa Madre yanked on her hair, jolting Miri with a sharp pain.

The Glick yanked again, this time so hard that Miri was knocked from her chair.

Miri fell forward toward the ground, raising her cuffed wrists in front of her to break the fall, but the fall never came. It was cut short by Santa Madre's grip. Miri's hair acted as a leash, keeping the young girl heeled beneath Santa Madre.

"This way you filthy, little ... Maggie ... This way."

Santa Madre, tearing clumps of hair from Miri's scalp as

she pulled, dragged Miri closer and closer to the heated rock at the back of the room.

Miri let out the beginnings of a scream, but held the rest of it in, for fear of retribution.

Stifling the pain and putting it, as well as the anxiety, aside became harder and harder for Miri with every meter further she was dragged along by Santa Madre. Every step closer, the temperature rose exponentially, and the smell of the moist fecal mess grew more gut wrenching. The smell was so thick, Miri could taste it at the back of her throat.

"Upsy daisy, Maggie." Santa Madre lifted Miri up to the rock by her hair with no concern for how badly it hurt.

Miri's forearms were the first thing to touch the surface of the heat rock.

It burned to the touch.

Miri recoiled, but Santa Madre was relentless, forcing her onto the rock as though she were a disobedient pet.

"It's time for your nap." Santa Madre let go of Miri's hair, but palmed the back of the girl's head, forcing it onto the surface of the rock. To Miri, it felt coarse, like sandstone. She couldn't tell if it was real rock, plucked from the Glyconian landscape and heated by the red lights, or if it was an elaborate fake that radiated heat from the inside.

Then she realized that it didn't matter, nor did she care.

It was hot, and blistered and chafed wherever her bare skin touched it for more than a moment.

Miri went limp like a rag doll, putting the burning sensation out of her mind, and let Santa Madre position her just the way the old hag wanted.

"That's better." Santa Madre lifted Miri's legs up onto the rock, leaving her in a laying position atop it. "Are you sss-settled now, Maggie?"

Miri said nothing, trying not to squirm on the rock and attract any more unwelcome attention from her captor.

Almost immediately Miri broke into a sweat. She was confident the rock was hot enough to boil her alive slowly.

"There, there," the old Glick clucked.

Santa Madre leaned over Miri, pressing the poor girl into the sizzling rock. The sagging remnants of Santa Madre's breasts filled Miri's face, suffocating her with the stink of an unwashed body and the leathery rubber of aged, mutant skin and fat.

The heat was merely uncomfortable next to Santa Madre's fleshy embrace.

Miri gasped for breath.

"There's nothing there for you, Maggie...." Santa Madre stood finally, having grabbed a soiled old scrap of a cloth from the other side of the rock, dragging it over Miri's body like a blanket.

"Milk's been out for a long time, Maggie...."

Miri wretched, holding the bile that threatened to arrive at the top of her throat.

The cloth may have once been a blanket. Its original colors had faded. It seemed to have violet and white lines in a diamond pattern, but the violet had faded to an almost-gray in most places and the white was dingy and yellow, stained with urine. Streaks of brown decorated one part of the fabric in the center.

Miri closed her eyes, leaving Santa Madre to tuck the edges of the blanket under her body, giving her something of a smelly cocoon.

Despite the filthy state of the blanket, Miri was surprisingly grateful for the shield between the heated rock and her bare skin.

"Maybe later ... the milk will come after you ... after you wake up...."

The young captive kept her eyes shut, hoping she'd be left alone, if just for a little while. Even if she did boil alive on that rock, it would be an easier torture to endure than what Santa Madre had been putting her through more personally.

Through her clenched eyes, Miri could feel cool tears run down the side of her face, leaving tracks of comfort on their way down.

The tears came slowly, and as they dripped from the side of her face and hit the rock, they sizzled for a brief second before evaporating completely.

What Miri hoped would be a brief respite was interrupted by the sound she looked forward to most in her situation: the door at the far side of the room sliding open.

That meant guards were coming in to take her away and give her a chance to breathe and recover before getting dragged back and offered to Santa Madre.

Miri's eyes cracked open, hoping to steal a peek at the guards who would carry her off, but she saw a sight she hadn't expected at all. A man was there in the doorway. It was a well-dressed Glick who wore a white suit and a pained look on the mask-like facade of his face.

"*Mi madre*," the man said, tenting his fingers together in front of him.

Santa Madre turned to see the man.

Miri wasn't sure if she should open her eyes and get a better view of what was going on, or if she should continue playing dead. She never knew what would draw Santa Madre's ire, and she never knew when Santa Madre would turn and see something that displeased her.

She opted to squint.

"What is-sss it, boy?"

"It's nothing." The man lowered his arms to his side, and then put them behind his back.

"Sshhh ..." Santa Madre brought a finger to her mouth. "You'll wake Maggie."

The man ignored the request and didn't flinch at the mention of the name Miri had been given by the old snake.

"I wanted you to know, Madre, that things have been put in motion. I've accelerated our timetable." The man in the white suit took deliberate steps closer to the monster he called mother.

Santa Madre cowered upon his approach, bending her knees and lowering her body. She curled her neck and head around, offering it to him to pet.

He reached out to do so but couldn't seem to bring himself to actually touch her.

"They'll pay." He pulled his hands behind his back once more. "They'll pay...."

Miri closed her eyes and imagined how sweet it would be if she could make them pay, Santa Madre and the Serpent in the white suit. She wished she had the power and the where-withal to stand up, right then, and strangle them both for what they'd done to her. Revenge would be a cool relief from the searing heat she couldn't react to.

Santa Madre let out a sniveling whimper.

"I've been watching you have your fun with your newest playmate." The Serpent motioned to Miri with a whole, scaly hand.

Santa Madre looked back to Miri as well. Miri shut her eyes the rest of the way, pretending to sleep once more. She could hear them carrying on though.

"You'll wake her."

"What's this one called?"

"Maggie...."

The Glick in the white suit made a sound that made Miri think he was smirking, lost in thought.

"That's what you used to call Maria when she was small. Hopefully she'll last longer than the others."

Santa Madre hissed angrily.

"*Cálmate*, Madre. *Cálmate*."

Glass shattered. Agitated, Santa Madre must have broken one of the teacups; smashed it against the wall behind the Glick dressed in white.

"It was nice to see you, Madre."

The door whooshed open and closed again. Miri risked cracking her eyes in hopes of knowing what to expect from the growling Santa Madre.

Screaming, Santa Madre swiveled around to look at Miri. Santa Madre bared her teeth and claws, shrieking shrilly.

Now she was upset.

XIX

With the curfew in full effect, Stelio City was as quiet as a tomb. Aside from the low, haunting rhythm of the local insect life and the rumble of power stations, there was not a sound to be heard.

The sheriff, crooked as he was, deserved plenty of credit. He kept a nice, quiet kind of town. Clean, too. Superficially at least. The only debris in the street was the blowing desert soil, twisting and turning in looping patterns.

Twelve and his underage entourage approached the city from behind, avoiding the road. Finding the secret munitions stash his "informant" had told him about would be a relatively easy thing. Evading detection in a town on lock down with three kids in tow, now that was a challenge that he relished.

To start, he'd shut Zeke's voice actuator off. The most his wrist computer could do was offer text screens full of easily ignored advice.

The second thing he did was try to instill in each of the children a sense of the gravitas of the situation; the fact that any of the three of them could die in the process of this diversion to save Miri.

None of them seemed to care, each resolute in their decision.

Twelve would have assumed the massacre of their families would instill some fear of mortality in them, but no matter how much death surrounds it, youth always sees itself as immortally invincible.

Since the kids were adamant about doing the work and Twelve was adamant about not taking them into harm's way at the fortress, the only thing left to do was head to town and let them play their part.

The group of them, the orphans of Nine Mine and the gunslinger from parts unknown, crept around the outskirts of Stelio City, where the lights were low, and marched softly through alleyways until they reached the main speeder trail that ran through the center of town. Crouching down at the corner, Twelve directed the kids to do the same behind him. Then, he peeked his head around the edge of the building, looking up and down the street.

The first building he made a point to spy was the jail and sheriff's office.

The porch was vacant and the lights inside were extinguished. All was quiet. Either the lawman was sleeping or ready to spring a trap, but the stranger doubted the latter. How would the sheriff know that their next play would be inside the limits of his city?

Frankly, in his years of bounty hunting and being a gunsel on the frontier, he'd never encountered a single sheriff this far out that was half as smart as he ought to be.

Twelve scanned the street for anything else out of the ordinary until his eyes rested on the brightly lit gambling saloon that he'd killed four Glicks in not two days earlier.

Even during a lockdown it was bright and lively, though he couldn't see any definite signs of Guerrero's men.

He dragged his gaze down the street, looking for the building that he'd been assured was there. And there it was. A small building across the speeder trail from the sheriff's office constructed of adobe. It had no windows facing the front, and there was only one door.

Crouched in front of it, dressed in blue jumpers, and trying their hardest to remain incognito in the dark, were a pair of Glicks.

Agents of the Serpent.

The gunslinger suppressed the urge to sigh. He still had to cross the street with a gaggle of kids without being detected.

Twelve got down low on his haunches and went back to the children, who'd hidden themselves behind the jail at his direction. When he arrived to them once more, he brought his finger to his lips, re-instilling the paramount importance of their continued silence.

Before they'd departed for Stelio, he couldn't stress enough how quiet they'd have to be if they wanted to make it through the night alive. To reinforce the point, he made a show of turning Zeke's volume down all the way, despite the wrist computer's protestations.

He knew keeping still and quiet was a difficult thing for kids at this age, or any age, really, but they'd been behaving admirably.

A feeling grew deep inside him, welling at the base of his chest. Was that a swell of pride he felt?

Anything was possible.

"Quiet now," he reminded them. "We're heading to the other side of the street. But stay close to me. We're taking the long way."

Doubled over, maintaining as low a profile as possible, he led them around to the back border of town. Clinging to the sides of buildings and the dark alleys between, they made it as far as the edge of the alley before the gunslinger heard the blustering whoosh of a hydraulic door opening and then closing again. A dozen sharp clicks of footsteps could be heard on the concrete some distance away.

Three buildings over, the night was so quiet that even sounds that low and unmuffled carried away into the night.

At the sound of a messy sneeze behind him, Twelve startled, a chill ran between his shoulders.

"What was that?" a slimy, slithering voice, softened by distance and buildings, called out into the night.

The gunslinger's attention snapped back, looking to the kids to see Lila, clutching her nose with both hands.

There was a choice to be made there.

Should they simply keep quiet and hope that danger would pass them by? Or should they make a run for it?

Discipline and a working knowledge of the odds stayed the stranger's hand.

The sound of the sneeze wasn't so distinguishable. It was a muffled, high-pitched noise in a cold, windy night. There were a thousand things that could have made that sound. It could have been the creak of a busted door opening. It could have been any kind of malfunctioning problem on a hundred thousand different things.

They'd wait.

They'd have to.

He kept the children back, close to the wall of the building, silent as ever.

More footsteps moved back and forth, and they could see the growing wisp of light from a hand light reflected two or three alleys away.

Then the voice came back. "Ah, it was nothing. Shoot."

The soft circle of light from the guard's lightstick, spilling around the corner, shut off abruptly, and they could hear a defeated pair of footsteps walk back up onto the porch they'd originated from. Each half of the door whooshed open once more, and the sound of danger was gone.

Peeling themselves from against the wall, Twelve and the three children resumed their quest to the outskirts and the other side of the street. Dodging this way and that and remaining as silent as field mice was no easy task, but they made it the rest of the way to the edge of the city.

From there, they circled down and around until they reached the speeder trail that bisected the town.

It was the one thing they'd tried so hard to avoid because they knew it would be watched, but they had little choice.

Crouched low on the side of the trail, they looked out over the ribbon of magnetic pavement. The stranger's eyes looked up and down the street once more, looking for any signs that they were being watched directly, or that there was anyone around to spot them.

The other side of the street wasn't more than ten or fifteen meters away, but it may as well have been a hundred. And instead of a speeder trail, it might as well have been a raging river of molten lava.

Cursing himself under his breath, the gunslinger wondered how they'd ever get across undetected, but then noticed the answer was right in front of him.

The kids had all taken to their bellies, flat as they could get, and were crawling to salvation on the other side. All three of them were halfway across before he even realized it. Following their lead, he began the slow process of getting himself to the other side.

By the time he'd reached the midpoint of the road, the kids had already made it.

The only thing that was left to worry him was the distant roar of a speeder turbine. Looking to his left, he could see in the black of the horizon two twinkling dots, growing larger and larger with every second, heading directly for him.

"Damn it."

Hopping up on all fours, he scrambled the rest of the way to the edge, chance of being seen be damned.

The speeder traveled at top velocity, well over a hundred kilometers an hour, whizzing by the stranger just as he cleared the trail. The wind of it nearly knocked him over into the group of children waiting for him on the other side.

Even at a distance, the screech of the speeder hurt their ears. It wasn't pleasant to listen to a speeder revving up at top speed. Those turbines could get loud.

But that was perfect cover.

The speeder pulled into the center of town, right near the small outpost they'd soon be investigating.

Resuming his hunched posture, Twelve ducked past the front row of buildings with the children behind him as they made their way to the alley behind, and on to their intended destination.

From the rear, their target had but one unguarded window.

With the kids down against the red adobe wall of the building, the gunslinger peeked in that lone window to find that it was opaque, black all the way through.

He tried scratching the black off like paint and was able to make just enough of a transparent slit to see the contents of the shed inside.

"This is it."

The room they peered into was packed floor to ceiling

with metal crates and plastic barrels. Each of them was marked with the familiar inverted triangle surrounding the silhouette of an explosion.

He'd been told that these were the bomb-making materials and crates of ammunition that the Serpent had intended to enact his revenge with.

And there was more than enough here to do the job.

Worried about the guards, the gunslinger gave the kids a signal to stay put and edged his way along the side of the munitions bunker. He wondered if there was some way he could neutralize the guards without being noticed. He needed to give the kids the best chance he could so they could give him the chance he needed for his damn fool plan to work.

As he inched his way to the front of the building, the stranger saw that neither of the guards were at their posts. Both stood in the middle of the street, conversing urgently with the pair of Glicks who had arrived in the speeder that almost ran him over.

Twelve strained his ears, trying hard to overhear anything important, but he could only make out words that elevated over the whine of the speeder turbines. He only picked up a few words here and there, phrases like "the Serpent" and "the plan."

In the heated debate, the Glicks argued amongst one another for a moment more, never suspecting that they were being watched. Finally, with their conversation over, one of the guards reluctantly got into the back seat of the convertible speeder, and the other marched back to his chair in front of the armory door, annoyed by something.

Sucking in his breath and pressing up against the wall as tight as he could, Twelve waited for the speeder to race away.

As they pulled off, the light from the speeder faded, leaving the gunslinger and his wards in darkness once more. Night covered the stranger like a blanket, making him feel warm, safe, and secret.

The guard's chair was just a few feet from the corner of the building on one side and the small steel door into the building on the other. The Glick closed his eyes, as though he hoped to catch more sleep in the middle of such a peaceful night.

But that's when the gunslinger made his move. In one fluid motion, before the Glick could protest, the gunslinger put an arm around his neck and another hand on the back of his head, tweaking until he heard a sharp crack. The weight of the man went limp beneath him, and Twelve knew that life had left him.

Easing him back into his chair, the gunslinger took his own hat and put it over the dead guard's face as though he were sleeping on the job. That would probably do until morning. The ruse would only have to last a few more hours.

Moving back out of the light like some sort of nocturnal predator and into the alley behind the building, Twelve had to set the kid's part of the plan in motion.

"You kids ready for this?" he whispered.

Nik and Amir both nodded. Lila was distant as usual, clutching her doll and saying nothing.

"We're gonna get you in this window, and I want you to barricade that front door with all the crates and boxes you can move," Twelve instructed. "Stack the boxes of charges as high as they'll go. Then I'll give you a power charge for my pistols. I'll rig it to blow on a timer, but you'll have to set it manually. You'll only have a couple of minutes of delay."

"What do we do after that?" Nik asked.

"I'll bring the dromids around to this side and have 'em

tied up back that way. You set the charge, climb out the window and run like hell till you get on the mounts, then head to our little base. You oughta be able to get most of the way out of town before the explosion, but you gotta go fast because they'll be looking for you quick. I'll meet you back there, no problem."

Nik's eyes masked their fear with a tinge of hope in the dark light. "And you'll have my sister."

Twelve grinned slightly, revealing a spark inside him he hadn't felt in a what seemed like a lifetime.

Pulling his laser blaster from his hip holster, the gunslinger withdrew two of the power cells in the handle. He still had two more cells for that gun. As a consequence, the time between recharges would be twice as long for his right sidearm. Hopefully the advantage gained from the explosion would outweigh the disadvantage he'd be at with the reduced state of his pistols. From a different pocket, he pulled out a small device that Zeke had helped him cobble together for the occasion. He used it to connect the two power cells together.

As soon as the children activated the button at the top of the device, they'd have about two minutes before the negative feedback in the power cells overheated. One would explode the other, causing a chain reaction that would end up blowing the entire building sky high.

Using his knife, Twelve cut the seal on the window, pulling it up and open wide enough to fit the kids through.

He helped Lila through first, then Amir went through.

Once the younger boy made it to the other side, Twelve handed him the rigged explosive. "Be very careful with it. As soon as you see the first ray of sunlight, that's your signal."

He trusted the younger boy to think more soundly than the older boy and to act more rationally.

"I know, I know. I don't want to die here. I heard you the first time," Amir said.

"And remember, you'll only have about two minutes."

"I got you." Amir turned, getting to work inside barricading the door with crates of ammunition.

Outside, that left only Nik.

"Let me come with you. I can help you kill some of those bastards." Nik's eyes were wide and dewy; youthful. There were no lines of stress or age on his face, and he had no blood on his hands.

"No," Twelve said.

"But why?"

"Killing isn't the answer to your problems, kid. I've found that most of the time it isn't the answer to my problems neither, but as much as I don't like it, it always becomes my solution. It's the only one I seem to know."

"But I could kill them. It'd solve my problems. It'd solve plenty of them." The boy's eyebrows came together, narrowing his eyes and stressing his point. It was plain as the red day of Glycon that the desire in the boy's heart was for revenge as much as it was the safety of his sister.

"It won't solve anything."

He could see the dejected feelings of sorrow and worthlessness fill Nik like a poison.

"Learn the lesson I never did, son. Learn the lesson I'm still not learning."

Nik turned his back, grabbed the edges of the window, and put a foot up on the side of the building, ready to pull himself in.

"It's not too late for you, kid. Use your head. Forget about all this killing nonsense. Think about your folks. You really think your father would have wanted you to be doing any killing on his account? Or your mother?"

Nik stopped and half-turned back toward the gunslinger, his head hung low. "You had a mother once."

A writhing sting grew in the gunslinger's heart, radiating through his body.

He bit through it.

"Stay here. Protect Amir and Lila as soon as you get out of this. More than ever, they'll need you. Not just now, but forever. More than any of your mothers ever could have. They're your family now."

The stranger choked back the lump in his throat, envious of the life the boy could have ahead of him.

"Leave the killing to the damned, son."

Reluctantly, Nik nodded his head. Turning back to the window, he climbed up over the lip and into the building.

The boy turned back to the stranger a final time, and, in a sad, soft voice that warbled in the night, said, "Get her back for me, mister. I'm counting on you."

"I know, son. I know."

When the gunslinger turned, he could feel the eyes of the children on his back and couldn't shake the pounding dread of a feeling that he was leaving them to their deaths.

XX

Shafts of cold blue moonlight peeked into the munitions bunker through the scratches in the opaque window. The smell of oil and ozone filled the cramped space, along with the musty odor unique to Glycon-Prime. The Glyconian bugs played their song, muted through the walls outside.

Amir and Nik took on the hard work of stacking the boxes of power charges and old-fashioned explosives against the door, leaving Lila to sleep fitfully under the window, cuddling her blood-soaked rag doll.

Just as the stranger had told them to, the boys placed the wired charge packs on one of the munitions crates right in the center of the room.

They sat down cross-legged around the device, using the crate it rested on as a kind of table, only half-worried the explosive might decide to go off all on its own.

"Do you think he'll make it?" Nik asked.

"As long as they don't catch us in here," Amir said, "I

think he'll do it. He hasn't led us astray yet. I'm more worried about what happens if the Serpent's men catch us in here."

"I guess if that happens we'll just have to push the button and run as fast as we can and hope they don't kill us. They'll have to run like hell just like the rest of us."

Amir rubbed his arms as though he were chilled by the night. "If they caught us, I bet he'd save us, too."

They descended into silence. They were tired and afraid of falling asleep. If they missed their cue, the entire operation would be foiled. And they'd probably all get killed.

A smirk appeared on Amir's face as a memory from his youth that seemed so far in the past bubbled to the top of his mind. "You remember that time Rafiq broke into Mr. Croker's dromid stable?"

Amir wondered how confusing that question must have seemed to the older boy.

Nik's grim frown turned neutral, edging close to a half smile. "The time when he got chased out by Mr. Croker blasting away at everything? Or the time he made it out with a dromid and did laps around town and couldn't figure out how to stop?"

"Both."

"Yeah, I remember. Why?"

Amir smiled again, broader this time, almost ready to laugh. "That was funny."

Nik's lips parted in a smile, and a brief spot of happiness opened up in Amir, like the sun peeking through a cloudy sky.

They spent the rest of the night talking back and forth of inconsequential things, working hard to stay awake and avoid the subject of their families and the permanence of death.

It wasn't long before Amir volunteered to keep watch so Nik could get a little bit of shut-eye.

And it wasn't long after that that the long reach of sleep tugged at Amir's eyelids, shutting them against his will.

The boy was drifted to sleep and in his dreams was taken to better times. In that neverland of Amir's slumbering subconscious, all the worries and dread of the real world faded. Transported into a cloudy soup of easier times and smiles, Amir could comprehend the black and blue streaks of midnight giving way to the gray of morning, and at the edges of the horizon a thin ribbon of orange light appeared.

And that's when he was jolted awake.

Sitting over him was Lila, poking him awake with her finger. The first rays of dawn created a band of violet light across the girl's face.

"It's time," she said quietly.

Groggy, the boys arose. The fear was chief in their heads. Amir could feel it the worst. A knot twisted and churned its way through his stomach, choking him up. "Nik, why don't you take Lila and get out of here. Take a head start."

"Are you serious? You want to do this alone?"

"We don't need all three of us to push one button. Besides, it'll be safer for Lila." Amir could feel the weight of responsibility drag him down.

"I'll stay. You take her," Nik said.

Amir thought he was hearing things. "What?"

"I'm faster anyway. And I'm bigger than you. Get her back to base and I'll do it."

In a firm but quiet voice Lila decided for them. "Amir, we have to go."

"Fine." Amir threw his hands up in the air, outnumbered and outvoted.

Nik offered a pained grimace to the younger boy. "You can beat me up for it later. Now get outta here."

With a swell of pride and fear, Amir cracked the window open, taking great care to be silent. Despite his effort, the window creaked loud and low like a bullfrog from Earth proper, sending a shiver of fear coursing through him. Then, the younger boy poked his head out of the window and swiveled it back and forth, looking out for bad guys in the dim purple haze of Glyconian dawn.

The alleyways the window looked out upon were deserted. Not a soul was around to question the children or their mission.

"The coast is clear," Amir reported.

"Let me give you a boost." Weaving his hands together, Nik created a step for Amir and Lila, helping them through the window one at a time. After, he stuck his head back out. "Get out of here, you remember where we left the dromids. I'm giving you a five-minute head start."

Amir gave Nik a respectful nod. "Thanks, Nik. And good luck."

"*Asra.*"

Amir and Lila obliged, running from the building, back toward their mount. Amir wished in his heart, hard and passionately, that they wouldn't get caught.

After helping the younger kids out the back window, Nik came back to the explosive device, marveling at it. He was amazed by the idea that a couple of power cells, a few wires, and a button to overload the whole thing could turn into an explosion that would destroy everything in the building and probably some of the next building, too.

With no way to tell time, the boy began counting. He didn't know how many numbers it would take to get to five minutes, but he could count pretty fast, so he picked five hundred, which seemed pretty high. When five hundred came, it'd be time to push the button and get out....

202, 203, 204, 205 ...

During his count, he took in the sight of the metal crates once more, stacked against the door and all around the room. They were of a thin make, light and durable, perfect for cheap shipping across the galaxy. Each of them was full to the brim with heavy ordnance and explosives.

445, 446, 447, 448 ...

These must be for his tanks, Nik thought. Taking a deep breath, he knew that when he got to five hundred, everything would be different. There was no going back from causing this level of destruction.

478, 479, 480, 481 ...

He wondered if Amir and Lila had made it to the dromids by now, or if they'd been caught by the sheriff, or even the Serpent's men. It didn't matter. As much as he wished he could extend their head start, he just couldn't. Miri's life depended on it.

496, 497, 498, 499 ...

500.

Nik swallowed, gulping down his fear. "Here goes nothing."

He pressed the button, activating the device with a beep and a whistle. A small red light turned on, and he knew that he only had moments to run. He dropped the device, dashed to the wall, and crashed through the window, hitting the ground below on his shoulder with a thud.

"Hey! You!"

Nik looked up, trying to locate the man shouting. The

sound came from off to his right, thirty meters down the alley. It wasn't a Glick, just some random resident of Stelio City taking their refuse out to the recycler. He wore a blue mechanic's suit and work gloves. Atop his head was a wide brimmed hat like Nik had seen in old vids.

The man froze, like a dromid caught in the lights of a speeder. "What are you doing there?"

Dread pounced on Nik, adrenaline ignited his flee response and, without a word, he scrambled to his feet and sprinted, hoping he'd find a way through the network of alleys in Stelio City and all the way to safety without getting caught.

Though he could no longer see the man, he could still hear his shouting voice echoing through the alleyways. "Get back here, kid! What were you doing in there?"

Nik took a fast left, passed two houses, and then made another right, the voice never stopping, though it grew more distant.

The mechanic's voice grew hoarse from shouting the alarm. "Sheriff! Sheriff Peters! There's something going on at the shack!"

From the corner of his eye, Nik could see movement. Like he'd been kicked in the stomach, the feeling that he'd been caught stung. He wanted to double over in pain, from stress and exertion, but he knew he had to keep going. Whipping his head around, never slowing his forward momentum, he could see what had appeared in his field of view: Amir and Lila were riding on the dromid, galloping along the outskirts of town.

"Get on!" Amir shouted.

The sting of failure melted, and Nik doubled his pace, heading for his comrades.

Amir shouted once more, "Come on! She's gonna blow!"

A commotion echoed from the speeder trail. Nik could hear the yelling behind him; the mechanic getting even louder.

Nik grabbed the side of the dromid and leapt on, behind the other two.

"Hyah!" Amir screamed, kicking his heels into the beast, which galloped through the dust on the way back to their home base beneath the satellite tower.

Nik twisted his head back, looking to see if the mechanic had found any help, hoping they wouldn't be in time to stop what was coming.

The mechanic stood over the lifeless Glick propped up in front of the stash on guard duty. That must have been Twelve's handiwork from the night before.

Nik turned his head back toward the horizon.

They'd done all they could, and he prayed that it was enough.

When the shouting started, Sheriff Peters tried his best to ignore it and keep his eyes closed in sleep. Like everything else, it could wait. But, subconsciously, his ears strained to hear, and through the thin metal walls of the jail the sound of commotion carried easily.

A voice he only vaguely recognized screamed itself hoarse outside on the speeder trail somewhere. "Sheriff! Sheriff Peters! There's something going on at the shack."

The shack.

Peters snapped awake instantly with a rush of anxiety. He knew what the shack contained, and it was his solemn job to make damn sure nothing happened to it. If anything happened to the munitions stored inside, there was no telling what Guerrero would do.

The Serpent had insisted on putting his own men to guard the shack, and the sheriff did his best to dissuade the townsfolk from getting too curious about it. As far as he was concerned, his job was done where Guerrero's stash had been involved.

"Hey!" Peters finally recognized the voice as belonging to Franklin, the town's mechanic. "What's going on there? You awake, fella? Sheriff!"

Stuffing the tails of his shirt down into his pants and smoothing his hair with his hand, the sheriff hit the button to activate his front door. It flew open and he could see Franklin across the street hovering over one of Guerrero's men at the door, who was apparently slumbering on his chair.

"Frank, what's all the hollering about? You're waking up half the town."

"Sheriff, you told me to holler if anything was amiss here, and I'm telling you, there's something wrong. I saw a kid not one minute ago running around behind the shack, and I come to check on it, and this here Glick is dead."

Peters chilled, the blood drained from his face and hands. "Dead?"

"Yeah. His neck's broke. I thought he was sleepin'."

"Damn it. Take a look inside, see that it's all correct." Peters coughed nervously. "I'll see what Guerrero wants to do about it."

The sheriff tarried in the jail's doorway, hesitating, not wanting to take a step farther.

Across the speeder trail, Franklin tried the knob on the hinged metal door and pushed, meeting significant resistance.

"What's wrong there, Frank?"

"It won't open, Sheriff."

"Pry it open."

Doing as he was told, Franklin grabbed the seam in the center of the door and pulled.

A bright flash, accompanied by an impossibly loud boom, knocked the wind from Peters, smashing him into the floor and into an instant pain that blasted every inch of his body with all-consuming ache. Flat on his back, a throbbing ring in his ears, he rolled over, trying to comprehend what had happened.

Pieces of metal had found their way into the sheriff's body in odd places. Each stung, but none seemed to hurt in a life-threatening sort of way. But one could never tell. His ears were filled with a relentless high-pitched ringing, and his field of vision was consumed by splotches of white and yellow burned into his retinas. His head throbbed.

Propping himself back up onto his elbows, he saw the crater left by the explosion.

Josef Guerrero's munitions stash was nothing more than a scorched hole in the ground, leaving Sheriff Peters to wonder how long his life was going to last, one way or the other.

XXI

G ripping his morning drink, Josef Guerrero loved to watch the sunrise. It was an invigorating feeling and one of the few joys he had left in his life since he and his mother had been mutated so horribly.

The orange band of light on the horizon grew slowly, burning off the violet gray of morning.

The Serpent took a deep breath of the dusty Glyconian air.

But it was the air that he hated. It was the chemicals in the air his body had reacted to that had turned him and his followers into what they were. They were mutants. Towns-folk across Glycon-Prime had spit on them and scorned them. The corporation that brought them all to Glycon-Prime took no responsibility for it and refused to make things better.

They would all pay for their disrespect.

And once they'd paid for that disrespect and the whole of Glycon-Prime was under his control, he'd set his every resource into reversing the effects of Glickdom.

He and his Santa Madre would once again be human.

At first glance, the man known as the Serpent didn't notice the fire rising in the distance, nor the column of smoke that followed it. It wasn't until the sound of the blast, traveling slowly from kilometers away, reached his ears that he knew something was wrong. He could feel the rumble of the explosion in the core of his being, vibrating his innards like a bass drum. The sound hit the windows behind him, and they rattled like a snake.

His gaze was drawn immediately to the spot of trouble in the distance. A pillar of smoke rose over Stelio City.

Then he began to wonder, mentally going through a checklist of places through the town that could explode, not because he thought an explosion of such kind was plausible, but because he did not want to think that any of the means of his revolt had been vaporized into oblivion.

Fury built up within him until the glass in his hand shattered, spilling its contents all over the floor.

Entering his office, he went straight for the communications console, barely noticing that the sound of the blast had disrupted the sleep of his mother. He'd drawn the curtains every morning so he could see her. This morning, she'd not stirred from her rock; the girl who had been her most recent companion rested on the floor, motionless.

The sound of the explosion had Santa Madre upright, looking around and grimacing, inhaling deep breaths as though a smell should accompany the sound.

Guerrero sighed and hit the button to close her curtain, then activated the bright blue light that connected him to his security chief.

"Yes, sir?" came a voice through the speaker.

"Get out there to Stelio City. Now. Send everyone. And

bring me the hide of that worthless sheriff. I want to know who it is that is trying to destroy our revolution."

"Yes, sir."

"Well, that's that then," Zeke said.

"Looks to be." Twelve watched on from his perch on the ridge as the Serpent's army mobilized from the stronghold below.

In the morning light, the fortress appeared to be even more menacing than it had the night before. The metal of its walls was scorched in places and uneven across the surface. In the brighter light, it was easy to see that it had been cobbled together from a hundred different scraps of tin and metal from a hundred different containers and bits. There was a side of an interstellar shipping container here, a scrapped hunk of spaceship there. With the muddy river winding lazily behind the fortress, the scene might have almost been idyllic.

The gunslinger smiled.

This whole place looked like a house of cards welded together, and he'd be the one to knock it down.

"I'm getting a lot of wireless data traffic," Zeke informed Twelve. "It would seem as though they're throwing everything they have at you."

"Not at me, at Stelio City."

"Well, you were responsible for the explosion, so, in a way, they're still heading for you."

Or the kids, he thought.

Slowly, the imposing door on the broadside of the fortress rolled open, revealing the Glick horde on the other side, heavily armed and ready to march.

"They're going to war," Zeke said. Speeders, tanks, mounted units on dromids, all of them trickled out of the opening in the fortress like water over the lip of a dam.

With the troops leaving en masse, slipping in and slipping out would be child's play. Sure, there would be plenty of guards still inside, and his informant mentioned more than a few guards on the way to Miri's cell that wouldn't be gone. There was no guarantee she was in her cell, though. The short odds were on her being somewhere altogether more imposing. As long as his odds for survival might have been, they got better with every Glick heading to town.

"Let's hope she's where she's supposed to be," Zeke said.

"Let's hope she's still alive." Twelve muttered.

"I thought hope was my job."

The throngs of Glicks were heading away from their fortress, toward Stelio City and a wild boz chase. Ignoring his wrist computer and confidant, the gunslinger rose slowly from his prostrate perch on the ridge into a crouching posture.

"It's now or never, Twelve."

"Shut up, Zeke."

"After you."

Twelve growled but kept moving. Keeping his profile low, he edged his way toward the muddy river below.

The temperature dropped lower the closer he drew to the rushing water, tinted red from the Glyconian soil. The smell of the river reminded him of sulfur, but he knew it was the smell of the water being over-processed up stream and then mixing with the alien soil.

Twelve's feet pressed hard into the soft mud, carrying him along as fast as they could take him toward the front entrance of the Serpent's fortress. Crossing his arms in front of him, he grasped the handles of his laser pistols and leveled them up to his sides, ready for action. The weight of the pistols' grips felt satisfying in his palms.

Guerrero's fortress was most ominous from the front. Getting closer, the gunslinger looked up at the front wall to see that it reached all the way up to the sky; the tall saw-toothed spires of scrap metal piercing upward like the gargoyled towers of a cathedral devoted to death.

Gracefully taking the tin-metal steps up to the door two at a time, the gunslinger was surprised to hear it whoosh open without him having to activate it.

In the space inside, on the other side of the door, stood a Glick, tall and lean with a snarl on his face.

That snarl turned to shock when he realized he was staring down the barrel of an intruder's pistol.

The Glick's shock turned to the slack face of death when the stranger pulled the trigger and sent an energy blast into the sentry's side, vaporizing a hunk of his chest and spinning him around to the ground with a violent thud.

"That's one down," Zeke said.

"I don't need you to keep score."

"Of course you do. It makes you feel tough."

Stepping over the body without another thought, the stranger came into the first hallway of the fortress, starting his run through the gauntlet of Guerrero's men.

According to the Glick he'd killed in the desert, Miri's cell, if she was there, was on the bottom floor of the outpost. It was their practice to leave her there to sleep, so that's where he'd head.

The walls on the bottom floor were constructed much like the exterior; tossed together with scraps of mismatched metal all the way around. The floor was a hard concrete, tinted pink, revealing its local origin.

A logo had been sloppily stenciled onto the metal in front

of the entrance in green paint. The head of a serpent baring its fangs inside of a black half-circle. Perhaps it was designed to strike fear and menace into the hearts of those who viewed it, but it did nothing but make the stranger want to laugh.

Suppressing that feeling, he moved on to the corner, knowing that his only chance of survival stemmed from stealth.

Back against the wall, the stranger nudged his head out beyond the corner, catching a brief glimpse of the long, narrow corridor beyond and two Glick guards marching straight toward him. He recoiled, snapping tightly back into place, raising his guns.

He paused for a moment, glancing at Zeke's display screen. Predicting his intent, Zeke flashed him a layout of the fortress and two red dots to approximate where the Glicks were.

"You there!" A voice called out from around the corner.

So they had seen him.

"Is that you, Bowker?"

The gunslinger cleared his throat loud enough for them to hear it.

The words, "Don't blow it," appeared on Zeke's screen.

"Bowker?"

The stranger said nothing.

"Bowker, is that you?"

For a long, quiet moment, the gunslinger held his breath, waiting for just the right moment.

He could hear the guards talking between themselves quietly.

"Go ahead, see what's going on," one of them hissed.

"You go," the other argued.

Zeke flashed the message, "Good luck."

Smiling, Twelve snapped around on his heels and leapt out into the open airway of the hall, blasting as he went.

The two Glicks flinched hard, reaching for their sidearms.

Twelve's first shot went wide, far over the heads of his targets. The second shot disintegrated the face of the Glick on the right.

The remaining Glick actually made it far enough to level his gun and fire a violet blast at the gunslinger.

As it blew by, the stranger could feel its heat sear the side of his arm, going by and doing little damage.

Re-adjusting his aim in mid-charge across the hallway, he centered his guns on the remaining Glick's middle and pulled both triggers. Twelve's azure blasts hit the guard square in the chest, throwing him backward with an incredible concussive force. The Glick's legs kept moving, bucking for a moment until he went still, collapsing flat onto his back, dead as anything.

The gunslinger's left shoulder slammed into the far wall of the hallway, ending his strafing momentum. Redirecting his trajectory, he took a step forward, then another, stepping over more bodies.

He was going to be leaving plenty of them in his wake.

The break in the hallway was an open doorway. Approaching it with caution, the gunslinger peeked his head around, checking it for danger.

Empty metal bunk beds crisscrossed the room. Even at a glance, he could tell that they were kept meticulously.

"Whatever you wanted to say about this Serpent, at least he runs a tight ship," Zeke said.

Each of the beds were made and whatever belongings there may have been were all stowed neatly in lockers. As far as he could figure, the entire building was devoted to the Serpent's private army of disgruntled Glicks, ready to attack the average Glyconian pioneers with lightning speed and discipline. It wasn't anything the gunslinger could have imagined that mutants on other frontier worlds would be capable of.

This seemed unique to the atmospheric cocktail of Glycon-Prime.

Twelve took a side step into the barracks, one gun pointed in front of him, the other covering the open door to his left.

Taking no chances, he spun around, looking for anyone left. As far as he could tell, the room was empty. Never lowering his guns from hip height, he walked through the room, back to front just to be sure.

"Perfect," Twelve said to himself.

"For what?" Zeke asked.

"For hiding bodies. It's too bad you're not a full-sized 'bot, else I'd make you drag 'em in here for me."

"Take my word for it, sir, it would have been my pleasure."

XXII

For ten full minutes, Stelio City had been in a full-tilt panic, and all Sheriff Peters could hear was a faint, ringing squeal in his ears. Voices around him shouted, and they all sounded as though they were coming in through a tin can and a string three kilometers long.

Directly across from his office, someone had blown up the Serpent's supply of ammunition, and the only thing he knew for sure was that there would be hell to pay.

Aside from the disorientation from the blast, foreboding festered in the bottom of his gut. He wanted as many answers as he could find before the coming storm of Josef Guerrero and his men.

What was left of the bodies of the guard and the town's mechanic had been blasted into the speeder trail. The remains were scorched and bloodied, and nothing was left of them but pounds of dead and shredded meat. Unfortunately, the blast hadn't affected his sense of smell, because Peters could easily pick out the pungent charring of smoldering corpses.

The sheriff had called out his deputy, Bradley, and had him set up a perimeter with composite fiber poles that shot beams of light to each other, establishing a visible line that would sting sharply if it was crossed by any unauthorized individuals.

Because of his own ringing deafness, Peters shouted at his deputy who was crouched over what was left of the Glick Guerrero had left to guard the shack. "Who is he?"

The deputy scanned the Glick's tattered corpse, looking for any identifying marks. His scanner, a handheld number that used a red ray, warbled back and forth as he waved it over the dead man's hands and face. "I don't have him on file, Sheriff. I'm pretty sure he's one of Guerrero's."

"I know that, damn it!" Peters shouted. "I want to know who he is and what in perfect Hades happened, or it'll be my neck."

"Funny you should say that, Sheriff, but his neck being broke is what killed him. Not the blast."

"That doesn't do me any good. You holler when you find out who he is."

"His name was Calhoun," a slithering voice from behind the sheriff called out loudly.

Peters spun around on his heels, directing his attention to the imposing Glick standing on the porch of his jailhouse. "Who are you?"

"All you need to know is that I'm the mouth of the Serpent, and I'm the one asking questions," the Glick said coolly. "Why did this man die, and why was our investment destroyed on your watch?"

The 'mouth of the Serpent' was imposing, built like a tank himself, wearing a black work suit made of synthetic materials common to Glyconian pioneers. Peters's eyes moved from his bulging, scaly neck and down across the green serpent emblazoned across his chest, causing a frightened twitch at the base of the sheriff's neck that radiated into his head. "I'm still trying to figure that out. And who are you, exactly?"

The Glick ignored the question. "You're going to have to come with me, Sheriff."

"What? I've got to deal with all this here in Stelio."

"I'm afraid not."

"What was that? You'll have to speak up." The sheriff cupped his hand around his ear, emphasizing the ruse that he'd missed that last, chilling statement.

"I was given orders that if the Serpent's property was disturbed that I was to bring you to him. 'If it's out of order in any way, bring me the sheriff,' is what he told me. As it is, we are blockading your city until our own investigation has been conducted, and we have found the person responsible for this."

The bottom dropped out of Peters's stomach. The only image his mind could conjure was being shot in the back of the head with an energy rifle and buried in a shallow grave in the middle of the desert. "That's all well and good, but I can't leave just yet, son."

"You'll be leaving just now, Sheriff, or with a single energy blast your deputy will be the new sheriff."

Peters inhaled sharply. "Let me get my speeder."

"No need. You'll ride in ours."

Peters gulped hard. "Bradley. You're in charge until I get back."

Deputy Bradley stood up from his position over the corpses, "Yes, sir, Sheriff."

The sheriff, uneasy on his feet, staggered toward the menacing Glick. "Lead the way."

The mouth of the Serpent wrapped his firm grip around

the sheriff's arm and yanked him back, pulling him forcibly around the corner of the jailhouse and down the alleyway leading to the back side of the town.

As they reached the end of the alley and the open space beyond, Peters gasped.

In his immediate field of view was an aging tank, hovering over the ground, its gun barrel aimed into town. The sheriff moved his head to the left and the right and his knees buckled beneath him when he took in the sight before him.

There was an army there, ready to blow Stelio City off the map.

He whistled incredulously.

His problems were a lot bigger than saving his own skin.

XXIII

The stairwell leading down into the bowels of the Serpent's fortress was cramped and dark, but it was the right way to go according to the map Zeke had cobbled together based on the information given to them by the informant and his own scans.

"You sure this is the right way?" Twelve asked quietly.

Zeke lowered his volume to match Twelve's. "No. But it's the best guess given the available information."

Twelve resisted the urge to roll his eyes. Then, guns akimbo, he took the stairs two at a time, stopping dead when he heard the voice of the Glick sentry, calling up. "Aban? Is that you?"

Since the bottom of the stairwell was a T-junction, the stranger couldn't tell which direction the voice came.

"Aban?" The Glick called out again, worry and curiosity straining his voice.

Tiptoeing down three more stairs, the gunslinger tightened his breath, listening for a clue and waiting for an opening to act.

Footsteps shuffled closer and closer to the edge of the stairs. Twelve pressed himself up against the wall, tightening the muscles of his body like a mongoose ready to pounce.

"Aban?" The Glick's face appeared around the corner and the gunslinger leapt.

Trying to be quieter than a laser blast, Twelve tackled the Glick. Wrapping his arm around the guard's thick neck, Twelve used his forward momentum to crack the man's spine in two.

The pair of them skittered toward the back wall, crashing into it hard. The Glick let out his last breath in an agonizing groan before the stranger dropped him to the floor.

No time was left to hide the bodies now. He was close to where the girl was and had to get out fast.

The basement was really more like a dungeon, dark and damp, of dark red outer walls carved of the Glyconian clay. The interior walls that made up the cells were a brushed metal. With solid, deadlocked metal doors protecting each cell and an armed guard stationed in the hallway, escape must have seemed impossible to a prisoner. But breaking out was a lot easier after having broken in in the first place.

Working to regulate his breathing, slowing it, the stranger stooped down over the fallen guard, running his hands over all the pockets, looking for the keycard or unlocking device that would open the doors and allow him to rescue Miri from her tormentors.

There was nothing about handling a corpse that caused any distress in Twelve. It was easy for him to imagine how the kids had been functioning so normally in the sight of such a massacre, but then he realized that was wrong ...

Thinking back to the morbid terror he'd felt the first time he'd encountered a dead body; he was more unsettled by the fact that it had become something so routine that it instilled none of those human feelings. It left an empty, gnawing hole in the middle of his gut.

Holstering one of his pistols, Twelve turned the corpse over. It dropped to the ground unceremoniously, and the feeling of all that dead weight leaving his grasp caused him to marvel at how little it tugged on his soul.

There, tied to a belt loop, was a black keycard with the Serpent's logo printed on it. Yanking the ring firmly, he tore the fabric of the belt loop, and the keycard was in his possession.

Zeke chirped digitally. "The keycard is on the same frequency as the doors. You should be able to open them."

"Thanks. I'd've never figured that out without you."

"You're welcome."

"Shut it. Let's just see if she's still alive." Twelve eyed the first closed door in the row of cells.

"Miri?" he said gruffly. He thought for a moment about how he could soften his voice to make it sound more caring and comforting. "Miri?"

There was no response. After these days of torment, it would be no wonder she didn't want to announce herself.

He directed his attention to the second cell door in the row. "Miri?"

Again, no one responded.

"Miri, I'm a friend, I'm here to spring you." He removed so much of the hoarse loneliness from his voice that he almost believed himself.

After days of torture, he probably wouldn't respond when called in such a manner either.

"We haven't much time, Twelve," Zeke reminded him. "I suggest investigating the cells and leaving."

"Who can argue with that?"

The door to the first cell swung open with a squeak. The

stall beyond was empty, but the gunslinger got a stark look at the conditions the young girl had been subjected to.

The cell wasn't more than two meters wide in either direction. A metal toilet was affixed to the back wall, and the bed was nothing more than a tattered pile of discarded blankets atop a metal slab. With the door open, he caught a full whiff of the body odor and fecal smells emanating from even the empty holding cell.

"Miri...?"

He opened the next cell and found that it, too, was empty. There were only two cells left, and he wondered if she was the only prisoner they'd taken and left alive.

The third door held a surprise of its own, though. Laying on her stomach in the corner was a scant female form, emaciated from captivity.

Half covered over with the soiled blankets, she might have been sleeping.

He called out her name again, hating himself for sounding like a faint canyon echo. "Miri?"

With his pistol aimed at the slumbering body, he approached slowly, calling out Miri's name once more, hoping she'd respond one way or the other.

The gunslinger closed the distance slowly, making sure to keep his body as far outside the door of the cell as possible, just in case anyone sneaked up behind him and locked the door. He couldn't think of anything that would be more infuriating than getting caught in so foolish a situation.

Sidestepping into the cell, he tried to keep his peripheral vision on the stairway. "Miri?"

His mind raced with worry. What if this girl was Miri? What if she was dead? What if his entire suicide mission into Josef Guerrero's stronghold was all for naught?

Worry did a backflip into his stomach.

He was close enough that he couldn't keep his back covered and reach out to help this poor girl, so he tried to keep his motions quick.

Grabbing the girl firmly with his left hand on her far side, he pulled, rolling her over. Just by touching her he could tell she was dead. Rigor mortis had set in, she was firm and hard, as stiff as a pine log.

The features of her death mask were pulled downward, telling the stranger that she'd died frightened and alone. But the sorrow on her face was somehow serene. There was a quiet strength to it that he admired.

But the wrinkles and features were not that of a sixteen-year-old girl. This woman was clearly much older, though many of the outward appearances belied that idea.

Lipstick had been smeared over her decaying lips. Her tangled nest of hair was pulled into two rough pigtails. The flesh of her neck had been badly burned. And down her arms, flesh was torn in scratched patterns.

Zeke emanated a scanning sound. "I do not believe this is Miri, sir."

"Me neither."

That it wasn't Miri was something of a warm relief to him.

If his information was good, and Miri wasn't in the last cell, there was only one place left to look.

But it was the last place he wanted to go.

Twelve took a moment to cover over the face of the nameless woman with the soiled blankets. A snap of sorrow filled him, swelling from his heart and leading up to the area behind his eyes.

As he stood up, a smile cracked along his face. Suddenly he didn't feel so bad about not feeling any pity for the man whose neck he'd broken not five minutes prior.

He hadn't felt anything in so long and now, standing over this poor woman's body, he knew why.

Zeke sounded again, then spoke. "We're running out of time."

The gunslinger snapped from his introspection. "I know."

The last cell in the basement was empty.

He was going to have to go up.

To the top floor.

Twelve remembered back to the advice his captive had given him. "You don't want to go there," the Glick had told him, wailing in pain. "If she's there, you should just let her die."

"Where?" Twelve had said, pulling back from the Glick.

"Santa Madre's terrarium."

XXIV

Josef Guerrero stood at the balcony overlooking the generous expanse of desert between his fortress and Stelio City. In the distance there was a billowing trail of dust following behind the fastest speeder in his fleet.

It would almost certainly contain the incompetent Sheriff Peters, brought by force by Colin Baltimore, his most trusted lieutenant and right-hand man.

Guerrero allowed his thin, serpentine lips to purse in concern. If the sheriff was being brought to him, that was a clear indication that his worst fears had been realized. That stockpile hadn't come cheap, and it figured into his plans more importantly than anyone could know.

Peters was an idiot, that much was clear, but that was still no excuse for what had happened. No one should have even known about his munitions stash, let alone know enough to blow it to kingdom come.

To say that this turn of events was disconcerting was to put it mildly.

The speeder grew larger as it zoomed in from the horizon. On Guerrero's deck was an aging Earth telescope that he'd acquired in his dirty dealings to gaze at the stars with. He desperately wished he could use it to get a closer look at the approaching speeder and its occupants to confirm his suspicions, but he knew the image would be inverted, useless to him. The only thing it would do was exacerbate his headaches, which had been getting progressively worse since his affliction.

Every time he thought of his transformation, his eyes darted to the red curtains covering the window into his mother's new life. Watching her had been difficult.

But giving her something to play with had made things easier for him, more amusing.

By the time Baltimore's speeder was close enough for Guerrero to see the occupants clearly, the Serpent had made his way off the deck and back into his top floor antechamber. He could hear the giant metal door beneath his perch slide open and he knew they'd be coming up the elevators shortly.

His antechamber was decorated in a fashion twice as decadent as his neighboring office. Each wall held a glass case containing a different Earth relic, each more expensive and lavish than those held next door.

The first was a display case with an ancient scrap of paper inside bearing the signature of the first Latino president of the United States of America. He'd been a relative of Guerrero's centuries prior. Sometimes, Guerrero would stare at the signature, wondering what it would have been like to have that much power. The changing nature of his mutation made his dreams of elective office impossible. No one on Glycon-Prime would ever elect a mutant to office.

But he didn't need an office. He had money, which was just as good. And he'd take over the entire colonized world for himself.

It was the only way to set things right.

The company shouldn't have been sending colonists out to frontier planets if they had known the risk of spontaneous mutation was so high. To him, the issues were as simple as that.

Black and white.

And that's just how he'd be dealing with Sheriff Peters; black and white. There were no shades of gray for failure of such magnitude. He would have to pay for what he'd done.

While he waited for Baltimore and Peters, the Serpent fixed himself a drink from a decanter on the table in the center of the room. High backed chairs and a sofa surrounded it.

Easing himself into his favorite cushioned chair, Guerrero sipped at his beverage, waiting for them to make their way to him.

When Guerrero saw Sheriff Peters appear in the doorway, he could feel his own features drawing tight with anger. Peters was led at the arm, roughly, by Baltimore, who shoved him into the room without grace, care, or manners.

Baltimore angled the sheriff in front of the chair opposite the Serpent, placed his hands on his shoulders, and shoved him down into a seated position.

Guerrero turned and did his best to not hiss when he spoke. "What has happened to the ammunition I entrusted you with, Sheriff?"

Fear punctuated the sheriff's stammering voice, music to the Serpent's ears. "I don't rightly know. It was blown up. I can't say more than that because more than that I just don't know yet. Your friend here snatched me up right in the middle of my investigation."

"How much do I pay you, Sheriff?"

Peters looked around nervously. Guerrero knew that he

did not like verbalizing the amount of his sale price. Perhaps he was embarrassed. "You ... you doubled my salary, Mr. Guerrero."

"And do you enjoy this raise that the fruits of my labor provide you?" Guerrero stopped to take a drink of his sweet tea. "And the lavish gifts I have sent as tokens of my gratitude for your complacency and service?"

"I reckon I do." Peters fidgeted, wringing his hands in his lap.

"Well, when you find me those responsible for the destruction of my property, I will double it."

Guerrero still had not decided if Peters was lying. Anything was possible. The only thing that mattered was that he found those responsible. If someone were onto his plot, then things could become very bad for the Serpent's army very quickly.

"Consider it done, Mr. Guerrero." Peters tightened his hands together, looking eager to please. "I'll get right back on it right away."

The Serpent stood up, turning his back on the sheriff who disgusted him so much. He preferred the view from the balcony. Then he chilled his voice, bringing it to a low and gravelly register. "Do not be so enthusiastic. You have not heard the other side of the deal...."

The gunslinger only had to kill three people on his way up to the top floor and Santa Madre's terrarium. And not one of them caused him any real trouble. The element of surprise was on his side. No alarms had been sounded, and with the Glicks at battle stations in Stelio City, the Serpent's fortress was not much more than a ghost town like the one they made of Nine Mine City.

"It should be the corridor on your right." Zeke kept track of their whereabouts so Twelve could focus on keeping them alive and disabling sentries.

The weight of the blaster guns in each of his hands gave him a confidence, a feeling of protection. Moving through Guerrero's complex at top speed, using those same laser pistols to end the lives of men, gave him an exhilaration he would have a hard time describing to the kids.

In fact, he wouldn't even try.

"According to the map I pieced together, it should be the first door here, down this corridor. But anything's possible."

"And the Serpent's office should be the next door?" From the stairway, the only thing Twelve could see were the control boxes for the doors hanging on the center of the wall.

"If the Glick was telling the truth."

"If. Then we're gonna have to make this quick and quiet."

"That would be my suggestion."

Twelve crept up the remaining stairs on the fronts of his toes, standing at the edges of the steps to keep them from creaking. When he reached the landing, he took slow, deliberate steps to the first door.

Even through the magnetic seal, the gunslinger could smell the harsh odor of Santa Madre, and as his nose became accustomed to the stench, he picked up finer notes in the horrendous aromatic bouquet. Sweat. Body stink. Feces. Sour musk that reminded him of a snake.

They'd definitely chosen the right door.

Twelve glanced down to Zeke, thinking to himself how lucky the computer intelligence was that it couldn't smell.

Standing at the door, the gunslinger took in a shallow breath and held it, hoping to keep the stink out of his mind.

Then, he passed the keycard over the control box for the door.

The box beeped, and a small light on the top of it flashed from red to green.

Twelve furrowed his brow anxiously as the door swooshed open, bracing himself for whatever shocking scene might lay before him.

But nothing could have prepared him for what he witnessed.

Even through the gunslinger's shallow mouth-breaths, the smell wafted through the opening along with a blast of warmth. He choked back his gag reflex.

With the eye of a seasoned professional he took in the layout of the room. His gaze began with the far end, where the only light in the room emanated. It was the blearing red glow of an infrared heater, making the room boil in a crimson, steamy heat.

The majority of the light was aimed down at a slimy lump of a beast curled up on a rock like a cold-blooded creature warming itself in the early morning sun. Between Twelve and the snoozing beast he assumed to be the dreaded Santa Madre he'd been told about, was a room full of odd curiosities. A table in the center of the room was laid out in a sort of tea party. An open kettle sat on a burner on a counter to the side of that.

The opposite side of the room was consumed by a mirrored wall, reflecting the scene before him. The way the image echoed in the light, Twelve knew it must have been one-way glass.

Someone must have enjoyed watching Santa Madre torture her victims.

The floor was scattered with other items the gunslinger couldn't imagine uses for. A soiled blanket. Three shattered pieces of a ceramic figurine. A makeup brush. Bent forks and spoons. A tube of lipstick. A stuffed caricature of a dromid, soiled and matted.

The room was littered with shards of debris from what seemed to be a hundred shattered objects that had outgrown their usefulness and no one had bothered to sweep up.

The one thing the room was missing, however, was the one thing he'd come for: Miri.

Unless she was hiding behind the rock or somehow on the rock, obscured by the snoring bulk of Santa Madre.

Pistols raised in both hands, Twelve took two small steps into the room to investigate further, just enough for the door to race closed behind him.

With the door closed, the light from the hallway disappeared, and the only draft of good air went with it.

As he took a few more steps toward the table, his eyes struggled to adjust to the dim red, his ears strained to hear any meaningful noise above the snoring, and his mouth and nose worked in tandem to dampen the horrid reek.

If Miri wasn't there ...

... but that's when he heard a sharp but muffled gasp from behind him.

Spinning on his heels a full hundred and eighty degrees, he turned to see a young girl standing at the door with her back to him, trying desperately to pry it open.

"Miri?" Twelve said softly, not wanting to wake the monster at his back.

The girl stopped her effort and turned to Twelve.

She anxiously covered over the sides of her face with the open palms of her hands.

"Are you Miri?" he repeated.

The girl, young, beautiful, and scared, did her best to avoid eye contact with the stranger, but for just an instant her eyes met his. Watching her cover her head and hair, he knew at once what the problem was.

He glanced back over his shoulder, ensuring that Santa Madre was still sleeping soundly, then turned back to Miri. Uneasy about doing so, he returned both of his pistols into their holsters on his side and gripped his serape at the edges, tearing a strip off the bottom of his front. It tore unevenly from one side to the other with a scratching rip.

Though it was soiled and dirty, leaving his belt and pistols exposed, he folded the scrap of cloth neatly and handed it to the girl.

"Go ahead. Take it. Quick." The gunslinger could feel dread crawl up his back and over his shoulder. He didn't like having his back turned to the slumbering demon.

He could see the confusion and fright on the poor girl's face, but he understood it. She'd been ripped by grief and abused for so long these last few days that any act of kindness would likely be met with mistrust. But after the initial hesitation, she snatched the cloth right up, wrapping it uneasily around her head. It wasn't a proper headscarf, but Twelve knew enough about the settlers from the Arab Station to know it would help put the girl at ease and convince her that he wasn't one of the bad guys.

Maybe she wouldn't trust him, maybe not yet anyway. But at this point he didn't need or deserve her trust, he just needed to get the hell out of there.

Miri looked up at him, truly locking her eyes with his for the first time. Her eyes were a deep, chestnut brown that seemed black in the red light, her nose, a button on her face, and her mouth a grim line above an elegant chin. All of her features were bathed in the red reflections of hot ruby light.

She tried to offer Twelve a smile, but the best she could

do was to struggle against her pained frown, until her eyes widened, staring off at something behind the stranger.

It took him a moment to find that curious, but when he heard a throaty hiss behind him, he knew trouble was coming.

A feeling he recognized as instinct flashed through his body, and he began to move without even thinking. His fingers felt it first, reaching for the handles of his laser pistols. Then the instinct took over his hips and feet, whipping his body around to face the danger. His head was the last thing that received the signal, swiveling around, trying to catch up to his body ...

... but its rotation was cut short by the slash of razored nails across his face. A sting jolted him from across his cheek, making him painfully aware of the mistake he'd made.

Twelve swung his pistols around, hoping to shoot the growling Madre, but she swiped his guns away as he pulled the trigger. A pair of brilliant blue laser blasts shot high, hitting the back wall of Santa Madre's domicile above her rock, exploding fragments of the faux-plaster into the air.

"What'sss it doing here?" Santa Madre shrieked, her voice hoarse, groggy from her nap. Reacting with the speed and strength of a banshee, she snatched his wrists, gripping them backward.

Off balance from his turn, the gunslinger had to fight to keep upright. Santa Madre was strong, stronger than he would have guessed. Watching her sleep lazily on the rock, he'd assumed she would have been slow but there was a primal force behind her.

With every coughing hiss she made, he knew she was more beast than human, and far less human than any colonial mutant he'd ever encountered, Glick or otherwise.

Wrestling back against the force of her weight, Twelve

managed to shift his legs around in front of himself so he could meet her head on. But her arms proved powerful enough to continue pushing him backward at his knees.

"Leave usssss alone...." Santa Madre angled the gunslinger back even further, gripping his wrists even tighter, and gurgling with fury.

Twelve had one choice, and it was a bad one in any normal fistfight, but it was the only one he had.

The gunslinger lifted his left leg and kicked it into Santa Madre's stomach. An experienced fighter would have never let him do such a thing, but Santa Madre was a primal beast, not a smart fighter. She had every opportunity to steal his balance from him, press the attack, and chew his face off, but instead took the kick and reeled backward.

But she didn't let go of the gunslinger's wrists.

She pulled the intruding stranger backward with her, but Santa Madre had no control of their fall.

Santa Madre hit the table behind her, crushing through it to the ground on her back, eliciting a guttural roar of pain from the top of her throat. Her scaly mass broke Twelve's fall, but in her falling she let go of his hands trying to use her arms to reach out for safe purchase.

During the descent, the gunslinger could hear the clatter of his laser pistols hitting the floor and sliding off to his right.

When they landed, Twelve did his best to roll off her, where he could free himself from the potential of her grasp. Through the debris of the table and the mess of the room he rolled in the direction he'd heard his pistols drop until he felt he was far enough away from her to throw his forearms underneath his body and push himself up to a standing position.

But Santa Madre stood, too.

Miri screamed.

Scanning the ground in front of him, he sought the location of his pistols....

Santa Madre snarled, foaming at the mouth, turning slowly in place toward the gunslinger, as though her rage were so all-consuming that she could barely move, letting it all build up for a final pounce.

The gunslinger could hear the rumble in her stomach and the gnashing of her teeth. A chill hit his heart when he realized with certainty that if he didn't finish her off, she would strip the meat from his bones and eat it like a buzzard.

The Serpent's mother made her move, pulling back like a snake about to strike ...

... the gunslinger spotted his laser pistol and reached out for it, diving toward it ...

... Santa Madre sprung forward, but there was suddenly something between her and Twelve.

Miri.

"No, Miri," the gunslinger firmed a grip around his pistol and raised it up, looking for a shot of Santa Madre, but Miri's back side consumed his view.

The young girl clearly held something in her arms that he couldn't quite see, but whatever it was it had stopped Santa Madre in her tracks.

"Maggie?" the creature said.

The gunslinger scrambled to his feet and saw what Miri had done.

The poor thing had taken one of the shorn metal legs of the collapsed table and used it to lance her tormentor. The table leg had pierced Santa Madre's belly, spilling tar colored blood down over her dress.

Santa Madre looked confused.

Her rubbery features slackened. Without the tightness of

anger, she looked almost human. Her eyes widened, glossed over with the wetness of tears Twelve wasn't sure she'd been capable of.

"Maggie ..." she repeated, damaged much more than the table leg could have wounded her.

Using the table leg for leverage, Miri stepped left, swiveling Santa Madre around with her. Then, the young girl pushed forward, doing her best to ram the beast back into her rock.

But Santa Madre still had fight left in her.

"Wicked ... filthy ... girl...." Santa Madre reached out, clawing at Miri, scratching the air, screaming, trying desperately to do what damage she could.

Though Miri pushed as hard as she could, Santa Madre stood her ground firmly, yowling in painful hurt and anger.

But it all stopped when an azure blast of light smashed into the Glick's chest. Santa Madre groaned, and the sizzle of her burning flesh overpowered the stink of the place. In more pain and with less breath, Santa Madre couldn't stand fast against Miri's force and ambled backward.

Twelve smiled grimly as he aimed once more, right over Miri's head, and again pulled the trigger on his laser pistol. Instantly, the second blast arced from the pistol and terminated in the face of Santa Madre.

The momentum the monster had blocked Miri from building gave all at once. Her body reeled backward, taking involuntary steps until she collapsed over the heat rock.

Twelve could see Miri shaking, still clutching her makeshift lance, keeping it held into Santa Madre's middle.

The gunslinger lowered his pistols, holstering them. "It's over now, Miri."

But Miri did not respond.

Zeke did, though. "We're well over our optimal time limit. We really must go."

"Shut up, Zeke." Twelve took a step toward Miri, reaching his hand up. He wanted to somehow comfort her, and his open palm inched closer to her back ...

... but no.

He pulled his hand back to his side, stuffing it into his pocket.

Twelve took a deep breath, hoping to soothe the situation with his demeanor. "Miri, I know this is hard, but we really have to go."

After a long moment, the girl sniffled and turned her head toward the gunslinger. "Go where?"

"To your brother ..."

"Nik?" Life and hope returned to her voice. "He's alive?"

"He is. And a couple of other youngsters besides. But they're in trouble, too. We gotta bolt, fast."

"Who are you?"

A hundred words passed through Twelve's mind, but only one of them came out. "Kelly," he said quietly. Then he repeated it, running the word he hadn't said in so long across his lips. "My name's Kelly. But that doesn't matter anymore. We've gotta go. Now."

Slowly letting go of the protruding spear, Miri turned to him and looked him in the eyes. The anger and fright had disappeared, replaced by the determination only found in survivors.

"Okay, Kelly," she said. "Let's go."

XXV

I really do not think you understand the gravity of the situation, Sheriff Peters," Josef Guerrero said, pacing the room as he scolded.

Peters said nothing.

"If you fail to bring me the heads of the men responsible for this," Guerrero continued. "you will be killed, Sheriff. And it would bring me great pleasure. But it will not be quick. Or pleasant."

Guerrero knew that he'd inspired the proper level of fear in the sheriff. The lawman's eyes widened, his jaw slackened, and his face bled white in terror. The Serpent knew that it was all in how he used the natural hiss of his mutated state and the intonation in his voice.

The Serpent grinned. All weak men find terror easily in the hearts of the powerful.

Peters swallowed his fear and grew arrogantly confident. "I won't fail you, Mr. Guerrero."

"I know you won't, Sheriff." Guerrero stood and walked

over to the door that led to his office, then beckoned Baltimore and the sheriff to follow.

At the nod of the Serpent's head, Baltimore snagged Peters by the scruff of the neck and pulled him across the lush carpet, out of the antechamber, and into the lavish office.

Guerrero paced the room, allowing a fury to build inside of himself, feeding into the image of angry power he wished to project. "Failure is not looked kindly upon by me. I may look a mutant, you and the people of your town might call me a snake behind my back, but my mind wasn't damaged in my metamorphosis. I'm no one to be trifled with."

Peters stammered. "I ... I never said you were."

Guerrero was glad to see that Baltimore hadn't removed his grip from the folds of flesh around Peters's chubby neck.

"You see, Sheriff, if you fail, I won't kill you. No. That would be too easy for you, letting you get away with failure with no chance to contemplate it. Your fate will be altogether more humiliating."

The sheriff's eyes widened, and his skin lost its rosy complexion, bleeding white. He knew what was coming. He'd heard the stories.

Guerrero hated using his mother as a bargaining chip, but after the stories of what she'd become and what she was capable of had seeped into town, she was impossibly effective at inducing terror. While it struck terror in the hearts of others, it stained the Serpent's heart with remorse. Her fate as a monster wasn't her fault. And her fate represented the very injustice Guerrero wished to fight against. But his mother had always taught him to use the tools at hand, so he banished his remorse and turned to the curtain that hid the plasti-glass barrier between his office and her terrarium.

"She's lonely, Sheriff Peters." The Serpent balled a lump of red curtain in his fist and dragged the curtain back. As furious as he could seem, nothing instilled fear like the thought of being imprisoned alone with Santa Madre.

Without looking at the sight himself, Guerrero turned to the sheriff with his back to the glass, reveling in Peters's reaction.

Narrowing in on the sheriff's expression, he knew the sight of Santa Madre was having the intended effect.

But looking up to Baltimore, Guerrero got the distinct feeling that something was wrong. Baltimore had seen Santa Madre a hundred times. He'd even overseen the construction of her sleeping quarters when she'd grown meaner and more feral. Why would Baltimore's features slacken in surprise and concern? He was neither being threatened nor frightened by Guerrero's mother.

But his face was contorted just the same.

Guerrero turned to look into the terrarium where he kept his mother. At first, the image he saw didn't process. Surely, she must have been sleeping there on her rock.

But no.

A makeshift spear stuck into her middle, like she was an animal slaughtered by a primitive and left to die. The Serpent zeroed in on more details he had no desire to see, focusing on the blaster burns that had hollowed out her chest and face. Blood thick as oil poured over the lip of Santa Madre's heat rock, collecting in an inky pool on the floor.

Guerrero hadn't realized that he was shaking.

In anger.

In shock.

In sadness.

The Serpent let out a long hissing scream that could be heard ringing through his complex.

When he finished, he caught himself against the plasti-glass of his mother's enclosure with an outstretched hand and tried to catch his breath.

His mind revved like a speeder turbine, working to put each piece of the puzzle before him together.

His mother was dead, and someone was going to have to pay. Suddenly, the failures of the sheriff didn't seem as important in the grand scheme. Something much more sinister was afoot, for whoever was responsible was surely the same person behind the explosion of his munitions. This was a coordinated attack against not only his revolution, but him personally.

It made no difference who was behind the plot, he wanted whoever it was that killed his mother to die.

Guerrero wanted to kill whoever was responsible person-ally and publicly.

His hoarse throat let out a croak as he turned to Balti-more and the sheriff. "Find whoever did this. I want them alive."

Sheriff Peters wiped the sweat from his brow and relaxed his body. Guerrero's eyes narrowed in on the relieved look on the sheriff's face. "Do not mistake this as a reprieve, Sheriff. If you fail to bring those responsible to me, you'll meet with a fate worse than they will."

The tightness in the sheriff's face returned, giving Guer-rero some small bit of satisfaction.

The Serpent looked up to Baltimore. His trusted advisor. His right-hand man. The only other Glick in the world who understood as well as he did what they were trying to accomplish with their new order of things.

Baltimore hissed, baring his sharpened teeth. For a moment, Guerrero wondered what Baltimore must have looked like before his mutation in the same fond way he thought back to memories of his mother, before all this …

Guerrero locked eyes with his lieutenant and felt the strain of saddened pain come through his voice. "Find them, my friend. Find them for me."

The gunslinger hit the accelerator on the stolen speeder, launching him across the expanse of Glycon-Prime's prairie. He flew far and fast toward the edge of the red desert, knowing he didn't have long before Guerrero's men would be on to him.

"So, can I call you Kelly now?" Zeke said to him, modulating his volume over the roar of the speeder.

"You know better than to even ask." The gunslinger shouted, adjusting his feet on the pedals in order to keep his speed down. Now that he was out of cannon range of the complex, he wanted to give the Glicks an easy chance to catch his trail.

"I just don't think your bounty license number is all that great of an inspiration for a—"

"Not now, Zeke." Twelve revved the turbine in low gear to make a loud grinding noise with the turbine to accentuate the noise of his escape.

He didn't make it a full five kilometers before the Glicks were on to him, bursting from their fortress in a speeder of their own. "There is a speeder on your trail now," Zeke informed him. "Heading right this way at top speed."

"And Miri?"

"Nothing on my sensors."

"Good." Twelve smiled and doubled the acceleration.

Who didn't love a good chase?

Looking back behind him, the gunslinger could see the pursuers Zeke had warned him about. There were three of them packed into a roofless speeder on his tail. One drove, the other two sat on the tops of the seats, holding their balance on the top lip of the windshield, leveling laser pistols in front of them.

Twelve turned his control yoke sharply to the left, adjusting his heading away from both Stelio City and the satellite tower that he and the kids had adopted as their home base.

A laser blast rocked the back of the speeder, spinning the rear portion out of control.

"Sir, we've been hit!" Zeke said.

"Will you shut up?" The stranger fought with the wheel to bring it back into a straight line, and, with his left hand, blindly fired at the speeder behind him.

Squeezing off five shots, he snapped his head around, the wind whipping his hair into his eyes, to see if he'd hit any of his targets. All of the blasts he'd fired had gone wide, dissipating into the growing dust cloud behind them and affecting nothing.

"All misses, Twelve. You're getting rusty."

The Glicks returned fire, rocking the back of the speeder up and down. The impact sent them fishtailing. Twelve overcorrected with the control yoke, veering him off his intended course.

"Shut. It. Zeke."

"Sir, yes, sir."

From the bank of the sludgy river, the stranger had told Miri to go as fast as she could along the shore until she reached a fork in the stream. Then, she was to turn left and travel toward the line of relay towers in the distance. Then, she was to walk and walk and walk until she came to safety.

The stranger hadn't given her time to process what had happened.

There wasn't any time to be had.

Ideally, she would have wanted to spend roughly forever trying to forget about the trials of Santa Madre before attempting anything stressful or strenuous. But if she ever wanted an opportunity like that again, she couldn't think about it.

She just had to go.

The man named Kelly had told her as much.

And he'd saved her. So who was she to argue?

When they had escaped the complex and reached the riverbank, she'd broken down in fear and panic and disgust, but he had done his best to assure her.

"As soon as you see me go, you just head out. Your brother is there. You'll have to take care of him and the rest of the kids the Serpent orphaned."

"Where are you going?" she'd asked him.

"To distract them. You find your kin and get out. Head south, don't come back this way, toward Stelio or anywhere else. Find a spaceport. The Corporate Authority will do right by you. They love money, but they've got a soft spot for kids on planets like this. I'll get the Glicks out of here."

As much as she agreed, as much as she wanted to get away, she couldn't help but linger, wanting to know what would happen to her rescuer.

A faint quiver in his voice, almost imperceptible, told her that he was holding something back.

"I'll lead them away. I'll give you the best kind of head start so you won't have to worry about them."

"What about you?" she'd thought to ask.

"Me? I'll be all right."

But he hadn't meant it.

Deep down, she knew he meant to get himself killed so that they could live.

But why?

Why risk yourself for a gaggle of strange kids? Whether it was one child or four, Kelly didn't seem the type to take unnecessary risks.

That's when her tears started all over again.

Something about the gunslinger made her sad.

Miri crouched low to the bank, watching until the stranger, heading in the opposite direction in their stolen speeder, disappeared. She waited until a second speeder, full of Glicks, burst out from the compound, heading in the same direction as her rescuer. She held onto her makeshift hijab with both hands, working to extract comfort from it after her days without it.

Laser fire was exchanged between the two speeders, but soon they were nothing but dots in the distance.

That was her cue to flee.

Lingering wasn't an option; if they caught her again, they'd surely kill her.

But that wouldn't be worse than what they'd already done to her.

She couldn't think about that, though. She just had to get to her brother and let him know what the stranger had done for her—for all of them.

One agonizing and exhausted step after another, she carried herself closer toward the one thing that had given her hope since the stranger had mentioned it in Santa Madre's house of horror.

It was the one word that played in her mind, repeating itself over and over.

"Nik."

XXVI

Sheriff Peters bound down the stairs three at a time, hot on the heels of Baltimore, each of them racing down to the armory. Peters hoped that there would be something there he could use to catch the killers of Santa Madre, and, in turn, catch the laser-wielding gunman who was surely responsible for the explosion in Stelio.

Short of breath, he found time to gulp uneasily at the thought that his life was forfeit if he failed.

The armory was a wide-open garage of a space that seemed hollow and empty. The life had drained out of it when Guerrero had ordered his men to occupy Stelio City. There were only a few speeders left in reserve and the Serpent's man, Baltimore, had dived into the closest speeder. It was occupied by a pair of Glicks in uniform that he barked orders at. With Baltimore secure in the passenger seat and brandishing his pistol, the Glick at the wheel revved the vehicle's turbine and sped out the impressive bay doors.

That left Peters alone in the warehouse, with the only two speeders left at the far wall.

Peters plodded toward the speeders at the back of the vast warehouse, cursing himself when he realized that the remaining speeders were in maintenance. Hoping they were fit for service, he picked the one that seemed the most put together and got in.

The engine turbine started with a puff of smoke, but started nonetheless, leaving Peters to make an overly complicated six-point U-turn to get it out of the hangar.

He swore with every turn of the wheel he made until he was free of the hangar.

The sheriff didn't like the idea that his days might be numbered if he failed to catch up. Perhaps they were numbered regardless, but it didn't matter. If catching these bastards would help save his life in any small way, he'd do it.

By the time Peters had righted the speeder and was heading the proper direction, the culprit and Guerrero's men had disappeared in a trail of red dust and Glyconian vapor that would be preposterously easy to follow.

Looking down, he scoured the control panel, looking for a sensor screen that might show him the locations of the speeders ahead of him.

Sheriff Peters was dismayed to find a gaping hole where that screen would go and dangling wires hanging down from the empty cavity.

"Damn it."

Cooling his head, he knew that wasn't the only thing he could do. He punched the accelerator and pushed a combination of buttons on the busy console that boosted his speed, overclocking the turbine's maximum acceleration by double.

Catching up was a matter of life or death. The threat of an exploding turbine was minimal next to the threat of Guerrero.

The red dust he chased thickened so much that he pulled

his shirt up over his nose and mouth and rifled through the console, looking for safety glasses of some sort to protect his eyes.

"Come on, cut me a break," he muttered to himself.

His heart skipped a beat when he reached into the armrest compartment between the seats and found an old pair of dusty goggles. He guided the speeder's steering column with his knee while he pulled them on and adjusted them to fit his head.

Though the lenses were smudged, Peters was still able to see better through the cloud. With his improved sight, he gunned the turbines and did his best to make short work of the distance separating his speeder and the Glicks pursuing the responsible party.

The moment he caught a solid glimpse of Guerrero's men in their speeder was the moment he pulled his laser pistol from his hip holster, aimed, and fired.

The sheriff's first shot was lucky, tagging the Glick in the back seat between the shoulder blades. His body went limp, slumped forward, and then the momentum of the speeder dragged his form back until it slid off and hit the soil below.

Peters swerved to dodge the corpse.

Up ahead, Peters could see Baltimore turn to watch what was going on and why his suppressing fire had disappeared. The sheriff took smug satisfaction in the look of surprise on Baltimore's face. Baltimore had been in the passenger side, blasting away at the murderer when he must have seen the blasts of azure light race by him from the wrong direction.

When Baltimore turned to see that his compatriot was dead and long gone, his face grew confused. It took him a moment to add up the equation of the situation.

Gritting his teeth and clearly enraged, Baltimore turned in his seat, ignoring his pursuit to open fire on Peters.

He shouted something back at the sheriff angrily, but over the singing turbines, Peters couldn't make out what he was saying.

Sheriff Peters could feel his heart pound in his chest. Now that he'd killed one Glick, he'd have to kill all of them to bring the stranger in alive.

Peters took in a sharp breath. If he left the Serpent's men to bring in whoever had killed Santa Madre, there's no telling how far Guerrero would carry his threats. The one thing Peters knew was that he didn't want to find out.

The sheriff had decided long ago that it was best not to take chances when his life was at stake.

He reached his gun up over the lip of the windshield once more and opened fire wildly in front of him, at the Glicks, the culprits, at everything, and at nothing.

Another blast rocked the back of Twelve's speeder, and he could hear the spinning gears and motors behind him make unnatural sounds, twisting and shearing from the force and the heat of the laser bolts.

"Damn it."

They hadn't yet hit anything else of importance, so it was certainly a lucky hit. No one could have made a shot like that on purpose in the dust his speeder kicked up.

Except maybe Twelve.

The bolt had managed to hit his turbine, and his speeder began to slow. He could feel a numbness originate in his middle and radiate outward. It was a full blast of unease.

"There's another speeder, sir," Zeke informed him.

"That's just what we need."

They were going to catch up to him and overtake him a lot sooner than he wanted them to, and there was still so much more of their time he wanted to waste to ensure Miri made it back to the rest of the kids safely. Maybe it was just a dream that she'd do it, but he had to give her the best chance possible.

Twelve craned his neck around and fired another volley of blaster bolts behind him indiscriminately into the direction of the Glicks.

While firing his last volley, the gunslinger noticed something peculiar. They were firing more at each other and less at him.

Who were they and why were they doing it? At the end of the day, did it matter?

Most likely not.

Whoever they were back there, they were probably just fighting over his corpse prematurely, hoping to get a better cut of whatever reward the Serpent would offer for the man who killed the infamous Santa Madre.

Though their infighting might have improved his odds, his need for survival against them had not changed.

Sputtering, his engine added a shower of sparks and acrid black smoke to the mix of red dust particles kicked up into the air by his exhaust, making it virtually impossible to see anything behind him. But he didn't need to see to point his gun and shoot in the direction he had come.

"You think she made it?" he said out loud.

"Unknown, sir," Zeke responded.

Firing off blue bolts of lethal light into the smoke, he hoped one of the blasts would hit a target meaning to kill him. Contorting himself around to both steer and shoot, though, meant he probably wasn't going to hit anything.

"That's not what I asked, Zeke."

Each pull of the trigger, every blast, felt as though it went wide.

The engine hissed and wheezed, and he could feel the drag of his momentum lessening against his chest. The wind running through his hair diminished drastically, and he knew the speeder wasn't going to make it much longer.

Zeke's accelerometer must have told him the same thing. The AI came to the same conclusion Twelve had. "You're going to have to do something drastic."

"I know." The gunslinger scanned the horizon in front of him. Flat, clear, and red, free of obstructions, he knew just what he had to do. "Hold on."

"I'm always holding on, sir."

"Good." Twelve jerked the wheel of the speeder all the way around and pulled the lever to switch the direction of the turbine to reverse. The centrifugal force smashed him into the side of the speeder door, and the resurgence of wind and force whipped his short hair into a frenzy.

"Good work, sir."

Despite the rapidly degenerating condition of the speeder and the clunking noises it made to protest, Twelve's maneuver had been successful, and he found himself speeding backward while facing his pursuers.

Never letting up on the accelerator, moving rapidly in reverse, he raised the laser pistol in his shooting hand up above the level of the windshield and waited for a clean shot.

He knew they were there behind him; he could still see random laser blasts flying quickly in his direction. Thankfully, none of them came close to hitting him or the speeder.

When the stranger could vaguely make out what he thought was the outline of one of the speeders, he squeezed the trigger repeatedly, launching a volley of cobalt lasers into the black smoke. On their way through, the bolts illuminated more details of his pursuers.

When the shapes became clearer, he knew exactly where he should shoot and let out another hail of fire in just the right spot. He couldn't know it for sure, but he was fairly positive he had blasted the driver of the speeder directly behind him.

He could tell his hunch was correct when, through the particle cloud, the Glick speeder veered off hard to his right and at top speed, leaving the dusty smoke. As the image of the speeder cleared through the haze, the stranger could see that he'd shattered their windshield. The driver was hunched over the steering column, pinning it to the left. The passenger, a fierce-looking Glick, had been shooting to the rear of his speeder and cocked his head toward the driver, panicked at the evolving danger of his situation.

Their speeder swayed and wobbled, the features on the surviving Glick's face widened in shock. He scrabbled back over the front seat and toward the dead man, doing his best to quickly leverage his fallen comrade's weight out of the speeder so he could correct its course and maintain pursuit.

Distracted by the scene, Twelve almost didn't notice the blaster bolt that came sailing forth through the blurry fog.

Another searing laser light appeared in the haze, lancing in the gunslinger's direction. Twelve could see it coming at him, but he was powerless to do anything. It flew straight and true, catching the front end of his speeder.

On its own, a single laser blast shouldn't have had enough stopping power to do any significant damage to the front end of the speeder. But a laser blast impacting the windshield, cracking it into a thousand different geometric shapes, caused the normally staid gunslinger to flinch.

His eyes snapped shut, the muscles in his hands and

arms contracted, and his head pulled away. Even for a professional, the biological urge to protect vital organs was a powerful response.

He pulled the control wheel sharply to the right with him, sending him into a ferocious spin.

Losing control caused the front end to smash into the soil, and the back end reared up into the sky before the entire speeder landed on its side. In that brief instant, the stranger couldn't tell what had happened to him, because he'd moved in so many directions all at once.

He could feel the impact, though. It started with his hands on the wheel and radiated from the front of his body to the back, like he'd been tackled by a lawman.

Somewhere along the way, he must have hit his head and been thrown from the speeder. There was a dull ache in the back of his neck and a sharp pain in his forehead.

All the noise of the world went quiet. The pitched sound of turbines wound down to nothing, and all he could hear was his own heartbeat.

Then, after a long moment wondering if he was dead, he heard a voice calling out from the desert, taunting. "Well, well, well, what is it we've got here? Just one guy? You don't look so tough to me."

The gunslinger tried to speak, to respond, to reach for his pistol, but no words or actions came. He tried angling his wrist toward him, but even Zeke seemed to be nothing more than a blank, lifeless screen.

Twelve reached up with his hands, trying to right himself into a standing position, but even that was too much effort.

"I'm just going to assume," the man hovering over him said, "that you're the fella responsible for all the problems we've been having in my little town."

With a groan, Twelve rolled over onto his belly, hoping

he could draw his limbs underneath himself to stand. He tried to talk but had to spit first. Blood coughed up onto the soil beneath his face. He forced a sly smile. "Who ... who are you again?"

"Me? I'm the sheriff around these parts, and you done pissed off the wrong men."

Finally, Twelve got an elbow up underneath himself.

But that's when he felt a meaty fist connect with the back of his head, and everything went black.

PART III
REVENGE

XXVII

The children, Nik, Amir, and Lila, waited anxiously in the ever-shortening shadow of the satellite relay tower.

"With any luck," Nik said, pacing about and tired with worry, "it's all over by now. And he's on his way back and Miri's fine and everything is all fine."

Amir stood slowly, scratching the back of his head. "You think it's been long enough?"

Lila sat quietly, watching the boys.

"It been a long time." Nik turned in place, kicking dirt with every step.

"Maybe a long time wasn't enough." Amir folded his arms in front of him.

Nik harumphed.

"They'll make it," Lila said, with a soft confidence. And that was the last word about it.

Despite their anxiety, a calm managed to seep its way into their bodies. The sound of Glyconian crickets lulled them into a quiet state of forced serenity. The boredom set in, and they scratched this and that into the dirt, barely talking in the heat. For what felt like hours, they waited, but that all came to a grinding halt when Amir pointed to a spot on the horizon. "What's that?"

Nik snapped his head in the direction Amir had pointed, seeing an ambling figure floating on the false water in the distance coming at them. "It's only one."

"You think it's a Glick?" Amir raised his hand to his brow and squinted at the approaching form.

"Could be," Nik said. "Quick, everybody hide!"

At Nik's command, the children scrambled to duck behind the relay station, clinging close to the ground. Even Lila, clutching her doll, hit the deck and crawled into the shadow of the metal utility box.

Nik crawled as low as he could toward his bedroll, reaching around for the family sword he'd spent his time clinging to. Taking it by the hilt, he knew that if trouble presented itself, he'd be ready. The adrenaline coursing through his body settled into his heart, bucking him up for any danger.

Lying there in the dirt, watching the intruding form approach, grasping the hilt of his family sword, Nik felt invincible. A feeling of power grew inside the boy, radiating from his ever-tightening grip on the sword.

The figure grew from a tiny speck to a medium-sized one. At the rate they came, he knew that whoever it was, was clearly on foot and not moving with much urgency.

Amir turned to Nik, his voice a harsh and harried whisper, "I wonder what's taking them so long. If they were trying to kill us, don't you think they'd have hurried it up?"

"Maybe," Nik admitted.

"Or maybe," Amir continued, wondering out loud, "they're just trying to scare us? What do you think of that?"

Nik tightened the grip on the handle of his sword, which in turn tightened the feelings inside him. "Anything's possible, Amir. But I'll tell you this: we'll be ready for what comes."

The figure grew slowly, and Nik even thought he saw it stagger once or twice. And that got him to thinking.

What would a Glick be doing all the way out here in the desert on foot? Wouldn't they come by speeder? And even if they did come on foot, wouldn't they have come by way of the speeder trail?

Then he began to wonder....

"Miri?" he finally said.

When Nik said that one, simple word, Amir looked closer, squinting harder. "I think ... I think it is. It's Miri!"

Nik shot to his feet and sprinted toward her, carrying himself across the red soil as fast as his legs would take him.

It didn't take him long to cover the distance, and once Miri saw him she got a second wind, regaining her speed to reach him.

"Nik!"

"Miri!"

They crashed into each other in a deep embrace, meeting on the slope of the empty landscape.

Neither child could control the river of tears flowing from their eyes. Neither had ever felt so comforted by the caring, familial embrace of the other.

"I never thought I'd see you again," Nik said.

"I thought you were dead. You got shot. They'd killed you," she cried.

They kissed each other on the cheeks, desperately, both wanting to feel the warmth of family they had been missing for so long.

Miri wobbled on her feet, about to fall over.

"Are you okay?" Nik, his arms still wrapped around her, caught her from falling. "What's wrong?"

"I haven't ... eaten ..."

Nik pulled her arm up over his neck and swiveled beside her, letting his own body be her crutch. "Come on, I'll help you. There's food at camp. And water. We'll get you better."

They covered the distance to the camp quick enough, but Nik could feel that she wasn't doing well. She'd lost weight since he'd last seen her, and he'd been so excited to know she was alive that he hadn't even acknowledged the bruised and battered condition of her body. She was burned and filthy, exuding a foul odor that no one cared about in the least.

At the camp, Lila stood quietly behind Amir, who jumped up and down, excited. "I told you he'd do it!"

But Nik had more important things on his mind. "Amir, she's not doing well, she's hungry, go get the rations out of the saddlebags."

"Right," Amir turned, immediately heading for the dromid's saddlebags.

"And the water!" Nik called out after him.

"Right!"

Amir did as he was told while Nik brought Miri around to the shade, sitting her down cross-legged with her back to the satellite column.

Approaching slowly, Lila dropped to her knees and curled up next to Miri, snuggling the older girl between her arm and her leg.

Amir brought over the half-empty canteen and vacuum-packed portions of ration paste, handing them both over to the battle-scarred girl.

Miri took them both gratefully. She twisted the cap off the canteen and drank thirstily. Then she pulled the lid off the ration paste, squeezing it into her mouth, ravenously swallowing every bite.

As she wiped off the food and water that had dribbled down her black and blue face, Nik smiled.

He was in disbelief.

The gunslinger had really done it.

Thinking on it, Nik's brow furrowed in confusion, and he blinked once, then again. "Wait. Where is he?"

Miri's voice was weak and warbled. "Who? Kelly?"

"Kelly?" Nik asked back. "Who's Kelly?"

"The man who saved me. Who killed Santa Madre. He told me his name was Kelly."

Nik turned to Amir, and they shared an exaggerated look of puzzlement, their eyebrows pointed inward and their mouths tightened.

Amir looked back to Miri. "He told us his name was Twelve."

"Maybe he was lying." Nik shrugged. It didn't matter what his name was.

"Who was he?" Miri rested her hand on Lila's back as she spoke, offering the young girl as much comfort as Miri was receiving.

Worry cracked Amir's voice, "He rode into Nine Mine just after those Glicks took you. He helped us."

Nik pointed to the cloth bandage around his arm. "He fixed up my arm, and then we told him about you. He said he'd help us get you back."

"What happened to everyone else?" Miri asked.

Amir looked away, unable to meet her gaze.

Nik felt something catch in his throat.

Miri turned her head to meet her brother's eyes, which were filling with tears as he explained what had happened.

"They had you blindfolded, so you couldn't see, but they're all dead. They killed everybody."

Nik tried to calm himself, taking deep breaths and doing his best to not hyperventilate.

Miri wiped the tears from her eyes.

Lila wrapped her arms around the older girl, and Nik planted himself next to her, hugging her from the side.

Amir seemed to be the only one unconcerned about the death behind them, worrying instead about what was ahead. "I wonder where he is. You think he's coming back?"

Nik closed his eyes, letting his distrust return. "If he comes back."

Miri's sobbing ebbed away with a sharp intake of breath. "Don't say that, Nik. I didn't even get a chance to thank him for saving me."

"What if he's in trouble?" Amir asked.

Nik stood up to join Amir in watching the horizon. "What sort of trouble could he be in? He's a professional. Remember? And besides, he's got Zeke."

"That doesn't mean he couldn't get caught," Amir said.

Miri ran her fingers through Lila's hair. "I'm afraid he probably did get caught. When he left me, he was stealing a speeder and trying to draw all the attention to himself while he sent me here. They chased him; two speeders full of Glicks."

Amir turned to Nik. "That would explain those crashes we heard echoing."

Nik brought his hand to his chin, rubbing it in thought. "Maybe we should head into town and see if there's any sign of him."

Amir cracked a grim smile. "I'll go. You need to stay here and take care of Miri. They probably won't recognize me by myself. I'm just one kid."

Nik took in a breath, ready to protest, but Amir raised a hand and cut him off. "No. It's fine. I can take care of myself. Trust me. She needs you now."

Begrudgingly, Nik shook his head, agreeing to Amir's plan. "Go see what you can see. I'll be here with the girls."

"Right."

XXVIII

When regaining consciousness and finding that his hands and feet were bound tightly, the gunslinger kept his eyes shut. It was his considered opinion that keeping his eyes closed and discerning as much about the situation as he could before opening them was a wise policy. Before anyone knew he was awake and aware, he could determine where he was and how to get away. He began by cataloging his surroundings.

First, he could hear a speeder turbine whirring directly to his left. The sound was deafening and more than enough to prevent him from learning much more than the fact that he was in a speeder. Wind whipped over him, but stayed directly out of his face, which told him the speeder was moving and he was probably tucked away neatly in the back seat.

Casually exerting pressure against the binders keeping his wrists close together, he could tell a lot about them, too. The cord was flat and about six centimeters wide; most likely plastic. That would mean he'd been captured by a lawman, since that sort of cuff was favored by lawmen on the frontier. No locks to pick meant no chance of escape, and they were mostly unbreakable.

A bare spot on his left wrist above the cord, a phantom absence, meant they'd taken Zeke from him. That meant they weren't as stupid as they might have looked, because a man with a wrist communicator was capable of calling all manner of help. Twelve put the chances at about fifty percent that they'd guess or discern just how autonomous Zeke was.

Zeke could very likely be his ticket out of there if he was still fully functioning and hadn't been damaged at any point between the chase and the capture.

Twelve heard the buzz and beeping of a communications panel over the spinning of the speeder turbine, but it didn't sound like Zeke at all. It was most likely a part of the speeder's console. That told him that whoever it was that had him in custody was about to talk to someone. Would the communiqué reveal that he'd been captured?

There was a connection tone, and someone on the other side spoke. Their voice was gruff and muted through the digital compression piped through the speakers that were laced throughout the speeder's interior. "What is it?"

"Is this the Serpent's man?" A blustering and arrogant voice yelled, over the sound of the air rushing past.

The gunslinger was quite sure that he was in the custody of the sheriff of Stelio City.

Damn.

"I represent Mister Guerrero," the voice crackled over the speakers.

"Good. This is the sheriff. Is Guerrero there? Put him on the line."

"Mister Guerrero does not talk over comm devices."

"Oh he doesn't, does he? Well you listen up, sonny, and you listen good. I've got him. I've got the son of a bitch that blew up that ammunition in Stelio. And I just want to make sure that me and the Serpent are square. I got him what he wanted and there's no need for anything more complicated."

"Where is Baltimore?" the voice asked.

"Baltimore?"

There was a wavering in the sheriff's voice. That told the gunslinger that who, what, or wherever Baltimore was, the sheriff had a problem with it.

"Mister Guerrero sent Baltimore after the man," the voice on the speaker continued. "I doubt Baltimore would give up the chase so easily, or that he'd leave the prisoner in your custody."

The stranger couldn't help but grin slightly. It sounded like the sheriff might be in a bigger fire than he thought he was.

"Well, uh ..." The sheriff stuttered, searching for an answer. "Well, this bastard I got in custody killed him. And the others before I got there. He would've got away with it clean if it hadn't been for me."

"Baltimore is dead?"

"Uh, yes. That's right. That's what I said."

Twelve could hear the panic in his captor's voice.

"And the man in your custody killed him?" the crackling voice asked.

"You got it. That's what happened." The sheriff found a confidence that hadn't been there before he'd formulated his story. "And you tell Guerrero I'm taking him into my jail in Stelio City. And if he needs me, I'll be there with this fellow in my custody."

"I'll relay the message." Twelve could hear the squiggling beep of a button being pressed to end transmission.

Then the voice of the sheriff picked back up, muttering angrily to himself. "Damn Glicks."

Shifting slightly in place, the gunslinger did his best to see if he still had his gun holster on, hoping the sheriff had been too stupid or rushed to remove it.

No such luck.

Like Zeke, his entire gun belt was missing. Hopefully the pistols were still on the front seat. The closer they were, the easier his escape would be.

If he could escape …

After hearing the sheriff's report, Josef Guerrero hissed lowly and stroked the spot on his chin where his Vandyke used to grow before his mutation.

Pacing a few steps back and a few forth on the lush rug of his antechamber, he made a deep sound of thought, exhaling a breath over his vocal cords. "You're sure this is the man who killed Santa Madre?"

The messenger cocked his head to the left. "I don't believe there is any doubt. And if he was responsible for Baltimore's death, then he's twice as dangerous than we could have guessed."

Guerrero felt a fury inside him at the mention of the danger of this man. How could one man be responsible for causing him so much pain? In one day he'd lost his mother and his most trusted lieutenant.

He thought he'd lost everything the day his mutation began, but this was bringing a new definition to the word "loss."

Had he paced any longer, lost in thought, the Serpent would have worn a deep groove into his padded carpet.

"And it is just one man? Not a small army?" he asked.

"So it seems," the Glick standing before him straightened further to attention.

His mind rifled through the possible courses of action like a computer searching for keywords across a hundred thousand files. No matter how often he tried a new search term in his memory bank, he couldn't come up with the correct one. Each file he pulled in the computer of his brain took him to a different possibility.

Was this man from the company that had brought them all to Glycon-Prime? Was it even a possibility for them to be aware of his plans by now? Could he have a double agent within his organization feeding them information?

Who was this man?

Guerrero took a shallow breath and held it for three paces. If it was the company, why would they have not raided his entire facility all at once? And if they were responsible, why would they risk blowing up his ammunition in one of their prized population centers? True, Stelio wasn't the most populous city on Glycon-Prime, but the company would never blow up their own citizens if they didn't have to. It didn't make business sense to bring them all the way out to the frontier only to kill them.

No matter which way Guerrero worked to decode the information before him, there was nothing to believe that this lone mercenary was involved with the company.

The Serpent's plan was safe.

Perhaps this man was a bounty hunter. There were plenty of people Josef Guerrero had angered enough to warrant having a price on his head. And that would explain the disregard for the lives of citizens. But again, it didn't make sense. Wouldn't he have made his move during the chaos of the explosion?

Guerrero's pacing took him back into his office, the messenger following close behind in case he was given a message to deliver.

Through the glass wall he could see the cleanup crew removing the signs of his mother's death. One scrubbed the blood from the rock. The other worked to clean up the other fluids.

Guerrero turned his eyes from the sight and looked to the other end of the room.

He scanned the room for other signs, some clue that might tell him why this thing had happened.

But it was the absence of something that tipped him off.

The girl.

"What happened to the girl?"

"What, sir?" the messenger asked.

"Nothing. Go out to Stelio City. If the sheriff has the man responsible for this, make sure he stays in custody. Have them erect the gallows, and we'll make an example of him."

"Yes, sir."

"And just in case he's onto our plan, we'll find out what this man knows about it before we kill him."

"Yes, sir."

"Prepare everything, and I'll be there by dawn to cause the death of this man personally."

"Yes, sir."

Guerrero's henchman fled from the room, frantically racing to heed his orders.

Still feigning unconsciousness, the gunslinger could feel himself pushed forward in his seat as the speeder slowed to a halt. The whining sound of the turbine slowing, coupled with the sheriff huffing his way out of the speeder, told him they'd reached their destination.

Twelve followed the sounds of the footsteps around the side of speeder and could feel the sheriff standing over him. Though all he could see was the red-black of the inside of his eyelids, he could subtly make out a different shade of black, telling him the sheriff was between his face and the blazing Glyconian sun.

Knowing what was coming, it took every ounce of willpower he had to not brace himself for impact.

Then, the sting of a slap across the face jolted him.

"Wake up, twinkle-toes."

The gunslinger cracked his eyes open slowly, hoping for his first good look at the sheriff. Unfortunately, with the noonday sun bright behind the lawman, all he could make out was his captor's fat silhouette.

The stranger faked a disoriented surprise. "Huh? What?"

"Keep your mouth shut and your hands to yourself. I am not in any mood today."

Peters reached down into the speeder with both hands and underneath the gunslinger's arms, pulling him up to a sitting position. Then, the lawman yanked harder, dragging his captive over the lip of the speeder until his feet dropped down to the ground.

The stranger went limp, doing the sheriff no favors.

"All right, hop."

Looking around, the gunslinger got his first real look at the ugly little sheriff and the surroundings. He was on the shoulder of the speeder trail right in front of the Stelio City jailhouse. Looking down either side of the street, the stranger could see the blockade of speeders and Glicks wielding laser rifles and batons. Across the other side of the street was the smoldering wreckage of the destruction wrought by the kids. Then, his eyes darted to the front seat, where he'd correctly guessed his gun belt and laser pistols would be.

Tossed casually beside his belt and guns was Zeke. The wrist computer's display was off, giving Twelve no hint one way or the other about his status.

Twelve bristled at the touch of the sheriff behind him, guiding him toward the jailhouse, but he didn't move. If he was going to get out of this, now was his chance.

There was just no way to make an escape that he could see. His wrists and ankles were bound. His guns and computer were out of reach and out of order. To say he was in a tight spot sold the whole situation short.

"I said hop, damn it!" The sheriff shoved the gunslinger forward, forcing him into a hop.

"Easy there," Twelve said.

"I said keep your mouth shut."

With nowhere else to go and no way out, the stranger hopped, once, twice, three times until he reached the porch in front of the jail.

The gunslinger tried to imagine new ways to escape, searching desperately for an angle he hadn't thought of. He was a hard man, harder than most, but he still didn't want to be left at the mercy of the sheriff and Guerrero.

They had no honor.

They were liable to do anything.

Peters came around his prisoner and waved his ID badge in front of the console in the frame, opening the door with a hydraulic snap.

"In," the sheriff commanded, shoving the stranger firmly in the back.

The gunslinger's reaction was automatic, you never act in a way that'll let you fall flat on your face, so he was forced once more to hop to his doom. He couldn't think of anything less dignifying that having to march like a rabbit to his own torture and death.

Sheriff Peters gave the stranger another good, hard push from the back, toward the first jail cell on the far side of the room. "That's going to be your home for the foreseeable future, buttercup. Better get comfortable."

Peters flashed his badge once more, this time at the console screen in front of the three-meter-by-three-meter metal box of a jail cell.

Seeing no way around it, the gunslinger raised his head with dignity and jumped twice into the cell.

Then, he hopped once, turning to face ninety degrees to the right, then once more, making a full hundred-and-eighty-degree spin. Each bounce of his feet stung his pride like a dagger to his back.

"You gonna cut me loose now?" the gunslinger asked.

The sheriff laughed. Then he engaged the button that slammed both halves of the bars that made up the cell door shut. "No. You're a dangerous man. You've killed half a dozen of Guerrero's men just this last week alone. I don't aim to get myself killed on account of you or anybody, so, no. I'm not gonna cut you loose."

"Fair enough." The stranger made his way over to the bare carbon-fiber slab that served as a bed against the side wall. Stiff and uncomfortable, it would have to serve well enough as home for the time being.

The sheriff sat down at his expensive wooden desk, kicked his feet up on top of it, and then whistled incredulously. "I tell you what, I wouldn't trade places with you for the world right now, fella."

Twelve sat down on the bed slab and set his back against the wall. Then, he tightened his jaw in firm silence. He would ignore every word out of the sheriff's mouth. It was a trick of lawmen and outlaws alike. If he listened, he'd get riled up, and getting riled up wouldn't help anybody, him least of all.

"You know," the sheriff wondered out loud, "the one thing I can't figure is this: who's paying you for this? You on a company contract? If you're on a company contract, that probably spells a whole heap a trouble for a lot of people around here."

The stranger closed his eyes, relaxing every muscle in his body except for his jaw, keeping his mouth shut. With his jaw clenched, he took in a deep, cleansing breath through his nose. With every breath he took, he imagined that he was pulling in the crisp air of a cool autumn day at sunrise on Earth proper. That's where he went off to in his mind's eye; a thicket surrounded by tall trees, turning brilliant oranges, reds, and yellows in the autumn twilight.

But the sheriff went on and on anyway. "I don't expect you are, are you? It doesn't seem like the company's style to send one man to take care of an organization like Guerrero's. Is there somebody in Nine Mine that had some money squirreled away, and they got out of there with their hide intact?"

The stranger made a point to take his next breath loudly through his nostrils, punctuating his silence with the sound.

"You better start talking, smart guy." Peters threw his hands behind his head, stretching out confidently. "Because I'll be honest, you're gonna tell one way or the other. If you don't tell me, they're gonna get you to tell them, and they're gonna be a lot less nice about it."

Twelve smiled, coyly.

"It's not those kids is it? The ones that came in through here trying to report things? Are they the ones who put you up to this?"

The gunslinger's face hardened stoically, as if it was carved from a block of stone.

"That's it, isn't it? Those brats are paying you to do this?"

There was a buzz at the door. Gauging by the worried look on the sheriff's face, Twelve could only assume there was more trouble coming for them.

That's when he let out a small sound, a breath of a laugh. That sound gave way to another, louder and more forceful form of laughter. Like a pot of water on the flame, they were the first bubbles of heat rising. Then, as the whole of his mirth gurgled over into a boil, he let out a deep, hearty belly laugh that pierced through the sheriff's calm.

Clearly unnerved, Peters got up and waddled his way to the door. There, the sheriff pushed the button, sliding the halves of the door away to reveal a Glick, most certainly one of Guerrero's men. He wore the same black uniform with a green logo on his front that most of the other soldiers in the Serpent's army did. With his body language, the tilt of his stance and angle of his elbow, the Glick worked hard to draw plenty of attention to the blaster on his hip.

He wanted to be listened to and probably wasn't used to it.

"What is it?" Peters tried angling his body in front of the door, working to block the Glick from entering the jail unbidden.

But that didn't matter to the Glick, who pushed his way past the sheriff and came in to inspect the gunslinger, bound inside his tiny cage.

"This is the man?" The Glick dragged his eyes over Twelve, inspecting every inch of the gunslinger.

The sheriff closed the door behind them. "This is him."

Twelve gave a smile and waved with his bound hands. He smiled like he knew something they didn't. "Howdy."

The Glick focused immediately in on the gunslinger, ignoring Peters altogether. "Why did you blow up our supplies?"

Twelve's smile broadened. "Seemed like fun."

The Glick hissed. "Just as well. Play your games. When the Serpent arrives here, he'll make you talk before your death."

"His death?" The sheriff seemed confused.

"We're erecting a gallows. We'll hang him as an example to the people of Stelio City. Mister Guerrero is coming to do it personally. He's very upset by the death of his mother." The Glick never broke his direct eye contact with the stranger as he spoke.

"He's coming here?" A note of terror quivered in the sheriff's voice.

"That's correct. The hanging is at dusk."

The stranger could already feel the nylon cord reaching around his neck, biting into it. It was rough and burned, crushing his throat and collapsing his windpipe.

He gulped.

Getting caught was one thing. Given enough time in any frontier jailhouse he'd figure out a way to escape or bribe a lawman or come up with some other plan.

A big, public hanging was just a tad more permanent. And it didn't quite fit in with his long-term plans.

Wondering about what his long-term plans might actually be gave him pause. An image of the children filled his head, and he wasn't quite sure why.

He turned his attention to the Glick in the doorway, trying to shake the images of the kids from his mind. The Glick, with the quiet fury of a small man with an iota of power on his face, looked at the sheriff and back at the gunslinger before pulling his laser pistol from the holster without a word.

He leveled the pistol directly at Twelve.

"Now hold on a minute there," the sheriff protested. "I'm not comfortable with anybody pulling any pistols in my jail-house but me."

Based on the Glick's posture, Twelve knew he wasn't actually in any immediate danger of being shot. There was no tension in the Glick's muscles, and his finger was held against the side of the trigger, rather than wrapped around it. In fact, Twelve could even see the Glick peering at the sheriff from the corner of his narrow, yellow eyes.

It was all a show.

And it was no surprise at all to a seasoned gunslinger when the Glick turned on his heels and aimed his pistol at the sheriff.

"Now hold on here. What is this?" Peters must have either been a complete idiot to have not read the Glick's body language, or he simply wasn't accustomed to reading such signs in the first place.

"I'd like your pass key, Sheriff," the Glick demanded through a smooth, polite voice. "I'm taking responsibility for this man's custody, and I don't want any of your blundering or interfering."

The gunslinger soaked in every word between the two of them, gauging what he could of their characters in case he could use it to escape. He had the Glick pegged as a mutant with "little man" syndrome, and nothing he said convinced him to renegotiate such an assessment.

"Now I caught this bastard, I can sure as hell take care of him." Peters boiled in place, his face flushed red, and sweaty condensation appeared across his forehead. "He's been cutting your people down like it's goin' outta fashion, and I'm the only one who brought him down."

The Glick raised his pistol up higher, from the level of his hip to chest-high, emphasizing his point. "Your pass key, Sheriff."

Reluctantly, the sheriff raised his arms in the air into a position of surrender.

"I don't trust you, Sheriff." The Glick stepped forward toward Peters. "Although you claim loyalty to our cause, any man who would take a bribe against his current employer is not a man to be trusted. And you're certainly not a man I trust. Besides, I have my orders."

Peters held a breath in. "Now, there's no need to—"

"Your pass key, Sheriff. Or I will fire." Taking another step forward, the Glick jabbed the sheriff in the chest with his pistol.

The Glick meant business this time. His finger had moved from the side of the trigger to the front of it. It was so slight a movement, Twelve doubted the sheriff had even noticed.

"Fine. Fine. Here you go." The sheriff slowly reached around the laser barrel embedded into his chest and fished his passkey from his right pocket.

"Hand it here. Slowly."

Peters handed the Glick the passkey.

"And now your weapon."

Peters let out an annoyed sigh, and for a split second it seemed as though he'd protest, but he thought better of it. Without a word, the sheriff grabbed the hilt at an odd angle, proving he couldn't fire it.

"Drop it to the ground."

The sheriff obliged, the belt and pistols hit the ground with a clatter. Once Peters had been disarmed, the Glick withdrew the barrel of the laser pistol from the sheriff's chest and backed up a full meter, then used the passkey to open the cell next to Twelve's.

"Get inside," the Glick motioned with his laser pistol into the cell.

"What? You don't have to—"

"Now."

"But ..."

"The Serpent will decide when you're free, if he can truly trust you or not."

Surrendering, the sheriff took the five steps into the jail cell, turned around, and the Glick slammed the door behind him.

Smugly, the Glick smiled widely. His thick lips weren't accustomed to smiling in their new state, giving the Glick all the sinister charm of a snake laying patiently in wait, ready to pounce. "Now," he said coolly, "we wait for the Serpent."

XXIX

Amir sat up high and straight on the dromid, clip-clopping its way down the speeder trail toward Stelio City. The boy wasn't the best or most accomplished rider, but he was able to get the beast to head in the right direction and at a decent pace.

Barely, anyway.

Alone in his thoughts, he fought to keep them from fading back toward memories of his family, of his father, of his mother, of the life he used to have. He tried hard to keep his mind grounded, staring at spots of fur on the neck of his dromid, separating out each tan hair and following back into the dromid's gray hide.

After a while, Amir and his mount finally crested the ridge that had prevented him from seeing Stelio City away in the distance.

The boy's eyes widened, stretching out at the sight laid out before him.

Stelio City seemed under siege.

There were speeders, tanks, and all kinds of artillery on

hover sleds, blockading the city at all angles. Around each piece of heavy weaponry, men from the Serpent's army milled about. There were hundreds of them, seemingly five soldiers for every one person in town, Amir guessed.

"Oh. Wow."

The young boy could feel the adrenaline coursing through him, and all he wanted to do was fight, even though he knew he'd lose.

But anything could have been happening down there. And if he'd learned anything during this whole ordeal, he had learned that he couldn't just charge into a fight without knowing the score.

"Come on, Bluey. We've got to see what's going on."

As the dromid resumed his leisurely pace down the speeder trail, Amir wondered the whole time if he was making the right choice. His own well-being took a backseat, though. He was more concerned with the well-being of the man who had saved them and had saved Miri.

That wasn't a debt he could easily ignore. His father always told him that you paid your debts, and that's what they would do.

"You think he's all right? I'll bet he is. He's the toughest man I've ever met. I'm sure they couldn't get him even if they tried."

The dromid brayed in response.

"You think he's down there somewhere?"

The only sound that came back to him was the clippety-clop of the beast's hooves.

"I really don't think they could have caught him. He's too smart for that." Then an altogether more depressing possibility penetrated Amir's mind. "I wonder if he just left us."

The boy couldn't fathom a single reason the gunslinger

would have to leave, but neither could he find a reason for him to stay. But then again, he couldn't think of a single compelling reason for Twelve to do any of the things he'd done. He had no reason to go, but he had no reason to stay. He had no reason to care about Miri, but he had no reason to get her to safety, either.

Amir was under no illusions. He knew the stranger owed them nothing, and they owed him everything.

The small, besieged town before him grew larger with each step the dromid carried him, farther and farther down the speeder trail. The closer he got, the more worry grew inside him and left him unsteady on his mount.

Once Amir caught sight of the mass of Glicks blockading the speeder trail, he pulled on the reins to slow Bluey's pace down to a simple trot.

By the time Amir had actually reached the Glick's barricade, Bluey's pace had slowed to a nominal shuffle. The beast's legs shook with every step as they approached the guards.

Amir could feel the uneasiness right beneath him, coming from the shaking animal. Bluey shook with all the fear of what was coming.

But Amir had to cast it from within himself and carry on regardless.

"Just act natural," he told himself.

"Whoa, there," the Glick in green and black raised his hands to stop the boy and his dromid. His eyes were hidden behind a pair of dark, black goggles, and the collar on his uniform covered his entire scaly neck all the way up to his chin.

"Yes, sir?" Amir tried to disguise his trembling with a soft innocence in his voice.

"What's your business here?" the guard hissed.

Amir blurted robotically, "I'm passing through. Just trying to get through to Saurian City."

"This city is closed."

"Closed?" Amir saw an opening to ask for the information he so desperately wanted. "What happened? Is everything all right?"

"Everything's fine. The city should open back up after the hanging tonight, so you may as well just turn around and come back tomorrow."

Amir grinned, relishing the ability to lie without getting in trouble. "My dad's not going to like that."

"I don't care, kid. Turn around and come back tomorrow."

Something tugged at the boy's innards. "A hanging? Who's getting hanged?"

"A terrorist. He blew up a building and killed many men. No one to cry over."

Amir felt a coldness wash over him, a deep spite that made him wish he could kill this Glick right then and there. His feelings pressed hard against his chest like a raging water and almost broke like a dam, but he choked that flowing feeling back down and simply said, "Oh."

"Now turn around and get this stinking dromid out of here before I get angry."

"Yes ... yes, sir."

Amir pulled at the reins, turning the creature around. Bluey was all too grateful to be leaving, having the armed guards completely out of sight. As they turned, Amir made mental calculations of the strength of the force surrounding the city and how in the world they'd ever be able to get through.

All he knew was that they were going to have to find some way to save the man called Twelve.

How else could they repay him?

Clicking his heels into the side of the dromid, Amir sped away as fast as he could to gather his reinforcements.

Amir wondered what he must have looked like to the guard seeing him fade into the distance. Perhaps he didn't give a second thought to a kid racing away on a dromid, turning into an ever-shrinking dot along the speeder trail.

Then he wondered what the guard would think when they came back to rescue the gunslinger they meant to hang.

Would they be so ridiculous then?

And they'd do it without laser guns. They'd have to since they didn't have any.

We'll teach you a lesson, old man.

We'll show you....

XXX

Josef Guerrero's speeder pulled up to the outskirts of Stelio City, and he wondered if the small town had ever seen as much comings, goings, and commotion as it had in the past few days. He felt much like he imagined the city did, uncomfortable with the hubbub. He did not like change, and anything that forced change earlier than he had prepared for angered him.

Before he'd left his fortress, he'd had to prepare himself mentally. No one could know or see the anguish he felt for the loss of his mother. He had to remain resolute.

Once his vengeful justice had been meted out, no one would question his right to rule again.

But, as he left the safety of his complex, he knew himself to be exposed and vulnerable, as though a knife might find purchase in his back at any moment. This man who killed his mother surely wanted to hurt him, and had, indeed, done so. The company wanted to hurt him. The sheriff and the humans of Stelio City held no love for him. Guerrero was beset on all sides.

For a man living in fear of treachery and betrayal, a lurking suspicion held shape constantly over his shoulders, and, like a phantom, vanished when it might have been seen. But a man like Guerrero could not worry about such trivial frivolities. The people of Stelio needed to see him strong and angry for what had happened to ensure that it would never happen again.

And then, after his insurrection had succeeded and he had an entire frontier world of his own to rule as he wanted, the people of Stelio would pay for this infuriating hiccup in his plans and for the death of his mother.

He climbed from the passenger compartment of his luxury speeder with an elegant, sure step, leaving it parked right in front of the jailhouse with his driver.

He could see up ahead on the speeder trail that the gallows had been erected, just as he had ordered.

The stage impressed him. It had been built quickly and efficiently, just as he liked, and the gallows arm and lever mechanism were things to be proud of. The machine of death was constructed from sheets of carbon fiber and fastened together with steel.

A white synthetic cord, fashioned of nylon, dangled from the top arm and ended in the tear-dropped loop of a noose, waiting for its victim.

The entire production gave Guerrero a thrill of satisfaction. It proved to him the loyalty and proficiency of his Glick brothers, and it represented the end of a thorn in his side.

Standing on the gallows were two of his men in their sharp uniforms, guarding a man whose hands were bound. He wore the garb of a typical frontier bounty hunter, dressed like a lawman who'd lost his way. Guerrero wondered if the man had a look on his face as smug as his posture intimated, but it was covered over in a traditional black hood.

Seeing that the sun was nearing its nightly sleep and the ceremony would soon begin brought a wide smile to Guerrero's thin, dry lips.

Full of renewed confidence, he stepped up onto the porch of the jailhouse and pressed the door buzzer, waiting for a quick response.

Both halves of the door opened with a thick, hydraulic whoosh, revealing his lieutenant standing on the other side. "Lieutenant."

"Sir."

The lieutenant stepped aside and let his employer enter the jailhouse.

Instantly, Guerrero saw the situation and, though initially confused, settled into the idea. There in the second cell against the back wall was Sheriff Peters sitting on the cold slab of a bed.

The sheriff rocketed to his feet, seeing his crooked benefactor enter the room. "Mister Guerrero, there's been some kind of mistake. You've got to let me out of here."

Guerrero hissed back at the sheriff. "Quiet, Sheriff. We will deal with you and your situation in a moment. There is much more pressing business at hand."

Peters sat back down on the bed, annoyed humiliation telling a story all across his face, burning his cheeks red. Guerrero smiled at this dejected display.

Guerrero turned back to his lieutenant. "So, the man on the gallows is the one who blew up my ammunition, killed my men, and murdered *mi madre*?"

The lieutenant hesitated before speaking, knowing full well how the Serpent had reacted to messengers of bad news in the past. "We believe so. He's definitely the mercenary type."

"A mercenary?" Guerrero was not convinced. "If he is a

mercenary then someone is paying him. Who is it that would be paying him to hurt me?"

"He did not say."

"Then I shall have a few words with him before we make an example of him."

"Yes, sir."

"And now we get to the next, less important, subject at hand: Sheriff Peters. Why is he in this cell? What did he do to earn such treatment if he did, indeed, capture this outlaw?"

"I do not trust him, sir."

"Nor do I, but what warranted his placement in the cell?"

"Call it a hunch, sir."

"Ah, I was almost hoping you'd reveal some bit of treachery so I could deliver a final punishment upon him."

As Guerrero spoke of treachery, the sheriff's eyes widened. That detail did not escape the Serpent's notice, who cataloged it for future use. Guerrero sighed. "A double hanging would have been a wonderful end to the evening."

"I'm sorry, sir," the lieutenant apologized.

"No matter."

"Now that you are here," the lieutenant asked, "what would you like done with him?"

Guerrero stroked his chin and smiled at the sheriff. "Well, Sheriff? If I were to kill you for stupidity, who would argue with me? Perhaps a double hanging would be good for morale after the death of my mother."

The sheriff stood up, coming desperately to the cell door, pleading for his life. "I can help. I'm loyal. You've seen how loyal—I brought that mercenary back for you, didn't I?"

"Maybe so ..." The Serpent walked around behind the hard wood desk he'd purchased for the sheriff. "Such a lovely desk, Sheriff, don't you think?"

"It's a beauty, for sure."

"And you like working at it? You like having something that old and expensive beneath your workspace? Something so valuable and a memento from our shared ancestry?"

"It's been nice. And I'll earn it. I'll do everything I can to."

"You know that it is my desk. When you sit here, at this desk, you are not doing your work. At my desk, you do my work. It was to serve as a constant reminder of your fealty to me. Something so old and venerated could only be used to do the bidding of someone such as I, and not the rabbled affairs of a frontier outhouse."

The sheriff fell to his knees. "I get that. Honest. I'm loyal to you. Haven't I proved it time and again?"

"Hmmm ..." Guerrero wondered further, but his thought process was interrupted by an ugly buzz from the door behind him.

The lieutenant looked to Guerrero for orders.

"Let them come." Guerrero nodded to his man.

The uniformed Glick walked to the door and pushed the button, and the door split open.

"Who is it?" Guerrero asked without looking.

A raspy, worn version of a voice familiar to him responded from behind. "Baltimore," it said.

Guerrero had been looking directly at the sheriff and watched the blood run from his face and the features go slack. When he heard the voice of his most trusted right-hand man that had been presumed dead, killed by the man on the gallows, he turned to the doorway to see if his mind played tricks on him. "Baltimore?"

Indeed, there in the doorway stood Baltimore.

Filthy, covered in dust, bits of Baltimore's clothes were blackened from laser burns and fire. Blood ran from his lip and a gory gash across his bald, craggy forehead. He clutched his left arm close against his torso, keeping pressure on a wound still flowing blood.

Though dismayed, the Serpent smiled grimly. Perhaps this day wouldn't go so badly against him. And perhaps he'd get his double hanging after all.

Twelve thought the view from the gallows had been right pretty before they'd shoved the black canvas hood over his head. The sun had been hanging low in the sky over the far edge of the city. The vast stretch of red desert beyond blended seamlessly with the red in the bottom ribbon of light in the sky, giving the illusion that he was staring at a painting with no horizon.

No wonder some folks loved living on the frontier. It wasn't the kind of sunset you'd ever get a chance to see on a fully colonized world.

Twelve took in a deep breath and enjoyed the scenery while he could.

There was nothing he could do to stop it, so the gunslinger had resigned himself to his fate. He'd drink in this last beautiful sunset. He'd take solace in the fact that he had died the way he lived. And he'd be comforted that he'd finally done an unselfish thing since everything had gone to hell in his life all those years ago.

He banished every ill and evil thought of his past out of his head. It was all over. Every scrap of it was an ancient history he never wanted to remember or relive. He'd certainly not let it go flashing before his eyes when they pulled the lever that would yank the floor out from beneath him.

Then the black hood came.

The guards forced it over his head, and he could feel his own hot breath reflecting back at him. It wasn't pleasant, but he withdrew into his own mind and the sounds of the goings-on around him.

He could tell that people were gathering. There'd probably never been a hanging on Glycon-Prime, let alone in a little town like Stelio City. Hanging was the preferred method of execution on the frontier, but since justice usually came at the end of a laser blaster, hangings hardly ever happened.

It made sense that there would be a growing throng of onlookers waiting to witness the spectacle.

The stranger wondered if they'd be told the truth about what he'd done, or if they'd be fed a line of propaganda from the Serpent or his men before they did the deed. No doubt it would be something to keep them in fear.

He wondered what it would feel like, to have his neck snapped like that. Would it be quick? Would he hear the crack of bone? Would he lose his breath? Or would there just be the sensation of falling and then black?

More important than anything, though, he wondered if there would still be a chance to escape.

They'd cut the binds on his legs because he'd refused to hop to his death and they didn't want to carry him, but his hands were still bound. With the hood covering his eyes, he was as blind as anything.

Escape was possible, sure, but the more he did the calculations, the more he knew his odds were less than good.

He'd lost track of time, but he knew time couldn't have passed that quickly since he could still see the black-orange blur of daylight through the dark canvas.

He wondered what Zeke would say, if he were around.

Most likely something like, "This is a fine mess you've gotten us into now, isn't it?"

Or, "You really know how to pick them."

For a bit of programmed data in a wrist computer, he really did have quite the personality. And then Twelve realized that the impossible had happened; he found himself actually missing Zeke.

But Zeke was gone and could offer no help in getting him off the rope.

All there was left to do was to count the minutes until everything ended or an opening presented itself.

Easy.

XXXI

For a man as saddened and stony as Josef Guerrero, it was difficult to be surprised, but the sight of the badly injured and limping Baltimore entering the jail was enough to offer a jolt of relief and surprise. Relief that his most trusted man was not dead, but surprise when Baltimore hurried to the sheriff in his containment cell.

Cowering at the back of the bunk, covering his face and body with his hands and arms, the sheriff whimpered as though he'd seen a ghost. "No ... No, you were dead. You can't be here."

"Baltimore?" Guerrero said again, perplexed.

Baltimore, holding his guts in with one hand and leveling a laser pistol with the other, limped to the sheriff's cell. Then, he fired three blasts inside.

The first two bolts hit the sheriff squarely in his middle. His body spasmed backward, and his arms flailed, exposing his face to a third laser hit, vaporizing it into oblivion.

"What is the meaning of this?" the Serpent shouted.

Baltimore dropped to his knees, letting his blaster skitter

to the floor. It was apparent that he was in pain beyond comprehension. Guerrero could hear him straining to talk. "He killed us. Tried to ..."

"Sheriff Peters?" the Serpent asked.

"Aye. We were after the man ... and Peters ... Peters came after us ... I don't think he ..." Baltimore gasped, groaned, and crawled toward a chair to pull himself into it.

Guerrero looked to his other lieutenant who stood there gawking and completely immobilized; stunned. "You there!" Guerrero shouted, "Why are you just standing there? Help him."

The lieutenant crouched down and grabbed Baltimore from beneath his arms and helped him up into the chair that sat on the other side of the desk that Peters used to work at.

"He ... killed us. He wanted to apprehend the man who killed Santa Madre instead of us. We were going to get him ..." Baltimore braced his stomach for the pain before coughing. He winced in agony before continuing. "... but Peters came from behind and opened fire on us. He killed Alhazred and Van Dyne ..."

Baltimore took another gasp for breath while Guerrero turned and looked to the sheriff's corpse, wondering what his replacement would be like.

"I'm sure he thought I was dead ... Our speeder turned over and exploded ... Then he took the man ..."

Guerrero looked back up to the lieutenant, barking orders through his lizard-like lips, "Get a medic, a doctor, anyone. Go. See to it that Baltimore gets all the care he needs. Spare no expense."

"Yes, sir."

The lieutenant scrambled out of the room in search of a doctor, leaving Guerrero and Baltimore alone with the body of Sheriff Peters.

"The doctor will see to it that you are taken care of, old friend. You will be made whole and strong once more, and then we will take our revolution to the next level. We'll rule this world and Santa Madre will be avenged."

"Thank you, sir." Baltimore's words were strained with pain.

"In the meantime, I will make sure that we take care of this man who has cost our cause so much. An example must be made."

"I understand...."

Guerrero stood up, standing straight and tall, proud of his men, and proud of his organization. Nothing could stop them now. Not this lone man. Not the sheriff. Not the company.

Not even the loss of his dearly beloved mother.

All he had left to do was kill this one last insect, and nothing would ever stand in their way again.

By the time the gunslinger's hood was roughly removed, a fair amount of time must have passed. Standing before him on the gallows stage was the ugliest Glick he'd ever seen in a fancy, expensive suit.

Behind the well-dressed Glick and down below the level of the stage was an impressive assembly of townsfolk and Glicks alike. Twelve wondered if there had ever been such a sight of desegregation on Glycon-Prime.

It was nice to know he could be useful in uniting the humans and the mutants in something.

His eyes focused in on the Glick closest to him. There was no trick in guessing who it was standing in his face.

"The Serpent, I presume?" Twelve asked courteously.

"So you are the man who has caused me so much pain and trouble over these last few days?" Guerrero smiled wickedly.

The gunslinger cracked a smile. "Well, you know me. I'm just trying to have a good time."

Guerrero brought his hand up and slapped the stranger across the cheek with the back of it.

The blow stung sharply.

"Killing my mother? That's what you call having a good time?"

The sting of the slap turned into a dull ache, and Twelve resumed his smiling. "That thing was your mother? I guess I can see the resemblance now that you mention it. She was almost as ugly as you are. I'd hate to see your padre."

The Serpent slapped him again. "So you admit it?"

Twelve smirked through the sting. If he could enrage Guerrero into stalling or making a mistake, maybe he'd still have time to come up with a plan for escape. "I never said that."

"Now you deny it?"

"I didn't kill her."

Twelve could almost see the thrusters firing in Guerrero's face. He was weighing whether or not the gunslinger was telling the truth or not. Since Twelve wasn't lying, he could tell the Serpent was confused but wouldn't back down. A death sentence had already been passed down, and Guerrero was the sort of man who wouldn't back down once his mind was set.

"Why have you destroyed my ammunition?" Guerrero changed the subject.

"Oh. That was yours? I'm sorry, I had no idea." The stranger couldn't help but smile again. The smile was met with another stiff backhand.

"Why have you terrorized my operation?" Guerrero insisted. "Who paid you for this?"

"Paid? You mean I could have made some coin raining on your parade? I wish I would've known."

This time, the gunslinger's winning smile was broken with a backhand, this one so vicious that his lip was split, dribbling a trickle of blood down the front of his chin.

Guerrero's face was flushed, the color rose up into the rubbery, pale green cheeks that had been smoothed out and pulled back during his mutation. "I say again, who paid you?"

The gunslinger smirked.

Guerrero slapped him again. "Wipe that wretched smile off your face!"

The gunslinger chuckled, growing that chuckle into another deep bout of laughter.

Through all the pain, and torture, and the specter of death, Twelve was going to find himself a sense of humor and keep it.

"Who paid you to do this?" Guerrero's fury rose and he slapped Twelve with a firm, open palm, then across once more with a backhand, then back again with his palm.

But the gunslinger never stopped his laughing.

The gunslinger would take solace in the fact that he'd caused untold amounts of anger in this Glick who took himself and his cause far too seriously.

Through his laughing, the stranger asked Guerrero a question of his own. "How did you do that? I've never seen a Glick angry enough to blush."

The stranger wondered if Glicks could foam at the mouth anymore, because he'd never seen one closer, but it didn't matter. The angry Glick balled one of his hands up into a fist and punched the gunslinger firmly in the gut.

It took the wind from Twelve's belly and replaced it with a deep fire, killing the laughter in him and knocking him to the ground.

Guerrero huffed in a rage. "If that's the way you want it, you'll have it. You don't want to talk? You won't have to. String him up!"

The guards standing behind him on the gallows, snatched the gunslinger roughly, picking him up from both sides, propping him uneasily back on his feet. Twelve tried with all his might to resist, squirming and struggling, but with the air forced out of him, he didn't have much strength left with which to fight their will.

Guerrero dusted himself off and tried to bring some modicum of dignity back to his posture. There was a crowd watching intently, and the Glick clearly couldn't afford to be made to look ridiculous.

Twelve thought it was too bad he couldn't do more to embarrass him. Had Zeke been there, he would have found some way to make the proceeding sillier.

The executioners dragged Twelve on his heels back to the trap door of the gallows, and, as though it were some solemn and ancient ceremony on Glycon-Prime, they gave him a moment to recompose himself before they readied the black hood to fit over his head.

The gunslinger sucked in air as best he could, trying to calm his breathing, but couldn't bring it in past the soreness in his gut.

"Put it on," one of the Glick guards said to the other.

The guard holding the hood nodded and raised the hood over the gunslinger's head.

Before the hood came down, something caught Twelve's eye. He noticed something unusual on the speeder trail on the horizon, and as soon as he unraveled what it was he was looking at, he could feel his spirit crushed. Everything he'd worked for was going to be thrown away.

The gunslinger did his best to clench his jaw and show as little reaction as possible. He had no desire to tip off the guards.

Or Guerrero.

Stifling his reaction was difficult, however, since the sight on the edge of the town was one of the most unexpected, frustrating, but somehow most welcome sights he could have ever imagined.

Charging toward the crowd at a full tilt were two emaciated dromids; the sound of their hooves beating against the magnetic strip of road was muffled under the low, conspiratorial chatter of the townsfolk assembled to watch the stranger's death.

Riding atop the fast-approaching dromids were two pairs of children. Or, rather, three children who were led by a boy who had only very recently become a man, raising an old-fashioned sword high above his head leading the assault.

"For Nine Mine City!" Nik screamed, shaking his father's sword like a warrior charging into battle.

Though he was glad to see all four of the survivors of the Nine Mine City massacre reunited, the gunslinger was surprised to find himself frowning.

He'd risked his life, which he was about to lose, to keep those kids safe. Hadn't they learned anything?

XXXII

Nik swung his familial sword high above his head, galloping toward the crowd on top of Tornado, the stranger's dromid. His sister, Miri, clung tightly to his back, ready to kick anyone away from their mount during their charge.

The sword was heavy in Nik's hand, and he could barely keep it lifted over his head, but he didn't have much of a choice. Like an animal puffing up its fur to look more menacing, Nik hoped to instill fear in those who might see him from the corners of their eyes. If nothing else, he hoped to be just menacing enough to clear a path through the crowd to the gallows before anyone realized he was just a kid.

They were bent on rescuing their savior, even if it got them killed. Nik looked to his left and could see Amir, with Lila seated behind him and clutching his middle, riding atop Bluey. His head swung forward and back to the sizable crowd assembled at the feet of the gallows stage they'd need to get through.

Nik's stomach ached with tension. It tugged at his

shoulder and the back of his neck. It bounced up and down inside him, in time with the running gait of Tornado.

Ahead, he could see plainly that Twelve was being strung up. By the time they reached the edge of the gathered crowd and the commotion began, the two Glicks on either side of the gunslinger were fitting the noose around his neck.

That wouldn't do.

That wouldn't do at all.

No less than a hundred people were gathered before the gallows, probably more than that, even. The dromids charged into them, knocking the back rows of citizens and Glicks alike over into the crowd.

Thinking it somehow appropriate to shout a battle cry, Nik screamed, "For Nine Mine City!"

The din of the oncoming charge must have finally hit the ears of those on the edge of the crowd, for they noticed something was going on and turned from the view of the hanging to see what was coming from behind them.

Imagining what the approaching storm must have looked like to the townsfolk, Nik almost wanted to laugh.

When those on the fringe of the crowd realized that they were in harm's way, they scrambled in panic.

Chaos erupted.

Members of the crowd dove into the edges of the streets, clearing a path for the avenging children and their dromids. Anyone who didn't find themselves clear of the dromids, found themselves kicked or sword slashed. Each of the Glicks in the crowd reached for their weapons. Laser fire burst in constant waves, but the blasts all seemed to miss the kids and the dromids, blazing by as quick as they could.

Nik swung his sword back and forth, trying hard to hit every Glick in his path. He didn't hit many, but his wild swinging served as a stark warning to any of the Glicks who dared to get too close, trying their hardest to force the kids off their mounts and away from their goal.

Looking up, Nik could see a Glick on the stage of the gallows in a fancy suit turning at the commotion. The Glick's eyes widened, and his mouth went slack.

"Get them!" the Glick on the stage shouted, spit shooting angrily from his mouth as he yelled.

But the children were closing the distance between them and the gallows faster than anyone could stop them.

The well-dressed Glick that Nik assumed to be the Serpent turned back to the executioners at the lever, shouting, "Hang him! Hang him! Pull the lever!"

Nik's dromid, Tornado, made the leap up to the gallows in one clear jump, blowing right past the Serpent and toward the stranger who was ever so close to dangling in his noose.

The Glicks standing to either side of the stranger heard their master's call and clambered to do the deed before the boy and his sword reached them.

On the platform, the dromid bucked wildly, and the only voice Nik could hear was that of the Serpent shouting, "Do it! Do it! Kill him!"

Standing at the mechanism to drop the trapdoor underneath the stranger, the Glick grabbed the thick lever to work it and swung it across....

Without thinking, Nik swung his family's heavy Bedouin sword at the rope above the stranger's head. He was terrified the blade would simply bounce off the rope, but it cut through the taut synthetic cord cleanly.

The Glick who had thrown the lever looked down at the trapdoor as it opened, but no body had fallen. The soldier glanced back toward Nik in shock, but that's when Nik swung his sword mightily, slashing the point of the blade across the Glick's face. The blade tore a gash into the

Glick's cheek, and a wave of dark blood sprayed into the air.

The mutant collapsed, hitting the platform with a thump.

Nik watched the newly freed gunslinger pounce on the downed Glick instantly, beating down on his face with the combined might of his bound fists, knocking the rest of the life from him. Twelve's hands ran down the exposed left side of the Glick until they found themselves inside the mutant's boots.

"What are you doing?" Nik shouted.

The stranger removed something from the boot. There was a pop, then a swish, which was accompanied by the flashing glint of metal.

He'd found a knife!

The gunslinger used the blade to slice through the bonds around his wrists.

Nik looked back toward the crowd, hoping to spot Amir and Lila there. It was easy to see them. On top of Bluey the dromid, they were a full two heads higher than the rest of the crowd. Amir had pulled tight on the left side of Bluey's reins and had driven him to gallop in odd sized circles.

In the split second Nik had to see Amir employing the tactic, he was confused by it, but understood it when he saw two Glicks, confused by the movement, catch each other in a crossfire as they aimed their laser pistols at the dromid.

In the growing din of chaos, Tornado grew uneasy beneath Nik, and Miri clutched him even tighter around the waist. He called out to the gunslinger, "We have got to go!"

The boy pointed to the sea of angry Glick faces beyond them, each one organizing the wherewithal to put up a more coordinated fight. It was as though they operated with a hive mind. Before, in the confusion, they had all reacted individually, but their determination to stop this attack grew. Two of the larger Glicks barked orders and began to assemble the Glicks in teams.

The Glick in fancy clothes, the one that Nik assumed to be the Serpent, undid much of the organization by shouting countermanding orders to the assembly in anger. "Get them! Kill them all!"

By that point, Amir and Lila, still firmly riding Bluey, made it to the stage. Bluey leapt up on to the platform with a leap no one would have thought the rail-thin dromid was capable of.

Nik's attention turned back to the Serpent, who wore rage on his face like a mask. "Come on! We've got to go!"

Nik, pulled in the reins around Tornado, trying to calm him, as he watched Twelve tuck something he'd taken from the dead Glick under his belt.

Standing there, Nik thought the gunslinger looked like a communications satellite being beamed information. He seemed to download everything he needed to know and made a short dash and a leap up on to Bluey, seating himself behind Lila and Amir.

"Guerrero," the gunslinger yelled.

The Serpent, standing at the edge of the platform, turned to Twelve and shouted, "You're dead! Do you hear me? You're not going to make it out of here alive!"

"Maybe not," Twelve said, coldly. "But neither are you."

That's when the gunslinger raised something from his hip in a flash, it was so fast Nik could barely see ...

... the dead Glick's pistol!

A violet bolt of light left the purloined laser pistol, and, with nothing more than a blink, it impacted into Guerrero's face. Suffering a laser blast at close range, the flesh and the bone of his skull was vaporized instantly, leaving a massive, gaping hole where the laser incinerated the molecules of his head. The smell of charred flesh and electric ozone hit them all in the face.

"We've got to go!" Nik shouted once more in desperation.

"Go!" The gunslinger shouted back at him, pointing beyond at the empty stretch of road behind the gallows. The barricade had gone unmanned so the serpentine guards could watch the festivities.

"Hee-yah!" Nik kicked his heels into the dromid who had become increasingly wary of his place up on the raised platform. Tornado's knees shook, but he showed a surprising amount of courage when the boy's heels dug into his side. He leapt right over the back side of the gallows, leading the retreat out of town.

With Tornado taking him and his sister in the right direction, Nik turned back to see the gunslinger, on the back of the other mount, emptying the power charge of laser blasts from his stolen gun into the crowd, thinning the herd.

Turning cold at the thought, Nik realized that the more Glicks they killed, the better the chance they had of escaping.

The last thing he ever wanted to be was a killer.

But this was different.

Tornado galloped past the unmanned barricade at the back end of town without a problem. Nik turned back around once more to see Amir, Lila, and Twelve leaping off the back of the gallows, following as close behind them as their beleaguered and overloaded dromid would carry them.

"I hope they make it," Miri said.

"Me, too." He called back to her.

XXXIII

On the back of the dromid, Twelve reached his arms around both children, snatching the reins from Amir. He wished that he could have had a moment to shake some blood back into his hands. They were dead from the lack of circulation and difficult to manipulate, but there was no time to worry about the painful tingling sensation shooting through them.

The Glicks were right behind them, furious. Some ran on foot, shooting wildly in their direction. Others scrambled back toward their speeders.

They were going to put up a hell of a fight.

Even though his dromid was overloaded, Twelve knew that if they were going to make it out alive, he needed to catch up to the stronger animal bearing the older children up ahead.

"Come on, boy," he said lowly to the staggering beast beneath him. The gunslinger dug his heels into the beast's side, urging more and more speed out of Bluey. The dromid responded favorably to the coaxing, moving faster and faster, breaking beyond the point of the barricade at the back end of Stelio City.

Turning his head backward, the stranger could see the crowd, a mix of Glicks and civilians, cresting over the edge of the gallows as a mob.

Some townspeople headed beyond the buildings in town, but some were heading back to their homes, hoping to avoid the coming violence.

Amir, sitting in front of the gunslinger, turned and opened his mouth to shout. "Give me your gun!"

"No! Keep your head down. I'll do the killing."

Snapping his head around, the wind blew wisps of hair across Twelve's eyes, and the trouble he saw behind them sank his heart. It was trouble. Big trouble. If he didn't upgrade their ride, the kids would certainly die. Aside from the rushing sound of atmosphere passing by his ears and the thick clippity-clop of the running dromid, the only other sound that filled the air was the speeder turbines spinning up to launch. An entire army of Glicks were back there, all mobilizing to kill.

Looking forward again, he'd gained on Nik and Miri considerably. They were likely within shouting distance, so he yelled as hard as he could. "Keep going! Get them to the next town!"

Nik angled back, looking at the gunslinger, straining to hear his words. "What?"

"Get them to the next town! They're counting on you! I'll catch up, meet you there!"

Amir, craned his head around, looking dead into the stranger's eyes. "What are you talking about? Where are we going?" he shouted.

"With Nik," Twelve shouted back.

"But you just said—"

"I said I'd meet you there!"

"Where are you going?"

Lila spoke up, her words cutting him deeply. She said loudly, simply, sadly, "Don't go."

The gunslinger smiled broadly at both kids, then, without a word of goodbye, slipped down off the back of the sprinting dromid, hit the ground, and tucked into a roll.

"No!" Amir screamed. His voice was a tortured cry, like he was losing another family member to certain death.

The stranger watched as the children rode on. The girls, each on the back of a different dromid, looked back at the man who'd saved them. He could see the pain in their faces until they faded into specks on the haze of the horizon.

It was almost as if they were losing a hero, but he knew that wasn't what he was. He was much less than a hero, but something more than that, too. Something darker, perhaps.

But it didn't matter.

Confident in the knowledge that the children were far enough away, Twelve turned back toward the oncoming army, feeling comfort in the weight of the laser pistol in his grip.

Standing straight and tall, he looked down at the power charge on his stolen pistol, hoping there was enough juice to go out right.

Only a half-dozen speeders were heading his way.

The tanks had broken off from the pursuit and were heading back toward the Serpent's fortress. The power vacuum after the loss of their leader must have been filled quickly, and one of the lieutenants must have had enough wherewithal to divide their troops. Throwing their entire revolution against four kids and a mercenary seemed absurd.

Sending a squad, on the other hand, seemed a much saner expenditure of manpower.

It would all be for naught though.

The stranger smiled. If only Zeke were around to help lighten the mood.

There were too many speeders full of Glicks to fit on the road at once, so they came at him in three waves, kicking up billowing clouds of vermilion dust into the air. They were close enough that it wouldn't take more than a minute, perhaps half that, for the first wave to reach him. Those were the Glicks who ran the hardest to their speeders, the ones most angry at the loss of their bold and feared leader, and the ones who wanted to make the stranger pay for what he had done.

The gunslinger raised his laser pistol in a firm, two-handed grip. His right index finger was wrapped around the trigger, while his left hand held the butt of the pistol and the whole of his right hand. He aimed carefully down the sight, extending his arms fully.

Floating toward him, growing ever larger on the other side of the gun's barrel, the first Glick's speeder bore down on him. The lone passenger stood up, raising a pistol of his own, smiling. The stranger knew why the passenger was smiling. It was a standoff, and it was natural to think that in a standoff between a man and a speeder that the speeder would come out on top.

But the stranger was perhaps something more.

The passenger fired twice in the gunslinger's direction, missing both times. The blue bolts sizzled into the speeder trail on either side of him.

Those two blasts didn't manage to throw his concentration, and neither did the next two misses.

Planting his feet firmly and carefully aiming, the stranger made sure he had the driver's head perfectly in his sights, drew his breath, held it, and squeezed the trigger once. Then twice.

His shimmering sapphire laser bolts flew straight to their target, exploding the windshield with the first blast and then the driver's unnaturally thick neck with the second.

The passenger's weight wobbled back and forth when the entire speeder rocked, out of control. Without thinking, the Glick gunman holstered his laser gun and clawed his way to the driver's side, working to take back control of the speeder. He pulled back the corpse of his companion and dove for the controls.

But it was too late.

The gunslinger brought his pistol back up and readjusted his aim.

Keeping a breath in his lungs, concentrating hard on making his shot count, he squeezed the trigger once more, then once again. The laser bolt took the Glick in the side of his torso and in the shoulder, blowing him over with the force of impact. His body rolled off the back of the speeder and hit the trail beyond.

When they caught up, the Glicks in the second and third wave would be forced to slow down and move around their fallen comrade.

Without moving his feet a centimeter, the stranger lowered his pistol and waited for the front speeder to slow to a stop, a mere five paces in front of him. He knew he'd have to move fast to make his escape, so he sprinted forward, tore the driver out of the speeder and hopped in himself.

The corpses wouldn't serve as much of an obstacle; he'd have to move even faster. Fortunately, the speeder turbine was already warmed up, so all he had to do was hit the accelerator and he was off.

As soon as he got up to speed, the first thing he did was

veer off the paved speeder trail and onto the dusty shoulder. He knew if he kept up at this speed on the road, he'd run into the kids at any moment. The last thing they needed was the remnants of the Glick army breathing down their necks.

If the children were going to have a chance, he'd have to lead the Glicks on a chase through the sticks.

The first volley of blaster fire from his pursuers arrived soon enough.

"Not this again," he muttered to himself.

Two bolts hit the seat next to him, sending a spray of upholstery and stuffing into the air. He pulled his laser pistol up and checked the power charge.

Empty.

"Damn."

The stranger pulled hard to the right on the control wheel while he crouched down, scrabbling for the Glick's dropped pistol. Grasping for it, he could feel another blaster bolt rock the back of his speeder. The wheel beneath his hands wobbled back and forth, sending him along a winding trajectory like a sidewinding snake.

Overcorrecting, he slammed the wheel all the way to the right once more, using the force of the turn to extend him just enough to grab the pistol.

Sitting back up straight, he corrected his path, heading straight for the hills in the distance, the opposite direction of the kids.

Another laser bolt smashed into the dashboard above and to the right of the stranger.

Then another bolt came.

Searing pain suddenly exploded from his shoulder. Since he still had feeling and use in his right hand, it must have been a graze, but that didn't minimize the burning pain one iota. It felt like he'd been branded with a heat stick, but he'd just have to work through it.

That was the only way to keep the kids safe.

That was his top priority.

That was the job.

And if there was a thing he was best at, it was focusing on the job. Just the job. Nothing more.

Another blaster bolt came, flying high over his head. Had the Glick who fired it adjusted his hand just a fraction of a degree, the gunslinger's life would have been over just then, and he knew it.

Twelve slammed the wheel all the way to the left, trying his best to get a look at the Glicks behind him. There were three speeders peeking from the front of the dust cloud.

Where were the other two?

Snapping his head over to the road, he could feel his stomach drop out from beneath him.

The last two speeders were there, on the road. They were still heading for the kids.

"Damn it!"

Though the pain it caused him to raise his arm was debilitating, he clenched his teeth, working through it, and leveled the pistol at his immediate pursuers.

He fired three times, missing each shot, then decided quickly on another course of action. Dropping the gun into his lap, he pulled up on the brakes and made a hard turn a full hundred and eighty degrees, putting himself on a collision course with his tormentors.

The world and its landscape shrunk down and faded away. He was no longer looking at a situation, or a group of men, a gathering of speeders coming to kill him—none of that. He was looking at a checklist, organizing it into a neat list of quick actions to perform.

The Glick at the helm of the lead speeder was the first item on the list. Then the driver at the wheel of the second.

Third would be the front gunman.

Assembling the list of actions in his head, the gunslinger left everything to instinct and a burning desire to delete each completed task from his list so he could move on with more pressing matters.

The Glicks came straight at him, double speed. Laser blasts glanced off the front end of the stranger's speeder, but he couldn't be bothered to notice.

Straining his laser-burned arm, he brought it up to replace his hand on the wheel, using it to steer. With his good left hand, he picked up his own laser pistol and aimed it around the side of the windshield.

His eyes narrowed as he zeroed in on his first target. It was as though he was up-close and personal with the Glick, watching him move along in slow motion. The Glick's hands clutched the wheel, his rubbery face contorted into a squinted glare, and his long, wide lips were set apart and open slightly. The gunslinger could almost see a bead of sweat open on the Glick's brow and descend down around his eyes and past the corner of his mouth.

Twelve was there, with the Glick, at one with him, breathing in time with him.

And at the height of that out of body awareness was when the gunslinger pulled the trigger.

He didn't need to wait for the result. His focus moved to the next target, the second driver. His skin was even scalier than the first target. His eyes were wide set, taking in the situation ahead of him. The ridge where his eyebrows must have once been was elevated greatly.

Twelve pulled the trigger and moved on.

The gunman in the front car was next. Twelve was right

to select him as his next target. The gunman hadn't had time to even notice that his comrade was down. He was perched up, crouching over the windshield, blasting away with his laser pistol. It was obvious the Glick's mind was on his target, not his companion. So, too, was the stranger's mind on his target and not worrying about the laser blasts coming his way.

Over and over again, the gunslinger moved like a programmed robot, picking a target, shooting it, moving on to the next.

There were no more misses.

He couldn't afford to miss, and then they were all dead.

It was as simple as that.

It was then, when the smoke cleared, and all of the speeders had stopped coming at him, and all of the Glicks were dead, that the gunslinger crawled over the edge of the speeder and took a step forward. But that first step forward was a doozy.

He'd been hit.

More than once, and he hadn't even noticed.

There was the searing pain in his shoulder that he'd already put behind him, but a laser blast had glanced the side of his left shin, and another had mangled his right side.

But he had to put that out of his head.

There were still two speeders heading for the kids, and they were a lot faster than a pair of dusty old dromids.

Clutching his pained side and dragging his left leg behind him, the stranger scurried to the closest of the downed speeders.

He wished he could just collapse in pain and let it consume him.

But he couldn't let himself fail.

Not this time.

The driver of the first speeder he came to had a significant portion of his head and face missing from one of the gunslinger's shots. His body twitched, stray signals from his brain sending out the last electronic impulses of his life.

With his good hand, the gunslinger reached in, pulled him by his arm, and dragged him over the edge of the speeder. The Glick's body hit the ground like a sack, crumpling on impact.

"Is that you, sir?" a voice called out from the passenger-side floor of the speeder.

"Zeke?" Twelve said, suddenly aware of the blank spot on his wrist.

"I'd recognize the grunts of your pained labor anywhere. Also your bio-signature."

"Will you shut up? We've got to get out of here."

Twelve reached down and grabbed Zeke, working as fast as he could to clasp him back to his wrist.

"You're badly injured, sir."

"What's that got to do with anything?"

Straining, the gunslinger hopped up into the cabin of the speeder. Then he hit the accelerator.

XXXIV

Galloping along on the backs of the dromids, the children were out of breath, and their hearts beat hard and fast. Each of them was filled to the brim with the anger and frustration of having to leave Twelve behind so soon after saving his life.

For their part, the tired, old dromids weren't faring much better. They were pack animals and not used to the sort of exertion and strain they'd been put through, but they were performing admirably. Even through all of that, though, the children could feel the hoofbeats beneath them become less frequent and forceful.

They were slowing.

Not much, but enough to tell.

The town of Viper's Gate was like every other frontier town on Glycon-Prime, only bigger. It had all the hallmarks of a Glyconian settlement, including the central main street that doubled as the speeder trail in and out of town. The buildings were short and squat, never higher than two stories, and made of light, synthetic materials that were easy to ship halfway across the universe.

By the time the children had reached the outskirts of the town, their dromids had slowed to a crawl, exhausted from their monumental effort.

Each of them, child and dromid, was fatigued, though it was as much emotional strain as physical. The exertion of riding a dromid was great, but the toll that loss took was even greater.

Amir and Nik pulled the reins of their mounts, pulling them to a stop in front of the Viper's Nest Saloon & Inn. Perhaps the gaudiest building in town, it was painted in bright colors and trimmed with lights spanning one side of the front to the other.

Without a word between each other, the children tied the dromids to the side of the building and entered through the front entrance.

The front door opened to the saloon, which was full of tables, chairs, gamblers, and drinkers. The bar doubled as the concierge desk.

Scantily clad women in faux-feather boas served as bartenders and waitresses to the crowd, an equal mix of humans and Glicks.

Frightened by the surroundings, and suspicious of every Glick that laid eyes on them, the dirty children huddled in a group on their way to the bar. They had all of their belongings strapped to their backs.

Amir carried a cloth purse in his hands.

The bartender, an attractive young woman wearing a low cut, metallic halter-top with her blonde hair swept up into a bun, looked down at the group of kids from over the bar.

Confused, she asked, "Is there something I can help you kids with?"

Amir made his way to the front of the group, clutching the purse like Lila clutched her ragged doll. "We need a room."

The bartender's face turned up into a smile before cracking into a round of belly laughter. "You're joking, right?"

"We can pay."

Amir dumped the contents of the cloth purse out on the bar, spilling a pile of credit chips they'd salvaged from their hometown.

The bartender stopped laughing.

Before long, they were being shown into a room by the very same bartender with all of her most sincere apologies.

The luxurious nature of the room was a stark contrast to the disheveled nature of its new occupants. The four children stood inside, looking around in every direction at its opulence, each wondering who would be able to go first in the steaming shower and lie in bed.

"If you kids need anything, just let me know," she said. "We can send some food up for you if you like, or anything else."

Miri turned to her, "We'll be sure to let you know."

"Are you kids sure you're all right? You all look a bit shook up."

Miri took a step toward closing the door on the bartender. "We'll be fine."

But that wasn't quite true.

Lila stepped between Miri and the bartender, raising her hands and her doll tight to her chest. "There is one last thing."

"And what is that, little one?"

"If a tall stranger who goes by Twelve comes in here looking for us, go ahead and tell him we're here."

"Sure thing, honey."

The bartender backed out of the room, closing the door behind her, leaving the children to their solitude.

They took turns in the steamer, letting Miri go first.

With the exception of the time she spent in the shower, Lila kept a constant vigil at the window that looked out over the street from their second-story room.

If the gunslinger made his way into town, she'd be sure to see.

Worry covered them all over like a blanket, keeping it close to their bodies and not letting any escape.

Amir asked Nik, "What are we gonna do if he doesn't show up?"

"We'll wait until he does." Nik said.

"But what if he's not coming?"

Lila, from her spot at the window, told them without looking away from the street, "He'll come."

That ended the conversation. The boys knew if they spent any more time talking about the stranger in the past tense, as though he were dead on their account, they'd upset Lila.

And probably Miri.

And themselves.

And that wasn't good for any of them.

The sun was down completely, and even though her view turned into nothing more than a reflection of herself, Lila didn't move from her spot at the window until she was ready to collapse into sleep.

The kids could no longer stay awake waiting for their hero, and they all crawled into the comfy beds, their heads drooped in tired sadness.

The boys took up one of the overstuffed mattresses, while the girls curled up together in the other.

Sleep took them quickly, and, in the comfort of beds they hadn't known in days, they slept in a field of tired, dreamless blackness.

XXXV

The morning sun crept in through the hotel-room window, slowly filling the room until the light roused the first of the children.

The band of red-orange sun hit Amir's face first. He stirred for a moment, keeping his eyes closed, not wanting to wake up from such restful sleep after a week of sleeping on the cold surface of Glycon-Prime.

Finally rubbing the sleep from his eyes, he opened them wide, shocked at the surprising sight before him.

Sitting in a chair at the edge of the bed was the man called Twelve. The gunslinger slouched in the chair, covered over in a layer of red dust, clearly in pain.

Their eyes locked, and Amir blurted out in surprise and wonder and relief, "You're here! How long have you been here?"

"Few hours." His voice was strained and quiet, but it was enough to rouse the rest of the children.

"Why didn't you wake us?" Lila asked.

"You all looked so peaceful there, just sleeping. I didn't want to wake you."

Nik spoke up. "We did it, just like you said."

"Did what?"

"We rescued you. No shooting. No killing. We learned your lesson."

"I'm so proud."

Lila crawled out of bed and over to the stranger, curling up in his lap, her doll in tow.

The pressure of her weight on him forced a groan from him. Twelve adjusted himself slightly, trying to find a position to sit in that didn't hurt.

Lila looked up at him and asked, "What's wrong?"

"Just a scratch. Nothing to worry about."

Miri seemed to be the only one thinking straight. "There's got to be a doctor in this town. Do you need a doctor?"

"I reckon. I'll go see him."

With all the strength he could muster, he stood, lifting the young girl out of his lap and depositing her on the bed.

"You kids stay here. I'll be back soon enough, just as soon as the doctor can fix me up."

The stranger took a few slow paces to the door, opened it with slow, deliberate care, and took two more steps before Lila stopped him with a word. "I love you, mister."

He smirked, but emotion overtook him.

A tear rolled down the side of his face, cutting a path in the red dirt caked there. He took solace in the sentiment just before his eyes rolled up into the back of his head, and he collapsed.

The last four surviving children of Nine Mine City organized a funeral for the stranger in the city of Viper's Gate. Zeke, resting on Nik's wrist, played songs he thought the gunslinger might have liked played for such an occasion.

At the funeral, Nik asked Zeke why the gunslinger did it. Why had he sacrificed his life to save them?

Zeke, a computer and easily mystified by the whims of humankind, had no good response. He did his best though, and the children seemed to understand.

At first, they weren't sure they could pay for such a funeral service, but Zeke opened the gunslinger's credit accounts to them. There was enough for a proper burial at the very least.

The whole world, let alone the town, was still so new that a cemetery had not yet been established, but with the death of the stranger, the mayor of Viper's Gate designated a plot of land just outside of town for the purpose. It was on a rise, overlooking the speeder trail that led into the town, all of it prime Glyconian soil.

For many years, the only grave marked out there was topped with a headstone that read:

Here lies the man called
KELLY TWELVE
Father of Four
His sacrifice was not in vain

ACKNOWLEDGMENTS

When I set out to write this book, it was to tell a story I've had in me for a long time. When it came time to sit down and start writing, I knew what course I was charting, but I wasn't quite sure how I was getting there.

A number of people were instrumental in getting me to the point of this book finding its way into your hands.

First, I'd be remiss if I didn't thank my family. They put up with all of my bad behavior as I'm working on a story or a book. And they deal with me sitting in front of my notebook, typewriter, or computer with a blank stare on my face, lost in my own world and completely tuning out anything and everything they have to say. It's a terrible way for them to live, I'm sure, and I have no idea how they can put up with having a writer in the family.

Next, I'd like to thank Mark Dago for sitting with me all those long hours at the library or the coffee shop, working on his latest story while I worked on mine. His help was immeasurable, as was the help of Andy Wilson and Mark De Leon, who read it in its early stages and told me when I was heading in the wrong direction.

On the next step of the journey to get this book into your hands was my writing group. The members of that group most influential on the course of this project were Janine Spendlove and Aaron Allston. They had no problem reading the book over and over again to tell me what exactly I needed to fix and make better. They managed to point out every blind spot I had. Through their effort, I was able to come up with a book that I'm proud of, and that I hope will entertain anyone who comes across it.

In between those steps came Kolbie Stonehocker, who went through every letter of this manuscript and helped me address things that I didn't even realize were wrong. And then Patricia Bailey took over and asked me, repeatedly, if I was an idiot.

Finally, many thanks must be conferred on my cohorts at Silence in the Library. Ron Garner, Janine Spendlove, and Maggie Allen have worked hard to build something in publishing they should be proud of, and I'm grateful that my books and stories get to be a part of it.

Bryan Young
Salt Lake City, Utah
May 2014

ABOUT THE AUTHOR

Bryan Young works across many different media. His work as a writer and producer has been called "filmmaking gold" by *The New York Times*. He's also published comic books with Slave Labor Graphics and Image Comics. He's been a regular contributor for *The Huffington Post*, StarWars.com, *Star Wars Insider* magazine, SYFY, /Film, and was the founder and editor in chief of the geek news and review site Big Shiny Robot! He coauthored *Robotech: The Macross Saga* RPG in 2019 and in 2020 he wrote a novel in the BattleTech Universe called *Honor's Gauntlet*. It won the League of Utah Writers' Diamond Quill for 2021, reserved for the best book of the year written by a Utah Writer. Follow him on Twitter @swankmotron or visit www.swankmotron.com.

OTHER WORDFIRE PRESS TITLES

A Hero Born
Michael A. Stackpole

Gunslinger: The Dragon of Yellowstone
by Ed Knight

Madrenga
by Alan Dean Foster

Our list of other WordFire Press authors and titles is always growing. To find out more and to shop our selection of titles, visit us at:
wordfirepress.com

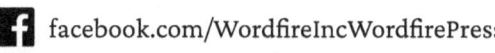 facebook.com/WordfireIncWordfirePress

twitter.com/WordFirePress

 instagram.com/WordFirePress

 bookbub.com/profile/4109784512